CW00968292

JAVA WATERS RUN DEEP

Part Cover Picture acknowledgement Ocean Images UK Ltd

JAVA WATERS RUN DEEP

Another airliner mystery with Peter Talbert

By

TONY BLACKMAN

This book is entirely a work of fiction. All characters, companies, organizations and agencies in this novel are either the product of the author's imagination or, if real, used factiously without any intent to describe their actual conduct. Descriptions of certain aircraft electronics and equipment have been altered to protect proprietary information. Mention of real aircraft incidents are all in the public domain.

All rights reserved. No part of this publication may be reproduced, stored in a retrieval system or transmitted in any form or by any means, electronic, mechanical, photocopying or otherwise without the prior permission of the author.

Java Waters Run Deep ISBN 978-0-9553856-9-8

First Published 2015
© 2015 by Anthony Blackman. All rights reserved.
Published by Blackman Associates
2 Thames Point
London SW6 2SX

Previous books by Tony Blackman

NON-FICTION
Flight Testing to Win (Autobiography paperback)
ISBN 978-0-9553856-4-3, 0-9553856-4-4
Published Blackman Associates September 2005

Vulcan Test Pilot
ISBN 978-1-906502-30-0
Published Grub Street June 2007

Tony Blackman Test Pilot (Autobiography revised and enlarged, hard cover)
ISBN 978-1-906502-28-7
Published Grub Street June 2009

Vulcan Owner's Workshop Manual
ISBN 978-184425-831-4
Published Haynes 2010

Nimrod Rise and Fall
ISBN 978-1-90811779-3
Published by Grub Street October 2011

Victor Boys
ISBN 978-1-908117-45-8
Published by Grub Street October 2012

Vulcan Boys
ISBN 978-1-909808-08-9
Published by Grub Street June 2014

Valiant Boys
ISBN 978-1-909808-21-8
Published by Grub Street November 2014

FICTION

Blind Landing
ISBN 978-0-9553856-1-2
Published Blackman Associates

The Final Flight
ISBN 978-0-9553856-0-5, 0-9553856-0-1
Published Blackman Associates

The Right Choice
ISBN 978-0-9553856-2-9, 0-9553856-2-8
Published Blackman Associates

Flight to St Antony
ISBN 978-0-9553856-6-7 0-9553856-6-0
Published Blackman Associates

Now You See It
ISBN 978-0-9553856-7-4, 0-9553856-7-9
Published Blackman Associates

Dire Strait
978-0-9553856-8-1
Published Blackman Associates

To Margaret, my long suffering wife, without whose first class ideas, enormous help, continuous encouragement and amazing editing skills, this book would never have seen the light of day.

Acknowledgements

This book could not have been completed without the help of specialist advisers. I should like to acknowledge with thanks the support and advice I have received. In particular I must thank John Saxon who not only helped editing the book but gave me lots of ideas and made certain my characters didn't try to do the impossible in and near Canberra and also Brendan Kelly who advised me on underwater searching and some forensic issues. I also received help from Richard James and Chris Payne. I must apologise to those who I inadvertently have not mentioned.

Despite all the help I have received, there will inevitably be inaccuracies, errors and omissions in the book for which I must be held entirely responsible.

Author's Note

This book is set a few years ahead and assumes that technology will not stand still but continue to accelerate at what, to some, seems an alarming rate. In particular the book is based on the latest communications systems made possible by the rapid advancement of cheaper rocket launchers and their ability to launch many satellites.

The other development targeted in this book is the use of unmanned aircraft which, in the commercial environment, is restricted not by current technology but by the need to get adequate regulation agreed worldwide. However in the military field where there is no such thing as regulation, unmanned aircraft are used worldwide and getting more and more capable.

Anthony L Blackman OBE, MA, FRAeS

About the Author

Tony Blackman was educated at Oundle School and Trinity College Cambridge, where he obtained an honours degree in Physics. After joining the Royal Air Force, he learnt to fly, trained as a test pilot and then joined A.V.Roe and Co.Ltd where he became Chief Test Pilot.

Tony was an expert in aviation electronics and was invited by Smiths Industries to join their Aerospace Board, initially as Technical Operations Director. He helped develop the then new large electronic displays and Flight Management Systems.

After leaving Smiths Industries, he was invited to join the Board of the UK Civil Aviation Authority as Technical Member.

Tony is a Fellow of the American Society of Experimental Test Pilots, a Fellow of the Royal Institute of Navigation and a Liveryman of the Honourable Company of Air Pilots.

He now lives in London writing books.

DRAMATIS PERSONNAE

Peter Talbert	Aviation Insurance Expert
Charlie Simpson	Peter's wife, Procurement Director Australian National Gallery
Mary French	UK Accident Investigator
Andrew Simpson	Mary's partner and Charlie's brother
Dominic Brown	RAAF Security/ASIO
Harry Brown	Chief Secretary in MOD
Philip Brown, Sir	Permanent Secretary for Transport
John Chester	Chief Pilot, Royal World Airways
Maureen Chester	UK Defence Minister
Mark Coburn	Inspector, ATSB
Derek Courtfield	WorldLink 's Australian Manager
Robert Covelli	Senior Inspector ATSB
John Dixon	Previous Office Manager, WorldLink , Canberra
Jill Evans	Peter junior and Francie's Nanny
Jim Forester	*Oceaneering* Project Manager
Jake Ginsburg	Air Traffic Controller, Brisbane Centre
Mike Goldton	Office Manager, WorldLink , Canberra
Simon Greensmith	UK Transport Safety Board Media Communicator
Tom Houseman	UK Accident Investigator
Margaret Johnson	ATSB recorder technician
Liz Mansell	Mike's wife and dress designer
Mike Mansell	Owner, Antipodean Airline Insurance
William Martin	Commander, Federal Police, Belconnen
Jerry Masterson	UK Accident Investigator
Roger O'Kane	Avionics designer, Independant Transport Aircraft Company
Vin Partridge	Secretary to the Australian Minister of Defence
Jeremy Prentice	Al Jazeera reporter
Kwok Qiáng	Chief Chinese Air Attaché, London
Charles Simon	Director General, UK Department of Transport, responsible for Safety
Sophie Schmidt	WorldLink Receptionist
Christine Smith	Defence Journalist, The Age
Geoff Smith	Minister for Foreign Affairs and Trade
Jack Smithson	Australian Minister for Defence
Gp Capt Buster Stone	RAAF Civil Air Traffic Liaison
Cliff Watkins	WorldLink Facility Manager, Canberra
Stephen Wentworth	Head Security, British High Commission, Australia
Frank White	ATSB recorder analyst
Laurence Williamson	Group Captain, Ministry of Defence
Jake Wilson	Perter Talbert's solicitor
General Max Wilson	Chief of the Australian Defence Force
Guan Jìng	UK Chinese Civil Air Attaché

ACRONYMS AND DEFINITIONS

Acronym	In full
AAIB	Air Accident Investigation Branch
ACARS	Aircraft Communications Addressing System and Reporting System
ADV	Australian Defence Vessel
ADF	Australian Defence Force
ADS-B	Aircraft position reporting to air traffic using ground stations
ADS-C	Automatic Dependent Surveillance Satellite Mode
ASIO	Australian Security Intelligence Organisation
ATC	Air Traffic Control
ATSB	Australian Transport Safety Bureau.
AUV	Autonomous Underwater Vehicle
CAA	Civil Aviation Authority
CSIRO	Commonwealth Scientific and Industrial Research Organisation, Australia
DME	Distance Measuring Equipment
DoD	Department of Defence (US)
EASA	European Aerospace Safety Agency
ELT	Aircraft Emergency Locator Transmitter
ETA	Estimated Time of Arrival
FAA	Federal Aviation Agency
FDR	Flight Data Recorder
FDSP	Forensic Document Services Pty Ltd fingerprint specialists
FIR	Flight Information Region
FMS	Flight Management System
GCHQ	Government Communication Headquarters
GPS	Global Positioning System
Intelsat	Provider of Geostationary satellites
JORN	Jindalee Operational Radar Network Over the horizon radar, Australia
MoD	Ministry of Defence
NRMA	National Roads and Motorists Association, Australia
NTSB	National Transportation Safety Board
NSA	USA National Security Agency
RAAF	Royal Australian Air Force
RAN	Royal Australian Navy
RF	Radio Frequency
ROV	Underwater Remote Observation Vehicle
TCAS	Traffic Collision Avoidance System
Transponder	Aircraft beacon which can be seen by Air Traffic---secondary radar
USAF	United States Air Force
UAV	Unmanned Aerial Vehicle
	Book Specific Acronyms
ITAC	Independant Transport Aircraft Company
RWA	Royal World Airways

CONTENTS

Search Area North West Australia

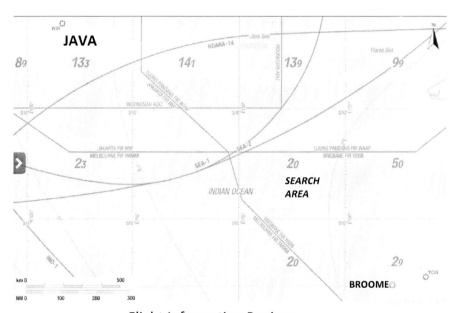

Flight Information Regions
Between Java and Western Australia

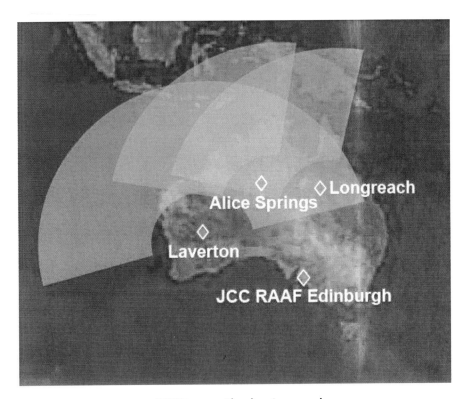

JORN over the horizon radar

Australian Defence Vehicle Ocean Shield

Prologue

Mary left the Talbert's home in Canberra and headed for the Deep Space Station near Tidbinbilla in her rented Toyota Yaris. It was just before Christmas and the sun burnt down from a cloudless sky. The temperature was already 30°C and the air conditioning in her rental car was full on. It was nine o'clock but there were very few cars on the road, which was a delight compared with her home in London. She had paid a bit extra to have a satnav in the car and she could see she was getting very close to the WorldLink satellite control site. The signs said CSIRO which she knew meant Commonwealth Scientific and Industrial Research Organisation but she was looking for a separate sign for WorldLink since she was aware that they had their own facility close-by, but not co-located with the CSIRO satellite centre. Finally, just as she thought she would have to go into the old CSIRO Space Station, she saw the WorldLink sign; the road led away from the Space Station and after a bit she found her way blocked by two pairs of large closed gates. On either side there was a high barbed wire fence which she guessed went right round the facility but the ground was hilly and she couldn't see the facility at all from the gates but only two satellite antennae.

Mary read and complied with the notice by the gates telling drivers to open their windows and to look in the camera on their right. The first gates opened and then as she drove through she was stopped at the second gates which had some red lights. She noticed another camera looking down, presumably at the car's number plate; the lights went green and the gates opened. She followed the winding road which went downhill slightly and finally saw a car park sign; the actual park when she got there was completely hidden from the entry gates and she parked in the only visitor's slot she could see, next to another Yaris and close to what appeared to be the entrance to a small single story flat-topped nondescript building with the two tall satellite dishes alongside. She could see a man's face looking out of a building window right in front of her which she guessed was an office. She got out of the car into the paralysing summer heat and walked quickly to get under the cover of a portico giving shade to the front of the building; she found herself looking into another camera as she entered into a keypad the four figure number which she had been given by the guy in the office in Canberra; the door opened automatically and she went into a reception area. It took a moment or two to get adjusted to the light and the air conditioning but after a moment she saw a smart looking blonde of about twenty five sitting behind a desk with a screen on her left.

"Good morning, Ms French. So you found us okay?" Mary nodded but wondered what would have happened if things had gone a bit wrong, like the planned car had had to be changed. "I'll tell Derek you're here."

Mary sat down in one of the two easy chairs while the receptionist was telephoning. It was cold in the building and she was glad she was wearing slacks and had put on a small jacket to go over her thin blouse. She looked around and there was nothing to show who owned the facility and that it was a key component of a brand new satellite world telephone system. It seemed completely anonymous and purposeless but she guessed that perhaps it was deliberate; nevertheless she did begin to wonder if she was wasting her time. Finally a man of about thirty five appeared, tall, brown hair wearing an open necked shirt, long grey trousers and sandals.

"Mary, good to meet you. I'm Derek Courtfield and I look after WorldLink 's interests in Australia. Shall we go into my office?"

He led the way and as they entered the room she realised it must have been Derek watching her as she had parked the car. There was a large map of the world on one wall but as far as she could see it was a standard Mercator's Projection with no special markings. The only other wall decoration was a picture of a vast deserted golden sandy beach with a sparkling Ocean behind. There was a large filing cabinet next to Derek's desk and the desk itself was clear except for a picture of Derek and a young lady with her arms draped lovingly round him who, Mary realised later, was the girl at the reception desk maximising her bosom with a well-fitting bra showing a large cleavage. She did a quick check and saw that Derek was not wearing any rings.

"Let me tell you what we do and then show you round though there isn't all that much to see." The accent was definitely from south of the Equator but perhaps tempered by some southern United States influence. They went into a large room with several large screens apparently controlled by two operators. "As you know WorldLink has a complete world communication system consisting of many low earth satellites and the facility here receives transmissions from the satellites as they fly by and sends responses as required."

Mary thought about this. "But surely you need to be connected to the internet."

"Of course. That is what the satellite dishes are for outside the building. They are connected to a geosynchronous satellite which has full internet connectivity."

"Couldn't you use a feed from Canberra?"

"The bandwidth wouldn't be wide enough. Canberra's internet connection isn't good enough to cope with what the City needs and what we need."

Mary looked around. "What happens in this room?"

"We have to ensure that our communication function is working correctly and of course to be certain that our internet connection is one hundred per cent. We are also looking for satellite anomalies and with so many of them we often have transmission and reception problems which need correction. We have a full time link to the WorldLink Control Centre in California."

"I thought a firm in UK called Camfen controlled the system?"

"It is their design and software but the physical control centre is in the States, actually in California. Of course Camfen monitor the whole system long term and as you know they are now a WorldLink company."

Derek introduced Mary to Cliff Watkins, WorldLink 's Technical Manager at the facility and he showed her the other rooms full of black boxes and the power supply room. "If the commercial electricity supply fails we have a battery driven back-up which comes on seamlessly and we have generators to keep the batteries charged. "

"Are there any other facilities like this one?"

Derek joined in. "Yes. One, in the States which is the Master and there is also a duplicate to this one but the location is very secret because we are frightened of terrorism. As you will have seen we don't advertise what we do here. In fact we've just had instructions to remove our WorldLink signs. We'll have to think of some other way of giving directions to this place."

They left the office and Derek looked at his watch. "Are you in a hurry? We could have a bite at the Nature Reserve and finish our talk later. We're not expecting any more visitors so I've asked Sophie to join us."

Mary looked a bit surprised when she realised that Sophie was the receptionist but Derek quickly explained as he made the introductions that they were engaged to be married.

They went outside and got into Derek's car which proved to be the Toyota Yaris next to Mary's car. As she watched Derek searching for his keys but not finding them, she suggested they used her car but Derek shook his head and turned to Sophie. "I've left my keys in my office. Let's go in your car, my love."

They got out and walked over to Sophie's car and ten minutes later they drove into the Nature Reserve and pulled up outside the restaurant. The room was fairly full and looking around Mary decided she would like to come back on another day and tour the Reserve. They sat down and ordered sandwiches each one of which, when they came, Mary judged would have been enough for two people. Suddenly they heard an explosion and everybody in the restaurant jumped. Mary felt an uneasy foreboding. "What on earth was that? It sounded very close."

Derek nodded but they carried on with their meal, though Mary felt some trepidation. The next thing they heard was the sound of two police cars and out of the window they could see that they were going towards the satellite centres. Then they heard and saw two fire engines racing along behind the police cars.

"Derek, we'd better go and see what's going on." Mary got up without waiting for an answer and the others followed leaving their uneaten sandwiches behind. They rushed to the car and Sophie drove back as fast as she could.

As they approached they could see smoke rising from the direction of the WorldLink facility and nearing the entrance gates police cars barred their way. It was impossible to see the facility but the smoke was coming from that direction and the two satellite antennae were no longer visible.

Chapter 1

Mary said goodbye to Derek Jones, a fellow UK accident investigator, and filed out from the Royal Aeronautical Society's lecture theatre in Hamilton Place. They had been listening to a well know aviation professor from Cranfield giving his analysis of the disappearance of the Malaysian Boeing 777 Airliner MH370 in March 2014 somewhere in the South Indian Ocean. The aircraft still hadn't been found and the lecture had in reality added nothing new to the discussion. In fact she wondered why the Society's Lecture Committee had agreed to the talk in the first place. Her own private view was that the aircraft was proving very difficult to find because the fuselage must have submerged intact with all the passengers and crew trapped inside; she based her view on the fact that so far no floating wreckage had been discovered though she was sure that eventually something would be found, probably wreckage or hopefully the aircraft itself.

She went down the steps on to the pavement and started heading towards the RAF Club in Piccadilly when, almost immediately, she felt a tap on her arm. It was Rupert Carstairs, one of the deputy directors of GCHQ, who she knew to be a high flier and very young for his position. She had formed a very close relationship with him when she was working there, even though she was very junior and at least ten year younger than he was.

"Mary, what a surprise. What are you doing here?" He paused. "You look as if you're heading for the RAF Club?" He looked at his watch. "Have you got time for a drink?"

She looked at him, immaculately dressed as usual in a grey suit, pink tie and diamond tiepin; she could even detect the perfume he used which she wasn't likely to forget. She had planned to meet her current itinerant roommate Andrew at the Club after the lecture but he had sent her a message saying he would be late and was going straight back to her apartment. However, as she had to return to the Club anyway to collect her coat she nodded her assent to Rupert's suggestion. "It'll have to be a quick one as I've got to get home."

They walked across Old Park Lane, into the Club and then up to the Cowdray Room which was almost empty except for a couple near the bar. She chose two chairs at the far end of the room and Rupert arrived with gin and tonics.

"Mary, what were you doing in the Aeronautical Society?"

"Oh, there was a lecture I needed to go to on that Malaysian aircraft that disappeared. It didn't help very much in solving the problem. Goodness knows what really happened. I'm not convinced it was a terrorist plot or that one of the pilots deliberately flew the whole plane, passengers and all into the next world."

"Yes, we looked at that disappearance and came to the conclusion it was probably an aircraft malfunction like the oxygen storage compartment blowing up. We didn't believe, for example, that the Captain would somehow kill the First Officer and then asphyxiate the crew and passengers. What did your lecturer say?"

"He was just explaining how Intelsat had recently reworked out yet again the path of the aircraft and revised where the fuselage of the aircraft must be resting but I believe there is now some doubt on the whole concept. Anyway enough of that, what were you doing in Hamilton Place?"

"I was making my way to the Underground."

She smiled her disbelief. "Are the taxis on strike again or is the GCHQ budget really hurting?"

"It was theatre time and they were full."

"Well what are you up to or can't you tell me?"

"Of course I can tell you as you are effectively still on our payroll. Anyway, you can guess. Three things Middle East, Middle East and Middle East."

"Must be very difficult to keep track of what is going on with all these new frequency hopping phones and commercial satellite systems."

"They still use the internet."

Even though she had left GCHQ she couldn't help herself keeping very interested in the place and what they were doing. "Not for local work, surely? Instant messaging for controlling people, weapons and the like needs to be a stand-alone system?"

"Yes, you're right there. For local work we must be able to read the terrorist traffic and read it quickly. It is very difficult. Luckily the earlier networks were all setup by European or American companies so we still get the info."

"Won't the local companies find any leaks that go back to you?"

"Maybe, but we've made back-up arrangements. We'll be OK more or less for a year or so. It's the new ones that are really troubling us."

"Well you had better be careful there are no Wikileaks."

"Yes, that's always a worry but everybody knows these days that all Governments are listening to everything they think might be important including other government traffic friend or foe, anything in fact that they think might be useful. What we don't want to lose is the key people who help us decode the communications." He looked at her. "Are you sure you wouldn't like to come back to GCHQ? There would be no problem about getting you a job."

Mary smiled slightly. "Well you had better not arrange it or it will confirm everyone's suspicions."

"Do I take that as a yes?"

"Certainly not, I was just pointing out a little local difficulty." She thought for a moment. "Thanks for the offer but I'm very happy with what I'm doing in my present job and learning a lot."

"I bet the manufacturers are very careful talking to you if they are trying to hide something."

She grinned. "I think they do know that I am very inquisitive."

They talked for a few minutes about her job and then Mary looked at her watch. "I must go in a moment. My roommate will be back soon."

"Hasn't he got a key?"

Mary looked at him thoughtfully and kicked herself for not guessing straightaway. "So it wasn't a coincidence our meeting was it?" She didn't wait for his reply. "You were waiting in the Society until we started coming out. You wanted to talk about Andrew and what he does?"

Rupert didn't bother to answer her questions. "Do you know what he does?"

"Of course I know what he does and so does everyone else. He works with WorldLink 's subsidiary Camfen. Why didn't you send your minions out to quiz me? Better still why don't you ask Andrew?" She got up to go and Rupert tried to persuade her to sit down again. "Rupert, I really must be off and, in case you hadn't noticed it, I'm not keen on the way you tackled your problem. If you've got some special difficulty with what he is doing and the way he is doing it you'd better ask him? I know very well, as you kindly pointed out, that I'm still subject to the Official Secrets Act but that doesn't mean that I have to answer all your questions."

"We could deport him."

"Now don't be ridiculous and try to threaten me. Go ahead if you want to. I'll join the NTSB if they'll have me. All you are actually doing is to make me wonder what he is doing that he hasn't told me. Anyway you know perfectly well you've got no reason to cancel his visa. Your real problem is that you don't like United States firms purchasing high tech firms in the UK which have security issues. Look, I'm not unreasonable. I understand you are worried about where that leaves GHCQ with private communication satellite systems. I take it you can't order Camfen to give you their coding information because it is now an American firm and so at the moment you can't read the messages."

Mary leant forward and gave him a kiss on the cheek which stopped him in his tracks and then she dashed off, picked up her winter coat, walked to Green Park underground station and caught the tube to South Kensington.

Andrew was already back, had put the heating on and had changed into a short sleeved shirt and slacks. They embraced and she decided to shower and change into some sexy panties, a brief pullover, short shorts and not bother with a bra. She went back into the apartment's living room where Andrew had poured two gin and tonics. She picked one up and sat down next to him. "I'm definitely not sure I ought to have another one."

She recounted her meeting with Rupert and Andrew listened carefully. "My love, what did you tell him?"

"Nothing, of course. Not that I really understand what's so special about your system and I'm not sure I want to know. Surely it's just another communication satellite system. However, the fact that Rupert took the trouble to contact me himself shows that the company you're working with must have some very special technology and your system is upsetting GCHQ."

"You know my position is very difficult here. My firm bought Camfen Satellites for a lot of money and they are technically responsible for the operation of our satellite system. Naturally we have asked Camfen to make sure that the messages can't be read by third parties and this has raised security issues with both our Governments."

Mary sipped the drink he had got, which luckily was not too strong. She and Andrew had hit it off from the moment they met. He was a native of New York and at the time had been working for Google but a rapidly rising competitor, WorldLink Inc based in Seattle, had persuaded him to join them. He was shuttling backwards and forwards from Seattle to London to monitor Camfen Satellites near Cambridge but it wasn't long after meeting Mary that they decided that he might as well stay in her apartment instead of staying in Cambridge when he was in UK; he travelled each day by train and took a taxi to Camfen. They both knew that their different nationalities might cause problems if they stayed together, particularly as she had been working in GCHQ with a high security rating. However they had decided to go for it and if they wanted to live together full time then they were sure they could work something out.

She mused over her meeting with Rupert. "I think GCHQ are finding it harder and harder to track terrorists and criminals as the technology keeps on introducing new systems, hardware and software. It's obviously very important for both our countries to be able to track all the terrorists and criminals but firms like yours don't help by having your own private networks and security."

"I don't know about the UK but we have to cooperate with the National Security Agency."

"But that makes GCHQ even more uncomfortable to think that NSA will know what's happening and they don't." She moved slightly away from Andrew. "If you think stroking my thighs like that is going to change the subject," she paused "you're probably right but sometime fairly soon we do need to decide where we're going, apart from bed that is."

***

Mary looked at her watch. Andrew had left very early to catch his train and she had a little time before she need leave to go to her office at the back of the airfield at Farnborough. She went to her desk and found the Aviation Week article she was looking for which discussed potential satellite communication providers; WorldLink was mentioned since it was already a global internet provider with its own satellite constellation. It was pointed out that the system WorldLink provided was different from Google's potential one as its system was designed by an offshore subsidiary company based in the UK near Cambridge which was responsible for the technology.

She tucked Av Week in her bag, went down to the garage and set course in her car to Farnborough. As usual she had to decide the best way to get to the M3 by looking at the traffic on her navigator and decided that at the moment the best bet seemed to be via the M4 and M25. As she approached Heathrow her telephone came to life.

"Mary, are you on your way?

"Jerry, of course. You're up early."

"Good. I've been up all night. You won't be going home to-night. How does Canberra appeal to you? See you shortly."

She turned on Radio 5 and heard a discussion trying to second guess why an Independant Transport Aircraft Company 990 operated by Royal World Airways had disappeared in the middle of the night after three hours out of Singapore on its way to Adelaide. It was difficult to separate the facts from the conjectures so she switched it off; she knew she would hear all the details soon enough.

She swung the car in to the car park, found a space and went up to her office she shared with Tom Wiseman. "Mary, have you heard?"

"Only that I'm off to Canberra but not much else."

"Well you've drawn the short straw. I'm off with Jerry to go to Singapore this evening. Your flight is 1400 from Terminal 5. Jerry's with the boss getting briefed. Apparently RW845 en route to Sydney just disappeared off the screen between Java and Australia."

"Not another Malaysian 370 or QZ8501?"

"Afraid so. Looks like once again that there will be complete loss of life with no survivors; there was a total of 254 passengers and 11 crew on board. However unlike the other two losses we're bound to find the answer. The aircraft was in touch with Air Traffic all the time and it had the very latest dual flight data recorder pack so that one of the recorders should have been ejected when it hit the water and be floating, transmitting its emergency signal. That's assuming of course that the aircraft hit the water south of Java. We'll know a bit more when Jerry comes back."

Mary sat down at her desk and switched on her computer. This would be her first trip without another accident investigator with her as she had only been with the AAIB for a few months. The organisation was meant to be being reorganised to be like the NTSB in the States with Aviation, Maritime and Railway safety all being rolled into one setup; she thought that the reorganisation was a good idea as it didn't make sense with current technology, and with such a high record of travelling safety, to have completely separate accident investigation branches with inevitable duplication of high tech facilities; however in spite of a new supremo being appointed it seemed to be taking a long time to happen.

It was Summer in Australia but the bag which she always carried in the back of her car enabled her to go anywhere at an instant's notice as it had all the clothes and accessories she would need for a few days. She wasn't sure what she would be doing there but knew Jerry would tell her. She looked at her watch and hoped he wouldn't be long but meantime she sent a message to Andrew breaking the news.

Jerry arrived holding print-outs in his hand and beckoned her and Tom into his office.

"It is a complete mystery at the moment. The aircraft, an ITAC 990 Royal World Airways Flight Number RW845, was flying from Singapore to Adelaide and its satellite secondary radar blip on the screen, ADS-C, apparently just disappeared. Everything was going normally up to then; the aircraft went from the Indonesian Flight Information Region, FIR, Ujung Pangdang to the Brisbane FIR at about 12°S 118°E. Brisbane Air Traffic Control had called the aircraft and passed the Adelaide weather, which wasn't too good, the moment the ADS-C icon was in their FIR. The position of the final ADS-C transmission was at approximately 13°30'S 119°30'E about 250 nautical miles off the Australian coast near Broome. What is so puzzling was that there were no unusual crew transmissions before the ADS-C icon disappeared.

"Because the accident occurred in Australian controlled airspace the Australian Transport Safety Bureau, ATSB, will be leading the accident investigation. As it's a UK registered aircraft ATSB have invited us to go to Canberra together with ITAC who manufactured the plane and Rolls Royce who supplied the engines. I'm going to Singapore with Tom because in this case the cargo is clearly the vital issue. It looks like there must have been an explosion, maybe a bomb. Royal

World Airways said there were no unusual system transmissions from the ACARS satellite communication system[1] which suggests that the aircraft had no system problems."

Mary thought for a moment. "Who's looking for the aircraft?"

"You should know." She had been a maritime Radar Navigator in the Royal Air Force and had had to submit her CV with her RAF career to AAIB when she had applied for her job.[2] "The RAAF are sending a Boeing P8 from Edinburgh Field, near Adelaide and also an Australian Defence Vehicle *Ocean Shield* which luckily happens to be at Garden Island south of Freemantle; it is able to leave almost straightaway for the crash location but it will still take several days to get there so, in addition as a temporary measure, a high speed Naval Patrol Boat will be going from Darwin. As I said the RW845 had the latest flight data recorders so, if they didn't manage to ditch and the fuselage sank, the rear recorder should be floating and transmitting. The P8 will obviously get there at least twenty four hours before the first boat but it will have to refuel at Broome before setting course."

Tom joined in. "Do we know what freight was on board?"

Jerry waved some of the papers. "Yes, or rather we know what should have been on board. RWA has sent us a load sheet from Singapore with a detailed analysis. We're having a look right now at any suspect items, like batteries. Of course ATSB are sending a couple of people there as well." He looked at Mary. "You'd better get organised to catch your flight."

Mary hesitated before she got up. "Aren't we checking at Heathrow?"

---

[1] ACARS sends aircraft system and flight operational reports to Airline via satellite if necessary
[2] See *Dire Strait* by same author

"Of course we are but we think it's more likely that the bomb or dangerous cargo will have been loaded at Singapore. If it had been loaded at Heathrow the chances are RW845 would have been lost before it reached Singapore, though of course nothing is certain."

Mary left the office and back at her desk she saw that the travel department had left her the eTickets for the journey; to her surprise she was going out business class but premium economy on the way home, presumably because that way she could get some sleep on the aircraft and start work straight away on arrival. They had also booked her in to the Novotel which she knew was right opposite the ATSB.

She sent a message to Peter Talbert, an insurance accident investigator who she had met a year or so earlier when she was a navigator in the RAF, telling him of her arrival; he worked in Canberra with his wife Charlie, a director at the National Gallery and who was Andrew's elder sister.

She put her laptop into her travelling bag and left her desktop computer primed with a utility so if necessary when she was overseas she could switch it on and operate it to collect data. She decided to get a taxi to Terminal 5 at Heathrow and leave her car in the AAIB car park. She finished arranging her bags and was finally ready to go. She noticed Andrew had acknowledged her earlier signal on her iPhone.

'Hope you sort it out quickly, darling. By the way, we've got a facility near Canberra. Would you like to see it?'

Chapter 2

We watched Mary French drive off to look at the WorldLink communication satellite facility; we had met a year or so ago after Mary had been shot down in an RAF P8 maritime reconnaissance aircraft in the Torres Strait.[3] We had got to know her very well and it was obviously very convenient for Mary to be able to stay with us in Canberra where both my wife and I worked so when she told me she was coming out to Canberra Charlie suggested that Mary could stay with us. She was a very attractive lady and I was very careful not let my appreciation of her finer points show in front of Charlie.

"Charlie, I don't know why she is so keen to go there. There's not very much to see."

"Andrew suggested it since she was going to be so close. Anyway how do you know? You've only been to the Deep Space Centre Visitors' Centre and never done the proper tour. She's a very bright girl as you are well aware and she probably has to report her visit to GCHQ."

"I wonder." I thought for a moment. "You know Mrs Talbert you may be right even though she doesn't work for them any more though I'm surprised she has got time to go sightseeing. She's meant to be working with the Australian investigators on the disappearance of that airliner south of Indonesia?"

"That's why she's going to-day. She told me they are waiting for the recorder to arrive from Broome so that it can be analysed by the Australian Transport Safety Board." Charlie looked at me carefully. "Why aren't you people doing it? It's a British aircraft that's disappeared."

---

[3] *Dire Strait* by the same author

I smiled at her turn of phrase. We had been married for seven years but she was still very much an American. We had been in Australia for two years where she was working as the Procurement Director of the National Gallery while I carried on my business as an aviation insurance investigator.

"It happened in Australian airspace, my dear, so the ATSB are in charge. Just as well really as we've just heard there were forty five Australians on board including a South Australian cricket team not to mention Americans, Brits, Qataris, Dutch, French, German, Russians to name just a few. Of course the UK investigators and the aircraft manufacturers are all helping."

"How come you're not involved? Mike Mansell always gets you to help."

Mike was an old friend who had started me off as an investigator. He had moved to Sydney from the UK to start what proved to be a flourishing aviation insurance business after he had married Liz, the Australian girl who had helped me win my first insurance case and who was now a first class dress designer.[4]

"Mike wasn't insuring the aircraft and I haven't been asked."

"What do you think happened?"

"I know no more than you do. You heard what Mary said last night. The aircraft took off from Singapore and after three hours with Indonesia behind them they established contact with Australian Air Traffic. Suddenly the ADS-C mark on the screen disappeared and all contact was lost. It sounds like a bomb or dangerous cargo; however a bomb is more likely as there would have been some warning with cargo, you know a smoke detector or fire warning which the pilots would have

---

[4] *Blind Landing* by the same author

communicated to Air Traffic and would have automatically been transmitted by ACARS and satellite to the airline."

"I don't know but I'll take your word for it. It sounds terrible. Is it going to be like that poor Malaysian aircraft that was never found?"

"Don't think so. The aircraft will be found this time because it has the latest crash recorders and one will be ejected and float. With any luck the water won't be too deep so it should be possible to get the other recorder and see the wreckage."

"Peter, I think it will be a bomb."

"Is that female intuition?"

"No, of course not but we've all been helping in the Middle East which makes us very unpopular with the Jihadis."

"You could well be right. I'm sure that is what ATSB and our Air Accident Investigation Branch will be trying to find out." I looked at my watch. "Time we were both at work. I'll drop you off if you like."

I worked all morning in my office in Marcus Clarke Street. I had various jobs advising airlines, unions and insurance companies on operational procedures and commenting on accident investigations from an insurance angle. In addition I had to prepare for some conferences where I had agreed to give talks. I took some time-off to look at *The Australian*; it had been printed just after Royal World Airlines had given some details of the passengers and there was a lot of discussion on the cricket team and the effect it would make to the league. The only other news seemed to be the Middle East and the continual bombing by aircraft and UAVs.

After a couple of hours my phone rang. "Jeremy Prentice here, you remember, Al Jazeera, QATAR."

"Jeremy I remember very well. All that nonsense of Al Qaeda claiming they had shot a P8 down.[5]"

"Well how about doing a job for us?"

"I'm an accident investigator, not a reporter."

"Well we haven't got a reporter we can trust with technical matters in Australia and we are very interested in this latest loss of RW845. There were twenty important Qataris on board. How about you keeping us up to speed on the investigation?"

"I'm not sure I should accept your request. I normally only work for insurance companies or airlines."

"Are you committed with this accident? Has anyone given you a contract?"

"Jeremy, as it happens I'm not committed but I'm expensive."

"We'll pay you fifty per cent above your normal charge. We trust you not to rip us off."

I hesitated. "Jeremy, let me think about that for an hour or so. Give me your number and I'll call you back."

"+974 3 4672 8933"

I put the phone down and considered the situation. Then I phoned Charlie and told her. She had no hesitation. "Half as much again above your normal miserable fee. Grab it."

"But it doesn't feel right."

"Look Peter, you've seen these so called experts being interviewed on TV. This time there will be a real expert."

"But I'm not sure I want to be on TV all the time."

"Nonsense. It will be good for our financial situation and the children's education fees."

"Yes, dear!"

---

[5] *Dire Strait* by same author

I put the phone down and rang Jeremy. "Jeremy. OK you're on but I will need a letter of authorisation and a journalist's pass."

"Of course. We will email you a contract and the other stuff and also post the paper work for those that don't like computer print outs. Can you send us the current situation as you see it? I suppose one possibility is that someone put a bomb on board."

I was still mulling over what I had just committed myself to when my phone rang and I saw it was Mary. She sounded desperate. "Peter, the WorldLink facility has just been virtually destroyed with a bomb."

I hesitated not knowing what to say and hardly believing what I was hearing. "Are you alright? Can I help?"

"Could you collect me or organise a taxi? Apparently my car has completely disappeared."

"I'll come straightaway."

I sent a message to Charlie and drove as fast as I could to the WorldLink facility. Two ambulances went by me the other way. As I approached I could see fire engines and police cars everywhere plus some other cars which looked as if they had come from the media. I was stopped by a policeman who said I couldn't go any further and so I explained why I had arrived. He got his telephone out and spoke to someone. "Well Sir, the lady you mention is being taken back to Canberra for questioning."

"Well I need to talk to her now." The policeman didn't seem very co-operative. "Tell your superior I'm not moving from here until I've spoken to her."

The policeman made another phone call. "There will be a policewoman coming here to take you to the lady."

I could see her approaching and went to meet her and was invited to go into one of the police cars. However to my surprise I found myself being interrogated by what looked like a senior policeman. "Now Sir, what brings you here so quickly?"

I gave him my card. "Ms French is staying with us and is a UK Government Aviation Accident Investigator. She told me about the explosion and as she no longer has a car I came to take her back to Canberra."

"Well we need to question Ms French first back in Canberra."

"When and where are you going to do that? She must be very shaken."

"We're going to our Headquarters in Belconnen very shortly."

"I'd like to talk to her for a few moments."

He hesitated for a few moments and then nodded and led me to another car where Mary was sitting looking a bit quiet; she brightened up enormously when she saw me. I went in and sat next to her in the back seat and the policeman sat in the driver's seat so he could listen to our conversation

"Peter, they're holding me here like a suspect as if I blew the place up. They think I had the explosives in the boot of the car. Apparently someone's been killed and another person seriously wounded."

I paused and considered the situation. "Maybe someone did put the explosives in your car. It was outside in the street all night."

She nodded. "Yes I suppose so but I might have been killed."

"I don't suppose that would have worried the person who put the bomb in the car."

"But why?"

"That's what everyone will want to know. Look, I'll come to Belconnen and rescue you the moment they've finished questioning you."

"They've taken my phone. You will have to phone them."

"Don't worry I'll keep in touch. If you need a solicitor get them to phone me. They have my card."

Mary look horrified. "Why would I need a solicitor? I've done nothing."

"It's not what you've done, it's what the police think you might have done. I'm sorry I mentioned it."

The police officer made it clear that it was time to move on. He gave me his card with his name, Commander William Martin, and telephone number so I could find out what was happening at Belconnen.

I drove home feeling very worried for Mary. My guess was that the explosives were in the back of her car or attached underneath and I could see the police arguing that she might have set a time delay when they went off to lunch. I drove back to the office and called Charlie bringing her up to date.

"But that's terrible Peter. Why would anyone want to blow up the satellite station?"

"Charlie, you've put your finger on the nub of the matter. Why would anyone want to blow it up? However we do have a starting point."

"Peter, this is not our problem. You are talking as if this thing is aircraft accident."

"My love, we've got to look after the girl or there could be a real miscarriage of justice. Andrew is your brother, think of what he would say if we did nothing. They are probably going to get married."

She made a grudging noise. "You're soft on that girl and I think she fancies you. When am I going to see you?"

"I'll go to Belconnen at about five if I haven't managed to rescue her before."

***

I left the office at half past four and drove to the Federal Police Headquarters at Belconnen and asked for Commander Martin. The lady at the desk made some enquiries on the phone and said he would be about fifteen minutes. I sat down and after about ten minutes he appeared and asked me to come up to his office.

"Mr Talbert, sorry to have kept you waiting. I've looked you up on the net so I won't bother to ask you any more introductory questions. I'm sure you appreciate we have a very serious situation here and there can be little doubt that the explosives were put somewhere on Miss French's car. Tell me. Did Ms French stay with you last night and where was the car?"

"Yes she did. The car was parked outside off the road in front of our garage. Surely you don't suspect her of getting the explosives and putting it in her car?"

"Mr Talbert, it's not quite as simple as that. We have to decide what was the motive for destroying the facility."

"If she did it she must have been a very fast worker. She only landed a few days ago and she has been staying with us all the time. During the day she has been working at the ATSB. Between them and us I'm sure we can account for every minute since she has been here. She could hardly have had time to buy some explosives and put them in the car."

"Again Mr Talbert, not as simple as that. She may have known that the explosives were on her car. She could have initiated the explosion before she left the car."

I thought about what he was saying and wondered what motive Martin thought she might have. "Well can I take her back with me or have you charged her."

"Yes, Mr Talbert she can leave here. However, we have taken her passport while we consider the situation. She must phone us every morning before 10am."

"I take it she did not ask for a solicitor? She would have rung me."

"No, she did not."

"You are aware this is not her first visit to Australia?"

"Yes, Mr Talbert. We have not been sitting on our hands. We know she was a celebrity last time she was here having been shot down by a Russian submarine.[6]"

"Well you know then she would be the last person to blow up the facility."

Martin made no comment but picked up the phone. Almost immediately a plain clothed woman appeared with Mary who rushed over and embraced me. She was going to start explaining what had happened but I held up my hand. "Come on, my love. Let's get you out of here. Have you got everything?"

"Yes, thank you. I've got my phone back but they've got my passport." She turned to Martin and in a moment her face changed from friendly to stern and efficient. "I need a receipt please for the passport, please." Martin started writing but Mary chipped in. "An official one please with the passport number clearly identified."

He looked at her, hesitated, but decided to say nothing. He pressed a buzzer and a policeman appeared with Mary's passport and a pad of forms. He copied the information to the form and then signed and stamped the form. He permitted himself to smile. "Will this do?"

---

[6] ***Dire Straight*** by same author

Mary looked at it and nodded. I thanked Commander Martin and we went down to the car. She got her phone out as we were driving away. "Oh Lord, Andrew has heard already." She started writing a message.

"Mary, call him first and let him know you're alright."

"He'll be asleep."

"I doubt it, if he is still in UK. He'll be talking to WorldLink on the West Coast."

She tried calling Andrew but apparently he was engaged so she started messaging again which couldn't have been easy with the car swaying from side to side.

"Peter, that's all I can do for the moment. Now I must let the ATSB know I'm alright. I told Mark Coburn, one of their inspectors, where I was going to-day and he is bound to have heard as I expect by now the media will be telling the world what has happened."

I heard her talking to an operator as clearly Mark was out. She shrugged and then started writing another message which I guessed was to Mark. After that she didn't say a word until we reached our home at Kingston by Lake Burley Griffin. Charlie greeted us and gave Mary a long hug. "Come on my love, sit down and have a drink before we eat"

"Water for me, thank you. May I use your phone? I need to sort out my car with Hertz and tell them the bad news."

We heard her telling the amazed lady at the other end that there wasn't a car any more. Hertz clearly needed some paperwork filling in and after a further discussion it was agreed that they would deliver a replacement car the following morning.

Mary started to tell us about what had happened. "I just couldn't believe it when the police started to think I was responsible. I got furious with them. I know the explosives could well have been put on my car somewhere but why would they think I would do it?"

I looked at her. "Not sure, but you are an obvious suspect. Did you notice that he said you had been shot down by a Russian submarine? I don't think that has ever been announced though there has been a lot of conjecture. He has obviously been talking to someone in ASIO. Just as well they didn't know you were employed by GCHQ as that might have complicated matters. They would have kept you in for sure for more questioning. Let's hope they don't talk to Dominic Brown of RAAF Security as he must be well aware from last time that you were not a 'run-of-the mill' RAF radar navigator."

She looked at me and smiled. "So? You're not suggesting that GCHQ would want to blow up the WorldLink system? Anyway we have a security arrangement between our two countries."

"You know security organisations never trust each other whatever they may say."

"Maybe, but they don't do indiscriminate killing. Martin told me that one of the engineers was killed and another was badly hurt." I nodded. "Can we see what the media are saying?"

Charlie switched on the TV and selected ABC News. Understandably the explosion was top news. As Mary had said an engineer had been killed and another was in a serious but stable condition. Apparently the Deep Space Centre facilities were not damaged as they were out of range of the explosion. The experts being interviewed were speculating on why the satellite station had been bombed. I never liked this type of interview as it was always pure guesswork before the facts were known but this time I did listen because I too wanted to know why the place might have been targeted. I didn't believe that GCHQ would have done it however much they disliked the WorldLink network for not being able to decrypt the transmission. After about ten minutes Charlie switched it off and made us sit at the table to have a meal. "Mary, did you have anything to eat at all?"

"Well we had a couple of bites before the explosion. I thought I would never eat again but this looks really good."

We ate in silence for a bit and then Charlie asked the question I wanted to ask. "Mary, how is Andrew?"

"He was fine when I left. He stays with me as you know when he comes to England which is pretty frequently. He's heard the news. I tried phoning him in the car but I couldn't get through so I sent him a message."

"Just as well or he would be very worried. Have you had a reply?"

She took her phone out and had a look and suddenly looked very pleased. "Yes. Would you believe it? He is being sent out here to have a look and talk to Derek who runs the place."

"That's great. He can stay here with you of course, if that's OK by you."

She smiled. "That definitely won't be a problem. Thanks, Charlie."

"Mary, how is the accident investigation going? Did ATSB know you were going to the facility to-day? Have you told them that you are alright?"

"Yes. As Peter knows I've sent a message to the guy I'm working with. The moment I get a car I'll go back there. With any luck they should be well on analysing the crash recorder."

"How come they have got it so quickly?"

"Well the RAAF P8 heard and located the flight data recorder that was detached and floated. The patrol boat picked it up and the moment it was within helicopter range of Broome it was taken there and then flown to Canberra.

Incidentally," she turned to me, "the P8 dropped a sonobuoy and heard the submerged flight recorder but the patrol boat couldn't hear it when it arrived twenty four hours later. Unfortunately it had it to go back before the Australian Naval vessel *Ocean Shield* from Garden Island could arrive. Luckily it is not too serious as the exact position of the wreckage is known."

Charlie carried on. "Well the sooner you get back to ATSB the better. By the way it must be a terrible place to park. I've been meaning to ask you. Where on earth do you park? You can't park in Northbourne Avenue."

"They have some spaces close-by in one of the apartment blocks."

I butted in. "What are you going to tell them?"

"About what? The explosion? What is there to tell? They will know as much as I do."

"May not be as straightforward as that. The media will be chasing the police to find out how the bombs got into the compound and they may decide to release your name. If you take my advice...."

Mary chipped in, grinning "Always."

"If you take my advice I think you should talk to Stephen Wentworth, you know the head security guy in the High Commission."

The phone rang and Charlie answered it. As she gave it to me she murmured "I told you this place was bugged. It's Stephen."

"Peter, have you got Mary French there? I gather the police are considering accusing her of bombing the WorldLink satellite centre."

"Why would they think she did it?"

"Maybe they've found out she was employed by GCHQ. I imagine that WorldLink 's system is not GCHQ's favourite, not that I know anything. Anyway we must talk later, same financial arrangements as last time. Let me talk to Mary."

"She's having a meal. Here she is."

I handed Mary the phone and Charlie and I couldn't help hearing her side of the conversation. Stephen was clearly arranging for her to go to the Embassy as soon as she could the following day and wasn't expecting an immediate debrief over the phone. She put the phone down and looked at me, forcing a smile. "You haven't changed. What excellent timing. Did you fix it?"

"Certainly not. It was bound to happen with your connections. The police found out about your previous time here and clearly had spoken to someone in ASIO. Goodness knows what conversations have been taking place with GCHQ and ASIO. Your name must be top of the pops. Presumably someone at GCHQ rang Stephen."

"Well it is all a bloody pain as far as I'm concerned. I'm trying to do a job of work and then this happens."

I suddenly remembered Jeremy. "Mary, there may be a problem. All that stuff about the recorders --- is it general knowledge?" I explained about my job with Al Jazeera. "You shouldn't tell me information that is not in the public domain or you'll get us both into trouble."

"Well I'll certainly tell you if there is stuff you shouldn't know," she grinned, "if that makes sense."

We finished our meal and Mary excused herself and went off to bed. Charlie looked at me. "Peter, there's something spooky about those waters south of Java. It's like the Bermudan Triangle. What do you think happened this time?"

"You told me not to get involved." She shrugged as if it was inevitable. "Obviously I will try to help if asked but as you pointed out it is not my scene. With regard to the destruction of the WorldLink facility, I'd love to be able to hear all the

Java Waters Run Deep

discussions between ASIO and GCHQ, not to mention the Federal Police and who knows, the politicians may get sucked in."

"I don't see why. Let's go to bed but don't get any ideas. It was fish not lobster we ate and I might get a headache."

***

In the morning Charlie and I left leaving Mary waiting for her car. Stephen Wentworth called at about ten o'clock and I went over to the High Commission.

"Peter, this thing is getting very serious. The Americans as well as the Australians are wondering whether GCHQ was involved. They think that GCHQ was so worried about not being able to hear the phone calls they decided to try and silence the system."

"Ridiculous. They would never kill people. Anyway is the WorldLink system actually down as a result of the bomb?"

"Very good question. No it isn't. As I understand it, the system is just short of coverage and less reliable."

"How do you know?"

Stephen smiled. "I have my contacts as well as you."

"Well I'm surprised they didn't tell you that if GCHQ had really wanted to silence the system in the Middle East they would have gone for a different satellite ground system in Europe or wherever it is. I'm assuming that the main control is in the States somewhere."

"You're right. That's what they did tell me though they said it would have been a lot harder to damage the other one."

"Stephen, I'll take your word for it. But coming back to Australia, who could have loaded the bomb on to Mary's car and when? And how did whoever did it know she was going to the WorldLink site? Maybe the bomb wasn't on her car."

"From what I've heard it definitely was. The car was blown apart. But you're right; assuming Mary wasn't involved who could have known?"

"What are the police going to do about Mary assuming they've now spoken to ASIO?"

"Don't know. Had the police known about her connection with GCHQ they would probably have kept her in Belconnen."

"I think your friend Dominic will probably have guessed there was more about Mary that meets the eye."

He smiled. "Well there's no doubt about that. When she wants to be she's very easy on the eye. Whether Dominic worked out she had a special clearance I don't know."

We talked some more and then I went back to my office. I found it very difficult to concentrate on my work as I kept trying to answer the questions that Stephen and I had discussed. And there was no doubt about what Stephen said, Mary definitely could be very attractive sexually; she was well endowed and I noticed that Charlie always watched me particularly carefully when she was about.

Chapter 3

Hertz arrived at the Talbert's house at ten o'clock. Mary filled in all the details and then signed for the replacement car. Another Hertz car arrived to take the delivery driver away and she then set the house alarm and drove to ATSB, parking the car beneath the designated apartment block in one of the allocated spaces. At the ATSB she showed her temporary pass and went up to Mark Coburn's office on the second floor; he was there at his desk and she went over to the other one in the room.

"Mary, great to see you. I was very worried when we heard the news on the radio and you didn't answer your telephone or messages. Very relieved when your message eventually arrived. Where were you when it happened?"

"We were having lunch at the Tidbinbilla Visitors Centre. Somehow I knew when I heard the explosion that it was at the WorldLink facility and we rushed back."

"I gather the bombs were probably on your car? You were lucky not to be killed."

"How do you know that?"

"It's just been announced on the radio."

"Did they say any more about me?"

"They mentioned your name and that you had been released after questioning."

Mary tried to put this unwelcome information to the back of her mind but realised she had better be prepared. "Can you tell the receptionists that I'm not in the building? If you get a direct line call can you do the same thing?"

"Of course. I'll talk to the guy who controls them."

Mark picked up the phone and soon sorted things out. Mary felt relieved and tried to concentrate. "Has the crash recorder arrived?"

"Yes indeed. They started working on it yesterday afternoon and were here until 2300 hours last night. They are still sorting out all the data but the cockpit voice recordings have all been transferred safely."

"Have you heard it yet?"

"Yes. It was amazing. A loud bang and nothing else."

"What about timing?"

"The recording stopped at the same time as the ADS-C return disappeared off the screen."

Mary felt horrified. "But that's terrible. How awful. What parameters are we looking at to find out what happened?"

"They are looking at everything."

"How are your people in Singapore getting on?

"It's a long job checking all the baggage. Your Jerry Masterson and Tom Wiseman are there as well as you know which should help."

"When I left they told me that the Heathrow end was being checked?"

"Absolutely correct. Checks are being carried out there as well."

"When will the print out be available from the recorder?"

"Later on to-day. They are not sure when. The main problem we have at the moment is that the media are giving us a hard time over the rescuing the bodies and in particular identifying the Australians. It's a very big task for us but we've liaised with Interpol and the UK are sending over a DVI[7] team to help as there were 136 UK citizens out of the 254 souls on board including crew. We've arranged with the airline to build two hangars in Broome to accommodate all the bodies. Speed is vital for quick identification. The airline is doing a great job getting dependants to send dental records, listing any special

[7] Disaster Victim Identification

identifying features and DNA samples if they can since it is going to take a long time and be very difficult to positively identify all the bodies. There's nothing more we can do at the moment until we can get a salvage boat on the spot but that doesn't stop the criticism."

"Well if it's OK I'll go to our High Commission and sign in if I may? Call me if anything breaks."

Mary sent a message to Jerry In Singapore explaining her situation in case he had read about the bomb and then she left for the Commission. Stephen came down to collect her and they went up to his office. "Mary, Rupert Carstairs has been on the phone. As you can imagine he doesn't like the inference by ASIO that GCHQ was involved with the WorldLink bombing and he is scared it will get into the press. He's also particularly worried that the media will try to connect you with GCHQ. He raised another point; apparently WorldLink are sending a man out here to ascertain the facts and he said you know him", he paused and smiled "very well."

"Stephen that's quite right. Andrew Simpson, he stays with me when he is visiting Camfen, you know the firm that designed the WorldLink satellite operation. How else do you think I was able to look at the place?"

"I did wonder. I was beginning to suspect GCHQ had sent you there."

"Nonsense. Andrew thought I would be interested."

Mary could see that Stephen for once was surprised. "That is an amazing coincidence, Mary. I'm not sure whether this complicates or simplifies the situation."

"Nor am I, though I'm glad he's coming out. And if you want a further coincidence Andrew Simpson is Peter Talbert's wife Charlie's brother, that's how I met him." Mary couldn't help smiling at the look on Stephen's face.

"Mary, that makes him an American?"

"Well of course he is. He's employed by WorldLink. I met him in the UK when he was over with Charlie and he came to see me and Peter get our decorations at Buck House. Mind you he was employed by Google then." She stopped for a moment. ""What we need to do is to find out who put the bombs on my car, though I don't know where to start. And, as Peter Talbert said, who knew I'd be going out to the place."

"Yes, that is probably the place to start. Who did know you were going out?"

"Andrew did and of course Derek Courtfield the manager here. Nobody else that I know of." She looked at her watch. "Stephen, I'll have to go soon. How am I going to get my passport back? Can you help me?"

"I don't know yet. When does your man Andrew get in?"

"At dawn to-morrow. I'm going to meet him."

"Well I think the police will be a bit perplexed when they realise your relationship."

"You think they might give me my passport back."

"Hope so. Quite frankly the Commission doesn't like getting involved in these matters unless they have to"

"Well I'm off now. I'll keep you posted."

Mary went back to her car and handed in her pass as she went out of the double gates. Back at the ATSB she went to her desk. Mark was there and together they went to Robert Covelli's office. There was a large screen on one wall which was connected to the internet and to the local networks; standing near it was Frank White, a studious looking middle aged man and he was holding a pointer. He waited until everyone was seated which took a little time as several chairs had to be brought into the office.

"We've looked at the parameters from the recorder and as far as we can see the aircraft systems seem to have been completely normal right up to the time of the noise on the flight deck mikes. The cabin altitude then suddenly increased to 39,000ft and at that point all the parameters disappeared. However, the recorder continued to run under its own power for another six minutes and thirty seconds. It then stopped, presumably when the aircraft hit the water and the rear FDR became detached from the aircraft."

Mary could see that everyone felt as amazed as she did. Robert burst out, "What about the ACARS messages."

"There were no messages."

Mary joined in. "How about the ADS-C?"

Frank looked at her, obviously not knowing who she was but nodded, clearly appreciating the question. "Yes, we've checked with Air Traffic and the ADS-C marker disappeared at the time of the depressurisation."

Mary replied. "Have I got this correct? There was a loud bang, the aircraft depressurised and the aircraft probably hit the water six minutes and thirty seconds later? What would the aircraft be doing during that time? It wasn't dropping straight down."

"Yes, that's right or it would have hit the water earlier. It might have been spiralling round and round. Probably hit the water quite gently. We've obviously no idea what direction it was going."

There was a moment's silence and Mary asked "When do you hope to get the other recorder?"

"Not sure. The P8 heard it when it dropped a sonobuoy but the naval patrol vessel wasn't able to hear it when it launched a hydrophone for some reason we can't understand; unfortunately it couldn't stay, not that it would have been able to investigate any further. The Australian Defence Vehicle *Ocean Shield* has just arrived and is starting to look for the recorder. The water is not too deep, luckily being south of the Timor Trough. However it is bound to take a little time."

"Well it will be interesting to see if we can glean something extra from it. There may be a time difference between the two recorders." Frank nodded and Mary carried on. "Presumably the ADV *Ocean Shield* will also be able to see the fuselage and wings, and engines for that matter?"

"Not my scene."

Robert interrupted. "Mary, I think you are getting ahead of the investigation. We shall be making a very thorough examination of the aircraft as soon as we can. *Ocean Shield* has an autonomous underwater vehicle (AUV) Bluefin-21 fitted with sidescan sonar which it is using right now for a preliminary search for the wreckage. We shall begin to get some details to-morrow, I hope, but we will need a proper commercial salvage vessel to recover the FDR plus the bodies and wreckage. Unfortunately the only one we can get quickly is the *Ocean Salvager* currently in San Diego but it is going to take another week before it gets to the accident spot. The UK firm *Oceaneering* is providing the search and rescue system with cage and tethered ROV which luckily is already on board the ship. As you know we thought that there might have been some illicit cargo with a bomb on the aircraft but clearly this now seems unlikely after listening to the flight deck recorder."

Mary looked at Robert. "Have we heard anything from Singapore?"

"Yes. They have almost finished looking at the cargo that was uploaded from there. They should have finished by lunch time to-morrow. Having your people there as well as ours has really speeded things up. London is also being checked, for what it is worth."

Mary was still searching for ideas. "Could an aircraft cleaner have put a bomb on the flight deck somewhere? The bomb wouldn't have to be very big."

"I suppose that's a real possibility. It would make the readings from the flight deck recorder understandable."

There was a general discussion for another hour or so but Mary heard nothing new. The briefing broke up and Mary drove back to the Talberts. Peter was home but Charlie was still at work. Mary put her head round the door in the room allocated as the playroom; Jill Evans, their part time Nanny, was looking after Francie while Peter junior was doing his homework; he started to move but Mary put her finger to her mouth making it clear he was to stay where he was. She suddenly felt Peter pressing against her also looking round the door.

"Peter, I don't think Charlie would like you pressing against me quite like that."

"Quite like what? I was only looking."

"If you say so. Don't get me wrong, it didn't worry me, in fact," she turned round and gave him a soft kiss and then quickly broke it off, "I rather liked it. Come on, get some drinks."

Peter returned with two glasses of white wine and they sat down on separate chairs. "Mary, how did you get on today? What did Stephen say?"

"Not a lot but the RWA accident seems really strange." Mary brought him up to speed.

"You haven't heard the recorder yet?"

"No Peter, but apparently there was just one big bang."

"It sounds unlikely but I suppose it could have been an explosion on the flight deck."

"That's what I thought. I wondered if a cleaner had left a package somewhere. Seems the most likely solution unless one of the pilots had wanted to commit suicide like the Malaysian 370," she paused and added, "but very unlikely."

"Mary, I've never been convinced on the Malaysian captain killing everybody but I suppose it's possible. Equally I don't believe a RWA pilot would blow himself up and kill everyone else on the aircraft. Glad I'm not involved except as an investigator. Far too difficult to solve."

Mary laughed. "That remark is absolute rubbish. You know perfectly well you'd just love to be in the thick of it. You're sulking because you haven't been asked."

"I'm not sulking but you could be right."

Mary suddenly looked at him. "I shouldn't have told you all that stuff. You can't use it with your Qatari friends."

"Don't worry. I'm not going to kill the goose that lays the golden eggs."

"I don't like being called a goose."

"Well believe me you're definitely not a gander."

"Talking of ganders, I'll go and meet Andrew to-morrow when he comes in at 0630."

"Won't he need a car?"

"I expect so but that won't matter. Has he stayed here before?"

"Yes, last year when he was with Google."

"Well hopefully he can find the place again as it will be difficult to leave the airport separately and meet up as I'll be in the car park. I'll remind him how to find you."

Charlie arrived looked at them both carefully, asked for a gin and tonic and went to get changed. The children arrived and Mary decided that work was over for the day.

***

Mary got up at dawn, looked at her car and decided to inspect it starting with the engine compartment. She checked the boot and then looked under the car as best she could. Seeing nothing unusual she set course for the airport and the car park. Andrew's plane arrived on time and he was soon through customs and immigration. They embraced and then Andrew went over to Avis to get his car. Having got his key and his instructions they decided, because it was still early, to have a coffee before going to the Talberts.

"Have you got your passport back? They must be mad thinking you did it."

"They've got to find someone and it is easy for them to make me the fall guy, or lady if you prefer. It certainly seems possible that the explosives were on my car somewhere though by chance Derek Courtfield had an identical car."

"You might have been killed."

"I know. I keep thinking about that. But that cuts no ice with the police as they have me initiating the explosion as we left for lunch."

"But why would they think you did it?"

"I don't know but I'm the obvious suspect. Luckily they let me go but I'm concerned they may have learnt a bit more about my previous jobs."

"But Mary, if they knew you were employed by GCHQ then that should immediately move you off the suspects' list."

"Not sure about that as GCHQ doesn't like private telecomm networks. ASIO are almost certainly aware that GCHQ can't read the WorldLink telephone messages."

"Well that's stupid. Apart from anything else, taking out our facility doesn't completely kill the telephone system anyway. Terrorists in the Middle East can still communicate. Anyway as you just guessed the NSA can read all the messages and phone calls so GCHQ doesn't have to worry."

"But Andrew, the GCHQ people don't like being dependant on NSA."

"Tough. Anyway, surely the Australian police have sorted things out by now? They should be looking for the person who put the bomb on your car."

"You're right. Anyway, it's lovely to see you but why have you come out?"

"WorldLink wanted me to talk to Derek and work out how we can rebuild the facility as quickly as possible."

"In the same place?"

"Why not? We'll make sure it can't happen again. And of course I'll have to see the police. They know I'm coming out. I'll go to our office and then see what they want."

They drank their coffee and made their way separately to the Talbert's house where Andrew was greeted with sisterly affection by Charlie.

"A fine mess you got Mary into. Lucky she wasn't killed."

"I know, I know but I'm not a clairvoyant. My first job will be to try to get her passport back. The police want to see me anyway."

"You better sit down and have breakfast or have you been travelling first class?"

"Hardly. I actually travelled Premium Economy. I need a shower more than I need food."

Mary showed Andrew their room and he opened his bag and started to unpack. She put his clothes in the wardrobe. He started to undress. She looked at him. "My love, I think it will be quicker if I don't stay. Don't make a mess." She left and joined the others including children for breakfast. Andrew didn't waste any time and soon appeared in a business suit. Mary could see he was impatient to leave.

"Andrew darling, slow down, relax and have some juice, or coffee or water. It's not going to matter if you're not at the front door when the office door is unlocked."

He sat down and Mary got him some Cranberry juice followed by some coffee. Peter junior and Francie watched them carefully as they ate their breakfast. Charlie hurried them along and packed them off to school. They then all left, Peter as usual dropping Charlie off at the National Gallery.

Mary drove to the ATSB and went up to her desk. Mark was already there. "Have you checked your email very recently? Your Jerry Masterson is flying in to-morrow as they've finished for the moment in Singapore. We were going to send two more people up there for a more rigorous check but there may not be much point now if it was a flight deck explosion."

"I agree. But Mark, if it was a bomb in the baggage hold or on the flight deck then surely the instigators would be claiming they did it?"

He nodded.

"Can I listen to the sound recordings?"

"Of course. I'll talk to Margaret Johnson who can arrange it. This accident is so strange. I'd love to know why for some strange reason the *Ocean Shield* also can't hear the other FDR with its hydrophone. However it has seen some wreckage with its *Bluefin-21*. We can't really start work until the salvage vessel arrives. Apparently the pieces of fuselage are quite large."

Margaret Johnson appeared and they went up to the room used for listening to playbacks from crash recorders. "Mary, let's listen to the Captain's speaker/headphones first and then the area flight deck mike. "

"If you want we could then listen to the first officer's side though in my opinion it just backs up the Captain and the area mike. How far back shall we start?"

"Can we start about ten minutes before recording finished?"

They put on some substantial headphones which were effective in cutting out external sound and they listened to the playback. The communications seemed normal between the pilots and the Indonesian and Brisbane FIRs until there was an enormous bang. After that there was nothing. Mary knew she was still very much a beginner in this type of accident but she felt horrified by the sudden cessation of the recording; she supposed that more experienced inspectors got used to such disasters and listening to the playbacks but she wasn't sure she ever would. She spent about an hour and a half in total in the playback room finishing by listening to the first officer's speaker/headphones.

"Margaret, thanks so much for playing all that. I expect my boss will want to go through it again when he comes in to-morrow."

"No problem. What do you think?"

"Strange that bang and then complete silence?"

"I agree. Sounds as if there was an explosion on the flight deck. Must have broken all the microphones."

"Margaret, I'm afraid a lot more besides."

Chapter 4

I was sitting in my office when Jeremy Prentice called. "Peter, ISIS has just launched a video on the net which you should look at. It claims that they put a bomb in the front of RW845 as a warning to the UK to stop interfering in the Middle East. If you go on YouTube and select ISIS and then RW845 you'll get it straightaway. Can you send us a comment as soon as possible when you've looked at it?"

"Jeremy, stand by. I'll just try and find it on my computer."

I went on to the internet. Amazingly in about thirty seconds I was looking at the latest ISIS video. "Jeremy, I've got it. I'll let you have my comments as soon as possible."

The video was not very long. An ITAC 990 in RWA livery was shown taking off and then a middle aged masked man appeared with a busy airport behind him; he was wearing a black track suit and spoke with a definite Australian accent. He said that the plane, its crews and its passengers were killed as a form of retribution for the ISIS soldiers being killed in the Middle East by the Coalition bombing. It finished by a threat saying that there would be more bombs on aircraft if the attack on the ISIS ground troops continued. I ran the video three times and then started drafting a reply to Jeremy.

'Jeremy, well produced video. Interestingly the ATSB here has not yet mentioned that there is a distinct possibility that there was a bomb on the flight deck so in some ways this gives an air of authenticity to the ISIS claim. Still maybe the media here got a whiff of the situation and ISIS heard the news.' I wrote a bit more, sent it off and then entered the time taken for doing the report into a special file on my computer and also printed the sheet out.

I tried to concentrate on my regular consultation work but I had barely settled down when Roger O'Kane of ITAC came on the line from Seattle. I had first met him some years ago in connection with a terrible accident at London Airport. He was the Independant Aircraft's chief system engineer.

"Peter, how's things? Got a job for you."

"What time is it with you?"

"9pm yesterday; I hoped you would be in your office. Are you committed on our aircraft that went into the Timor Sea?"

"Sort of. Al Jazeera asked me to keep them up to speed and write articles."

"We want you to look after our interests. We've just seen the ISIS video which claims they put a bomb on the flight deck. However we don't trust that lot and it is just possible it might be an aircraft problem."

"You've got a very good bush telegraph. It's all breaking news."

"We've got a man there helping ATSB and for that matter you seem to be well informed."

"Pure chance. I suppose I can represent you as well since I'm more of a reporter with Al Jazeera but if you've already got a man here why do you need me?"

"Our man will find the facts but you are much better at working out what actually happened."

"Thank you for that though it's not really my job. I'll need full accreditation as usual, plus contract."

"Good. That's a relief. You'll have everything by your to-morrow morning. Have you got any ideas?"

"Not yet for discussion."

"Good. From you that sounds hopeful. All the best."

I messaged Charlie to tell her the news and unusually she mentioned Tiffanys instead of a new dress from Liz Mansell in her reply which sounded ominous. I also messaged Mary who came on the phone. "Peter, that's good news. We make a good team. Can I tell anyone?"

"Not yet please. Let me call Robert in a moment when I've sorted things out.

I thought some more about working for ITAC and Al Jazeera and came to the conclusion that it shouldn't be any problem. I called Robert and explained about ITAC. Robert didn't seem to be worried. "Well Peter, you won't be getting any special confidential information so there won't be a problem. Would you like to come round and discuss things this afternoon?"

"That would be great. See you later."

I first went to meet Stephen Wentworth for a pre-planned chat over lunch at the Psychedeli on Barry.

"Stephen, what's happening in the big World? The Middle East seems as confusing as ever and the EU are still being stupid, annoying the Russians by encouraging all its immediate neighbours to join NATO."

He grinned. "I don't think you've got that latter bit quite right though I do know what you mean. Not everyone would agree with you however. But you know everything out here is not sweetness and light even if no outright killing is taking place. China is still arguing with Japan on who owns what on various islands. Then North Korea is continually firing weapons off into the Pacific and verbally attacking South Korea; it's amazing that the two countries can be so different, politically and technically. In addition to all that, all the countries out here are spending a lot of money on defence, even the small ones who can't afford it."

"Where does that leave the UK?"

"We're just watchers and thankful that we are not involved. Trade is the big UK issue out here. Since the shooting down of the P8s everything has gone very quiet, thank goodness. Don't want to go through anything like that again. "

"I'm now involved with the loss of RWA's ITAC 990 in the Timor Sea."

"That will be a bomb, won't it?"

"Not sure. It's a possibility and as you will have seen ISIS is claiming they did it. Not convinced yet. It could be an aircraft problem. It seems a rather unusual accident. I suppose that's why ITAC were looking for extra help and came to me, not that I can contribute much at the moment."

"I would have done the same in their position. You have a reputation for discovering the unexpected."

"Look, I'm not doing the accident investigation, that's the ATSB's job. I will just be trying to protect ITAC's interests."

Stephen looked at me and smiled. "Of course, whatever you say, Peter."

"Stephen, I mean that. Incidentally I haven't seen the technical intelligence summaries covering the Far East recently. Has the UK stopped producing them?"

"Certainly not. The summaries are bigger than ever. I suppose I didn't think you would still be interested. I'll put you back on the distribution list."

"You don't mean that do you? Surely you can't list me when I'm not in the Commission?"

"Your name isn't shown, just a number."

"Well your systems are nothing to do with me, thank goodness, but I do try and keep myself up to date with technology, particularly as it is advancing at such a rate. I find it helpful to know where the latest products are being made."

Stephen took a taxi back to the Commission and I walked to the ATSB on Northbourne. Robert came down and took me up to his office.

"Peter, they can't find the second recorder. It seems to have been removed if that is possible. Probably doesn't matter but we wanted to compare the two machines."

"Removed? That doesn't make sense. Where is the second FDR attached? Was it fitted?"

"Good point. We're busy checking that right now. On the face of it, not being fitted seems to be the only explanation. With regard to the actual accident, has the grapevine told you what seems to have happened?"

"Very roughly. There was a loud bang on the flight deck and after that everything stopped. Six minutes and thirty seconds later the recorder was ejected from the fuselage when it hit the water."

"Well *Ocean Shield* has just started sending us pictures of the wreckage. It has found two large pieces of the fuselage but so far not the nose section and the wings. We're waiting for *Ocean Salvager* for a more detailed inspection and for it to lift the wreckage and bring it ashore."

"What about the second FDR?

"I told you, *Ocean Shield* can't find it. As far as we can see from the pictures and talking to the Independant engineer it should have been attached to the front bit of the fuselage which we have found but it wasn't there. We need *Ocean Salvager* and its ROV to be certain."

"That sounds ridiculous."

"I agree completely. Anyway from a priority point of view we'd like to get the fuselage pieces ashore to see if we can see what might have happened and from a social point of view, we need to rescue all the bodies and try to get them identified."

"Yes, that will be absolutely vital. But tell me Robert, what messages did the airline get from ACARS?""

"None at all. Everything seemed normal."

"Well when did the ADS-C disappear?"

"Just before the big bang."

"And the plane descended fairly rapidly after the bang but making no transmissions?"

"Yes. We only know how long it took before the aircraft hit the water because the FDR had its own battery. Of course we've no idea of the path of the aircraft as it descended. It looks as if the pilots were incapacitated."

"What's your next move?"

"Inspection of the wreckage will be absolutely vital, particularly the front fuselage when we find it."

I thought about the situation. "Have you spoken to the RAAF?"

"No. Why would we do that?"

"Just in case they were operating in the area and would know something."

"I'm sure they would have told us."

We chatted a bit more and then I went back to my office. I sent a report off to Roger O'Kane in Seattle and also another non-technical summary to Jeremy Prentice in QATAR.

I thought again about Mary's request asking me to try to sort out who and why the WorldLink's facility was destroyed. I sent Andrew an email asking for Derek Courtfield's mobile and when it came I called him. "How long has WorldLink had an office in Canberra?"

"About eighteen months. I started it when it was decided to build our satellite operational facility."

"Who was the manager then? I gather you only changed to Mike Goldton quite recently."

"Yes, you're quite right. His name was John Dixon. He resigned. I think he had got a better job."

"Can you give me his contact details? I wondered if he could help or have any ideas."

"No, I'm afraid not. He just disappeared and apparently changed all his emails and telephone numbers."

I felt rather frustrated with my lack of progress on the WorldLink facility so I decided to try to find out a bit more about what happened to the ITAC990 on RW845. I rang Jake Ginsburg at the Brisbane Air Traffic Centre for an appointment and after some changes in his diary he fitted me in for the following afternoon. I tidied up and went home.

Mary was already back but only had the information which Robert had told me and had nothing new to report. She had heard about the ISIS video but hadn't seen it so I ran it quickly for her on the TV.

"Peter, do you reckon it's genuine?"

"No idea but they seem to have cottoned on to the idea of a bomb on the flight deck very quickly."

"How come? We haven't told them. I'm sure you didn't. You never tell anyone anything. You're like Poirot, you like a denouement right at the end."

"Mary, the problem is that once the recorders have been read there are a lot of people who know what's going on, in and outside the ATSB; some government employees for example. And let's face it, some people are getting retainers or sweetheart deals from the media though no-one ever talks about it. Nothing is secret once two people know about it."

Andrew arrived shortly afterwards and told us he wouldn't be going back to Seattle for a week or so. "There's not a lot more I can do here as Derek has got everything under control with the builders. However, the problem is that Derek is getting married shortly and going away on honeymoon for a couple of weeks and I can't leave until I am sure that the rebuilding is all under control."

"Talking of Derek, is he an Australian? Who recruited him?"

"I've no idea. Why do you ask? You don't suspect him, do you?"

"I like to know all the facts. Can you find out for me his background? It is just conceivable he was paid to do the job by some organisation."

Charlie butted in. "Peter, you'd suspect your own Mother!"

"Not if she had a watertight alibi. But talking of Derek," I turned to Mary, "you were incredibly lucky not to be blown up in your car. Why didn't you take your car to the restaurant?"

"Derek reckoned we hadn't finished talking and hadn't looking at everything. In fact we nearly did go in my car as Derek had left his keys in the office. I offered mine but Derek got Sophie to take her car to save him going back in."

"Who is Sophie?"

"She is WorldLink's very glamorous receptionist at the facility and the one Derek is marrying. He had a picture of her on his desk and she is well stacked, to coin a phrase."

Andrew chimed in. "That's not very ladylike, my love."

"I would have thought you'd have no problem with that but maybe you prefer big boobs." Andrew wanted to interrupt but Mary just grinned. "She didn't look too ladylike. When I first saw the picture I didn't recognise her and I was surprised to see it on his desk. She had her arms round him and, in my opinion, wasn't about to let go."

I changed the conversation and asked Andrew if he had heard from the police.

"Nothing I'm afraid. It just doesn't make sense. Apparently the explosive used is very common and is readily available."

I asked Mary what she had been doing. "Not a lot. We're waiting for *Ocean Salvager* to arrive and inspect the wreckage. I might as well go home but the police want to see me again to try to determine when the explosives were put on the car."

"Surely it must have been when you were in the ATSB?"

"It would have been a huge risk for whoever was doing it because they would have no idea how long I would be."

"I expect there would be a very strong magnet tied to the explosives so that it would have only taken a few seconds to put the packet under your car. If the guy was wearing a uniform there would have been no problem. If you had come back he would have said he was muddled on which car he had to work on. Anyway when are you planning to go and see the police?"

"To-morrow sometime."

Charlie and I went to bed before the other two. She turned to me. "Come on, my love. I know you after all these years. You've got some ideas on both the aircraft loss and the explosion. Out with it."

"Not really. I'm off to Brisbane to-morrow to talk to Air Traffic but so far I've made no progress on the explosion."

"Why can't you talk on the phone?"

"I want to see what the controllers see. It may give me some ideas."

"Alright as long as ITAC pay for your ticket."

***

Jake Ginsburg met me in the lobby of the Brisbane Centre and we went for a coffee.

"So you're involved with the loss of RW845, Peter? Any ideas what happened? Do you believe the ISIS video which claims that they blew it up?"

"It's clearly a possibility. ATSB are working very hard and will to be able to start landing pieces of wreckage when the salvage ship arrives from San Diego."

"I thought it was a bomb or dangerous cargo in the baggage compartment."

"That's what they all thought but apparently listening to the voice recorder there was a loud bang just before everything went wrong which isn't really consistent with a bomb in the hold."

"So maybe it was an ISIS bomb on the flight deck after all?"

"My view is that the ATSB can't come to any conclusion until they find the front fuselage. They have all the other bits of wreckage."

"Well I'm not sure we can help you. The record shows the ADS-C return moving steadily towards Broome and then the return just disappears. What would you like to see?"

"Can I see the play back and then maybe you can show me in real time what the air traffic looks like between Java and Broome."

We went into the playback room and Jake asked the technician controlling the records to run the actual flight. We lowered the lights slightly to get a better view on the screen. There were quite a few flights going both ways across the water all sending their ADS-C returns so that they marched steadily both ways across the screen. Jake pointed out the RW845 return. He asked the technician to freeze the plot just before RW845 disappeared. I looked at the screen and there no other returns anywhere near RW845.

"Peter, you do realise that not every aircraft on the route had ADS-C?"

"Isn't it compulsory?"

"Not yet, so there will be aircraft that will only appear on the screen as their ADS-B returns are received by the ground station at Broome; ADS-B is compulsory but of course it doesn't use satellite technology. Let's replay the last fifteen minutes."

I watch the returns near Broome and sure enough ADS-B returns were appearing and disappearing at about 200 miles from the coast depending I guessed on the aircraft altitude.

"Peter, I did some research and there were aircraft ahead and behind RW845 which did not have ADS-C and they had no problems."

"Would they be close enough to see RW845?"

"I wouldn't have thought so. Mind you it was pitch black that night with no moon so I suppose the navigation lights might have been visible forty miles ahead. ATSB have asked the same question and we have given them the flight number of the aircraft behind RW845 so that they can ask the crews."

We ran the playback frame by frame and watched as the return disappeared.

"Peter, remember the ADS-C is not transmitted continuously to the satellite so the aircraft will have been damaged after the last transmission on the screen. Shall we go and see the actual flights taking place in the area right now?"

We walked into a darkened area where the air traffic for Western Australia was being controlled. Jake took me to stand behind the controller looking at the area between Java and Broome. It was fascinating to watch the 'icons' marching across the screen and we could hear the controller handing over aircraft going north and accepting aircraft going south entering Australian airspace. The work load was highest dealing with the aircraft without ADS-C before their ADS-B returns appeared.

We stayed for about thirty minutes until I felt I had seen enough. We went back for another coffee.

"Well Peter, did you get any ideas?"

"Not really. It horrifies me that the sky between Java and Broome could be full of aircraft and you would never know."

"Peter, that's not true. Every aircraft must tell air traffic what their flight plan is."

"What about military aircraft?"

"They file flight plans like everyone else."

"Even if they are on exercises?"

"Well that's different but they are normally well below the airline traffic."

"Jake, are you sure?"

"Well you had better go and check with the RAAF what they were doing that night."

"You are right. That's exactly what I will do."

I thanked Jake and got home about 8pm. Charlie and Mary were watching the television.

"Peter, do you need feeding and have you solved everything?"

"No thank you, my love, I ate something indescribable on the plane. As for Brisbane, there was nothing new."

Mary looked at me. "Peter, do you have any new ideas on what might have happened?"

"Is that ATSB asking, AAIB or just you?"

"I'm not sure I like the concept of 'just me'."

"Well whoever it is asking I did think of a few things that might be worth exploring. I want to talk to the RAAF for a start. But what about you, how are ATSB getting on?"

"Not very fast at all. They are still looking for the front fuselage but have found the wings and engines. There will be an enormous amount of work required identifying bodies."

***

In the morning when I got to my office I called Group Captain 'Buster' Stone who I had met some time previously when Air Traffic Services were giving routine briefings on their latest systems.

"Buster. I'm involved with the loss of that RWA aircraft in the Indian Ocean north of Broome. I wondered if there were any RAAF exercises in the area at the time."

"Not that I recall but I'll have a look. Wait a moment." There was a pause. "Peter, I must be getting old. Yes, there was an exercise, Spoonbill. It was a joint one with the Navy but all the aircraft were below 15,000ft coasting out."

"Or they should have been. Presumably they had transponders, ADS-B, switched off.

"Yes, they didn't want to make it easy for the submarines."

"Have you been following the news on the accident?"

"Wasn't it a terrorist bomb on the flight deck? That's what the video I saw said."

"Possibly but nothing is certain. All very strange. I wondered if your people had seen or heard anything."

"I can send a signal asking but I'm sure if anyone had seen anything it would have been reported."

"How about radar?"

"We share with Air Traffic Services. However you may be in luck as JORN was operating that night because of Spoonbill. You know our Jindalee Operational Radar Network. We can see well over the horizon, ships and aircraft."

"I never thought of JORN. Is it any good? I know the politicians claim it's wonderful after all the money that's been spent on it. Can it really see over the horizon?"

"I'm not sure what I'm allowed to tell you with regard to detailed performance but it's the best radar of its type in the world. We have the advantage of lots of space here in Australia so, as you know, we're able to have three of these radars, each one nearly two miles long, at Alice, Longreach in

Queensland and the third at Leverton in Western Australia. They might have seen something."

"How can I check?"

"You need to go either to Edinburgh Field by Adelaide where the raw signals from the radar are processed or perhaps better to RAAF Williamstown where the information is integrated with the National Air Traffic System. But don't hold your breath; it's not like ADS-B."

"Will the processing have been stored?

"Oh, yes for sure. Tell you what. I'll do some phoning and call you back."

I looked up details on JORN after Buster had rung off. It was claimed it could detect missiles as well as aircraft and even ships but the radar polar diagram had to be manipulated. I wanted to dig into the system a bit deeper if I could but I got I involved with an aircraft at Tampa, Florida that had had to abandon take-off due to flying through a flock of birds. The aircraft overran the runway slightly and damaged the airfield lighting installation. ALPA had rung me to protect the pilots' interests as the airfield authorities were suing the airline and the airline was blaming the pilots for not stopping on the runway. I was emailing some questions to the FAA on the Tampa bird monitoring and dispersal procedures.

Before going home I called Buster and asked what was happening.

"Peter, I'm afraid we can't help you any further."

"Buster, I don't understand. Why not?"

"I'm not at liberty to say."

"Wait a moment! If I understand you correctly you are saying that you won't help me any further but you clearly could?"

"Peter, no comment."

I went home my mind buzzing trying to understand what was going on. Mary was still with us and so I related my conversation with Buster to her and also to Charlie who couldn't see the difficulty.

"My love, it's quite clear what's going on. Something that the RAAF thinks is very secret was discovered by their funny old radar and they don't want anyone except them to know."

Mary nodded. "I agree. Maybe it affected RW845. We could ask ATSB to lean on the Department of Defence."

"Mary, hold on. You don't like me telling Al Jazeera what you tell me and I'm not sure I want you telling AAIB my private thoughts."

"But surely there's no comparison? One is a media issue and the other is a safety issue."

"Well give me twenty four hours while I talk to Stephen."

"Can I come too?"

I detected that Charlie definitely did not think that that was going to be a good idea.

"I'd rather be just one to one, Mary." To my surprise she just nodded but maybe she also realised that Charlie didn't fancy the two of us going off together somewhere.

"Well don't be too long with Stephen as I may be going back home anytime and I'd like to know what he said or suggests."

Mary said goodnight and Charlie and I went up to our room.

"You got the message then."

I looked at Charlie and couldn't help smiling. "It wasn't too difficult. Did you notice she got it as well?"

"Oh yes, my darling, I noticed alright. She's nothing if not smart. I'm not convinced that she and Andrew will make it the way she carries on. She's got a soft spot for you, if that's the right phrase."

I decided that no comment was required even if it was a contradiction in terms. I definitely didn't think it would help relaying the way Mary looked at sex.

Chapter 5

Mary was at her temporary desk in the ATSB the following morning when the telephone rang from WorldLink.

"Ms French, it's Mike Goldton here. I've tried to get hold of Peter Talbert but must have the wrong contact number. Andrew Simpson told me that he wanted to contact my predecessor here, John Dixon. I've just found a street address in an old file which may be correct. The file also has his references which I'll send along as well. Can you pass it all on to Mr Talbert? I'll email it to you."

"No problem."

A few moments later she got the email and looked at the address. To her surprise it was in Belconnen, not too far away from the police station. She glanced at the references which Mike Goldton had scanned in and saw that Dixon had been in the Australian Army retiring as a Sergeant. She forwarded all the information to Peter.

Andrew rang and said that he was at the police station and Commander Martin wanted to see her again. She looked at her watch and decided to grab a sandwich in the Mall; from there she went to her car and drove to the police station. She managed to find somewhere to park and went to reception. Andrew had been looking out for her and they did a bit more than a perfunctory embrace as Commander Martin appeared. They went up to his office. "Ms French, Andrew Simpson here has been explaining your relationship and how he encouraged you to look at the WorldLink facility. However we still cannot rule out that you might have had an interest in destroying the facility."

"Why on earth would I want to do that? You know my background as an RAF Navigator and as an accident inspector."

"Yes we do but we have been advised that you might have been specially allocated to the aircraft that was shot down."

"Well I don't know where you got that idea from."

"You seem to know Mr Peter Talbert very well."

"Of course I do. He is an insurance accident investigator and we needed to find out who shot our aircraft down. You people were hiding a submarine which didn't belong to you and it needed Talbert to sort out what really happened to our aircraft as well as to your P8. No wonder I know him." She thought Martin looked a bit uncertain after her outburst and so she ploughed on. "Please stop wasting my time and let me have my passport back. We're trying to help your ATSB find out what happened to that airliner and I will need to go back to the UK in a day or so."

Martin trotted out his party line. "I'm afraid I'm not in a position to let you have your passport back yet, quite the reverse. We've now checked your car and it was definitely the one that had the explosives."

Mary looked at Martin with some contempt. "So, what if someone did put some bombs on my car. You can't really believe I would blow up the facility, killing and injuring people. Who do you think I was working for? China, Russia or maybe you think the UK now goes around killing their allies?" Again Martin looked discomfited and uncertain. "You've been reading too many spy stories."

Martin looked furious but before he said anything Andrew decided to chip in. "My love, I think you need a solicitor. Clearly the police have no grounds for keeping you or your passport but are doing so because they are at a loss to find someone else to blame to satisfy the media. We have the same problem in the States."

Mary could see that Martin took great exception to Andrew's remark, probably because there was some truth in what he said; he started threatening. "We are considering restricting your movements, Ms French."

Mary was getting cross. "Please don't start that game on me." She stood up and Martin asked her to sit down. He disappeared presumably to do some consultation and came back after ten minutes accompanied by another more senior policeman judging by the rank markings on the uniform. "Mary French we are charging you on the grounds of conspiring to blow up the WorldLink facility. You don't have to say anything at this time."

"OK if you want to play hard ball. Give me a phone and I'll get a solicitor."

She phoned Peter who was aghast at the development. "Alright I'll get someone to come straight over if I can."

Peter phoned his solicitor, Jake Wilson, who promised to send someone straight over to Belconnen if he couldn't go himself. Peter thought for a moment and then decided to ring Stephen at the High Commission.

"The police are being really stupid, Stephen."

"Yes, Peter but they are being chased by the media."

"Can't you ask your friend Dominic if he really wants ASIO and their detailed relationship with GCHQ to be discussed in public? To accuse Mary is quite ridiculous. "

"Problem is that some of the people really believe GCHQ might be involved."

"And kill people? Nonsense."

"I agree but that's what some people think. I'll talk to Dominic. By the way he's now based in ASIO."

Peter thought for a few minutes, then packed up his things, called Charlie and picked her up on the way home. He told her what had happened.

"Peter, you can't be serious? The police aren't that stupid."

"I think the media are causing trouble and the police want to show they are doing something."

They were in the middle of sorting the children out when Jake Wilson phoned.

"Peter, they are keeping her in overnight. I can't ask for bail until to-morrow morning."

"Will you be able to get bail?"

"Don't see why not. They've got her passport so they shouldn't need money."

"I'm surprised Commander Martin actually charged her. I thought he was sensible guy."

"In my view it's his boss the Assistant Commissioner that's calling the shots."

"What if the police say she needs to be detained because of National Security? I don't know how much she told you but they might."

"That would make it much harder. However the media would love it. I can see the headlines 'police charge a beautiful woman spy.'"

"Jake, you did notice then?"

"Couldn't help it."

"Was Andrew Simpson still there when you arrived?"

"You bet. He told me he was leaving to get some clothes for Ms French."

"That makes sense. I expect he'll be back here soon. Call me in the morning when you've got news."

Peter was just putting the phone down when Andrew appeared. He was fuming and Charlie rallied round selecting some things for Mary. Peter suggested he went by taxi and bring Mary's car back here or return it to Hertz. He went off almost immediately. Charlie brought Peter a drink. "What a mess. What are you going to do?"

"Me? What can I do?"

"Hire a detective to find out who put the explosives on Mary's car."

Peter looked at her. "Yes, I could do that I suppose. "

"Peter, I recognise that look. You've got some other ideas."

"Well I was thinking of taking a day off to-morrow. How about you taking a day off as well?"

"That's sound lovely. What have you got in mind? Can we go back to bed after we've got rid of the children?"

"That does sound a really great idea but that wasn't exactly what I had in mind."

"That's unusual." She thought for a moment and then looked at her diary. "Alright if you need me I'll make an excuse. Let's have some supper."

"Not before I've been over to Fyshwick and bought a couple of metal detectors from Garretts; I must go straightaway before they shut. By the way you will need trousers and walking shoes or boots to-morrow"

"Splendid, can't wait."

Chapter 6

In the morning Andrew left for his office and we drove out to the WorldLink facility or what was left of it. It seemed deserted except for a grey Toyota. "We can't get in there, Peter."

"We don't need to. But we need to meet the lady in the Toyota."

We drove up to the car and an athletic looking lady got out of the car. I introduced Christine Smith to Charlie. "You remember, a journalist on the Age."

"No I don't remember. I can't keep track of all your female" she paused and smiled "acquaintances."

Christine looked at me. "Alright then, why are we here and why did you need me."

"We are looking for the trigger that exploded the bomb that blew up the WorldLink facility."

"But I thought that British girl who was shot down in the RAF P8 sometime ago was the culprit. They've charged her I think."

"Yes, you're quite correct. The police are holding her at the moment but we're trying to get her out on bail."

"What's it to do with you?"

"It's a long story. I'll tell you sometime."

"I like long stories. Sometimes they can make good copy."

Charlie chipped in. "Another female acquaintance."

"Alright but tell me, why are we all here?"

"There's not much doubt that the explosive was on Mary's car but it must have been triggered by someone and the only thing I can think of is that it must have been done from outside the facility."

"Who is Mary?"

"The British girl in custody who drove into WorldLink. I'm sure she didn't do it so there must be a trigger somewhere and I'm hoping it's still around here. I'm proposing to have a search and we need you here in case we find the trigger as an independent witness."

"Well surely the police should be looking for the trigger, not you?"

"Yes of course they should but I can't tell them what to do. It would be a waste of time as they think that Mary did it."

"They should be searching here for the trigger, not you. And they should be searching her and wherever she is living."

"She is staying with us and they certainly haven't been looking in our place."

Christine thought about the current situation. "But you may have got the trigger from the girl and already planted it for me to see you 'find' it."

"You're right, of course. It's a possibility but in fact it's not like that. I really have no idea if we will find a trigger. You can write the story as you like. For the moment would you mind just watching what we are doing? I hope we're not wasting your time."

"Not a bit and if you find the trigger and it's not your Mary's it will be a real scoop."

"Christine, of course the police might still say what you said, that if we find anything it is because I put it there but hopefully they won't say that." I turned to Charlie. "Let's take a walk."

"Why should we do that?"

"I'm trying to see where one has to stand so that the entrance to the facility is visible but the watcher can't be seen."

"That's not going to be easy because of the ground and anyway the facility has been flattened."

"I think we can make a good guess. We had better put some hats on or we will get roasted." Suitably clad we walked about a quarter of a mile upwards and right towards the facility. "This spot is good. Look, you can see what's left of the facility here through the barbed wire fence."

"But you can see the facility from the other side of the gates further down and it is more open."

"I know but the watcher would be obvious as well. Here there is a rough track so a car could be parked without being seen. In fact cars have been parked here, look at the ground." There were tyre marks where the weight of at least one car standing on the soft ground had left its mark. "Let's use our detectors starting from the fence and walking away from it for about twenty yards. You start this end I'll go to the other. We should meet in the middle."

Charlie looked at me. "What am I looking for? What does the trigger look like?"

"I'm not really sure but if we are very lucky we might find a small metal box with a switch on it."

It took us an hour with Christine watching every move before we met, very nearly in the middle of our planned search area.

"I'm afraid we didn't have much success there. Let's have some water. We've got lots of bottles in the car."

We went back to the car and I started its engine to keep cool; I found some plastic drinking glasses and we drank warm water but there were no complaints as we really needed it. "I think we should now try in the shrub beyond where we've just searched. Our watcher, if there was one, having triggered the bomb, obviously wouldn't have waited for it to go off. Once he had pressed the button he probably threw the trigger away; I'm sure he wouldn't have wanted to keep it. Of course, if he was really smart he would have kept it and disposed of it as soon as he could elsewhere but I have a theory that the whole operation was amateurish. He was probably standing by the fence making sure the car was parked close to the entrance. He then triggered the bomb and drove off. It was a miracle that Mary wasn't killed going to lunch or on the way home. I can't believe he planned to kill anybody; my guess is that he just wanted to damage the facility and remove the masts. Problem is that if he was a real professional he would have put the trigger in his pocket and got rid of it somewhere else but as I said my bet is that he was an amateur. Anyway I think it's worth having a look."

Charlie volunteered. "Great. I'll help you again."

"Good but your trousers won't be improved. There are some nasty prickly bushes about."

"It will save time if we both have a go."

This time I drove the car up to where we had been searching and as before we started from each end of the area I had chosen but now we had to fight our way into the rough shrubs. As before Christine was watching us both very carefully, presumably to make certain I didn't produce something out of my pocket. As we approached one another in the middle Charlie's machine sounded excited. I took over with my machine and confirmed that there seemed to be something in the middle of the bush. I went back to the car and got hold of a walking stick; while I managed to hold back the branches of the bush Charlie pointed out a small metal box the size of a large matchbox with a recessed button guarded by a shield on one side and a rotating knob on the other; she lifted it out with a clean handkerchief that I had given her before we started searching. Christine who had been watching all the time with a camera and a notebook came up close so as not to miss anything. I went back to the car and got Charlie to hold the device in her hand resting on the handkerchief and took two photographs with my phone, getting her to turn it over with the handkerchief for the second shot. Then with the handkerchief I dropped the device into a large padded envelope which I had optimistically brought with me in case of success.

"Let's go over and have lunch in the Tidbinbilla Visitors Centre."

Sitting down I looked at my messages. "They've refused Mary bail on the grounds of security."

Charlie looked very concerned. "What are you going to do?"

I looked at Christine. "If I give you the trigger can you get it checked?"

"But Peter, there may be fingerprints. I'll be sent to gaol."

"There is a firm that does that sort of thing. I know the firm is in Sydney and not Melbourne but Forensic Document Services Pty Ltd, FDSP, in Sydney can check the trigger for finger prints; make certain they give you a set of fingerprints as well as a set to go with the box. Then you'll need an organisation to tell you about the capability of the box itself."

She looked at her watch. "I'd better be on my way because the police will want the trigger the moment they read my article and I want the box looked at before the police. I'll get the paper to put FDSP on stand-by. It may be quicker to fly."

I gave Christine the envelope with the trigger and she rushed off to her car.

Charlie looked at me. "But what about the police and Mary?"

"Well I imagine Christine has got enough for to-morrow's paper. The police will be very keen to get hold of the trigger and the fingerprints the moment they read her article. I think they will find it very hard in the circumstances to hold Mary and her passport unless they are going to accuse me as being an accessory."

"You're not going to be the flavour of the month in Belconnen."

"Well they should have looked for the trigger themselves but they were convinced that Mary and possibly GCHQ in some way were involved so they didn't consider other options. This will be quite a scoop for Christine I imagine."

"Peter, I'm more worried for you. The police don't like looking like fools."

"Well I did warn them they were wrong."

"That makes it worse, my love."

We finished our meal and made our way home. Andrew arrived having worked all day checking the specification for rebuilding the WorldLink facility. We all went to bed early which is just as well as the phone rang at 5.30; it was Christine. "Peter, I've had the police on demanding the trigger. Someone must have read the first editions or maybe the internet. They didn't sound too pleased."

"Did you get the fingerprints copied?"

"Yes, thank you and I got the trigger photographed and x-rayed as I thought it best not to tamper with it."

"Hope everybody was very careful not to blur the prints or the police will be furious though they will have the set that FDSP took. When are they collecting the trigger?"

"In a few minutes. They tried to tell me that I should have handed it in straightaway and I said I was going to hand it in to the Canberra police station in the morning as it was too late last night."

"A likely story! Did you tell them about FDSP?"

"Yes I did to reassure them that they will at least have one set of prints."

"How about the X-Ray?"

"Peter, come on! Of course not. My newspaper article talks about you, a friend of the girl being detained and an aviation insurance investigator, and what you decided to do to help. How you worked out what must have happened though you have no idea who did the bombing. I also reminded the reader that the girl being detained was the one who was shot down in the P8 but I didn't tell them that you were also involved."

"How did you know?"

"There were some notes in our database about you. There was also a query saying we should find out why you got a CBE at the same time as Mary got her OBE. Why did you?"

I put the phone down without answering her question and Charlie pushed me from her side of the bed. "You might as well get me a cup of tea. My bet is the phone is going to ring."

"I'm not so sure. Commander Martin or his boss will be involved and I don't think they will start that early. They will need to think what to do."

I got Charlie a cup of tea and then went back to lie down but in fact Charlie was right. The phone did ring continually as various media reporters tried to get me to give interviews but I refused them all. I considered taking the phone off the hook but I was frightened if I did that they would come round to the house.

In fact the police did not ring before we went to work but I stopped at the petrol station on the way in to buy two copies of The Age. My picture was on the front page with Charlie, both of us carrying metal detectors, and there was another picture of me gingerly lowering the trigger into my envelope. It was 1030 when the phone rang. "Commander Martin here, Mr Talbert. I am in two minds whether to congratulate you on finding the trigger or accuse you on not giving us the trigger having got it from Miss French. However, we think that is unlikely, bearing in mind all the circumstances, that you were involved, though we would like to take your finger prints. We have decided therefore to drop all charges against Mary French and give her back her passport. However you should have given us the trigger straightaway and not given it to Christine Smith."

"She was going back to Canberra and it wasn't convenient for us to deliver it. You've got it safely, haven't you? May I come and collect Ms French?"

Martin grunted agreement and I set course for Belconnen where I found some photographers trying to get into the police station and take pictures of Mary. I asked for Martin and when I gave my name I was asked for a set of finger print. When that was over I was shown into a small waiting room and after about fifteen minutes Mary appeared holding a sack of clothes. She embraced me lovingly showing signs of relief and I slowly disengaged.

"Peter, I've read The Age. You were brilliant."

"Thank you. Have you got your passport?" She nodded. "Let's go." I turned to the receptionist "Is there a back entrance for Miss French?"

He looked uncompromising. "Yes, but she will not be allowed to use it. All visitors must use the front entrance."

"Are you telling me that the police want the Full Monty of publicity and are keen for me to go outside with this lovely lady and have our pictures taken and be interviewed." I made as if to move out but he indicated that I should wait and he started telephoning. His phone rang back and then he turned to me. "It is alright for Miss French to go out the back way. Commander Martin has suggested that she uses a special exit that we have which goes into this side street."

He showed me the exact location and agreed to take Mary there while I drove round. I managed to get into my car without any problem though I guessed looking in my rear mirror that one reporter had finally recognised me from my photo in The Age. However he was not quick enough to follow me though I was so busy looking backwards I got slightly lost. I finally found the unassuming little door and Mary appeared.

As we drove home Mary started stroking me which I well understood in view of what she had just been through but her hand dropped down and I was pretty certain Charlie would not have approved where it was going. "It was most unpleasant there, Peter, though they tried to be as kind as they could."

"Mary you are not making it easy for me to drive."

"I'm only saying thank you. "

I made no reply but where her hand rested on me didn't actually feel like a thank you.

"Mary, must you rest your hand there. We'll have an accident. Maybe you could thank me some other time." I tried to change the conversation. "When did you know they were going to release you?"

"Someone stuffed a copy of The Age underneath the door of my cell at about 0530 with your picture on the front page. Who is Christine Smith?"

"You sound like Charlie. She's a newspaper reporter of course. She specialises in aviation and modern technology."

"Well she did a great job."

As we approached the house I saw what I guessed was a reporter and photographer outside. Mary rapidly took her hand away. We got out as quickly as we could keeping well apart and went in through the back door so that we could keep the reporter away by using our side gate. However we could not prevent them getting some individual shots of both of us as we went in.

Once inside Mary went to her room to have a shower. She appeared wearing only a towel round her middle and carrying some clothes which she was going to put in the washing machine. "I can't find the softener."

I went over to help. She smelt of perfume and I had to press against her to reach the softener which was no hardship. Her towel fell off and instead of moving away I found myself holding her and stroking her breasts. She started rubbing her bottom against me and I could feel myself responding in no uncertain terms. It took a superhuman effort not to undo my trousers; somehow I managed to pull myself away. "Mary, for God's sake put that towel back on. Andrew or Charlie could arrive at any moment."

She picked up the towel, put it in the washing machine, started it, found a smaller towel which barely covered anything and came over to me. "Is that better?"

"Mary you are impossible and making it very difficult for me."

She kissed me slowly and stroked me gently at the same time. "I want to thank you. It seems such a natural way to do it."

I managed to back away.

"What about Andrew?"

"That's different. He's absolutely lovely and we love one another but you and I would just be pure sex. You know I've always fancied you."

"Most people would class anything we did together as impure sex. Why don't you go and get dressed?"

"Alright, if you don't want my thanks. Maybe some other time."

She disappeared and I heaved a sigh of relief. The temptation had been enormous but it would have been madness. I looked at my watch and decided the best thing would be to go back to the office. Mary reappeared wearing a jumper and very brief shorts just as Andrew and Charlie appeared; apparently he had picked her up on the way home.

Andrew rushed over and embraced Mary and Charlie surveyed the situation.

"Peter, did you know there are two reporters outside?"

"No, I didn't. There was only one when we came in."

"Did they get any snaps?" She nodded. "That's nice we'll have a full family group in the paper to-morrow. What did you say?"

"Absolutely nothing of course."

"Splendid. I was about to go back to the office but it can wait."

"Good. You can get us all some tea."

Mary joined in. "Andrew would prefer coffee." He nodded. "Black with one sugar and I'll have Earl Grey."

I shuddered, went into the kitchen and returned with the orders on a tray. Andrew turned to me. "I've read the paper. You did a great job. The police are looking rather stupid."

"It's easy to criticise but I had the advantage over them as I knew Mary didn't do it."

Chapter 7

In the morning when Mary arrived at ATSB Mark told her that Jerry was with Robert Covelli. "Glad to see you here. We've read all about you in the papers and seen your pictures. The police seem to have really screwed up. What's it like being in prison?"

"It wasn't really in a proper prison but it was most unpleasant. I'd better go up and see Jerry."

Mary went up to Robert's office and was welcomed by both Robert and Jerry. "Well young lady, you've really been hitting the headlines. Robert here has been bringing me up to date. Why on earth did they charge you? I know the bomb was allegedly on your car but why would they think you would do it?"

She didn't bother to answer the question but looked at them both. "How are things going? Are we making any progress?"

Robert looked thoughtful. "Not really. *Ocean Salvager* won't arrive for a couple of days but the ADV *Ocean Shield* still can't find the crash recorder. However it has found a lot of the wreckage. We will need to look at what we've got and, when we can, bring bodies and wreckage up to the surface. That way we should be able to tell why the plane disintegrated."

Mary looked at Jerry. "Isn't that going to take some time? Maybe I ought to go back to UK?"

To Mary's surprise Robert made a suggestion. "Have you ever seen these ROVs operating and the recovering of wreckage?" Mary shook her head. "Well if you can stay here for a day or so we can take you out to the *Ocean Salvager*. We will have a helicopter ferry going out to the salvage vessel from Broome on a regular basis. Obviously we will get the wreckage on-shore as soon as we can because we must try to determine why the aircraft broke-up but you'll be the first to see the wreckage and maybe it will be obvious what happened."

Mary was very keen to go and Jerry agreed she could stay and possibly go out with him when the time arrived. She sent a message to Andrew breaking the news. On the way back to Kingston she went into the Centre to buy a warm waterproof jacket and arrived in time to greet Peter junior and Francie just home from school.

Later Peter and Charlie appeared and a decision was taken to order some pizzas. Mary decided what flavour Andrew would like and he arrived at the same time as the motor cyclist with the food. They sat down and Mary explained to Peter and Charlie what was happening; Peter focussed on the situation straightaway.

"Mary, that's great news. You can help me with Al Jazeera."

"I thought we agreed I wasn't going to tell you anything, or not much anyway?"

"Well surely it depends what the cause of the accident was."

"Peter, we don't know yet."

"Well I agree a bomb on the flight deck sounds a very real possibility but I would have thought that whoever did it would be claiming victory by now. I'm sure that's the way they would see it. I'm beginning to wonder if the accident is due to something else, something entirely different. The sooner we see the wreckage the better."

"What do you mean 'we see the wreckage'? You are not involved for a change. If you want to do something useful you can try to find out who put the bomb in my car."

"I'm not sure I like that remark, Miss French, since I'm retained by Independant however," Peter turned to Andrew, "Any news? What are the police doing?"

"Not a lot as far as I can see. They seemed to lose interest when Mary left. I think they enjoyed having a beautiful lady as the mysterious bomber locked up in their cells."

Mary joined in. "Well they may have enjoyed it but I didn't. The sooner you find out who did the damage the better."

Peter looked at Andrew. "Did you have good security for the facility?"

Mary interrupted. "Absolutely. I had to tell Andrew the car registration and he told me to go to the WorldLink Canberra office and get the key code for the door. They were working late and I just managed to see the guy there before the office closed."

Andrew managed to get a word in. "I sent Mary's picture to the Canberra office as well as the car reg."

Mary suddenly realised that all her movements had been known to the WorldLink Canberra office. She looked carefully at Peter before speaking. "You bastard! How long have you suspected without telling anybody? You're not seriously suggesting that the WorldLink people were involved?"

Peter smiled. "Known, suspected? About the office? I think you're jumping ahead. I don't know anything. I'm just wondering whether we're missing something."

Andrew looked at Peter. "Are you suggesting that it is the guy from our office that planted the bomb?"

"Well it could be or someone very close to the office. It had to be someone who knew when Mary was going out and knew about her car."

Mary thought for a moment. "But I didn't tell anyone where I was staying."

"But they knew the car registration. Did you tell WorldLink where you were working?"

"Yes, of course. I told the guy how they could contact me. Anyway Andrew had given them all the information."

"So they could have put the bomb on your car in the ATSB car park."

"I suppose so but wouldn't that have been a bit obvious?"

"Not if the person was wearing some sort of uniform, NRMA for example repairing car."

"NRMA?"

"Like our AA."

"Peter," Andrew looked really worried "you've given me a problem. How are we going to find out if the guy is bent?"

"Perhaps you should tell the police."

"But I've no reason to suspect him, Mike Goldton by the way."

"Would you like me to talk to Commander Martin? Mind you he won't like being told what to do."

"I think that would be very good, if you don't mind."

Mary watched Peter pick up the phone and dial Belconnen. He got through to Martin and Peter started to talk about WorldLink, their office and Mary. He quickly had to go into listening mode and then hung fairly quickly; he looked at them all. "I got a flea in my ear. Martin told me in no uncertain terms that his people were already sorting things out and he didn't need my help." Peter looked at Andrew. "Things should be a bit clearer in the morning. By the way how long have you been employing Mike? Do you have his references?"

"Can't answer that question. All before my time. This is my first visit here as a WorldLink man."

Andrew looked at Peter. "But why would anyone want to destroy the facility? It makes no sense."

"Have you got competition? What are the technical and financial implications of losing the facility?"

"Could be disastrous if we don't get a replacement running soon. This network is a huge investment for the backers of the project and we are relying on getting a large influx of new users transferring from other providers. If the network does not perform properly we could fold."

"Were you insured for bomb damage to the facility?"

"Don't know but I've got the go ahead to rebuild the facility and the builder starts work to-morrow clearing the site. Camfen are contracting in the UK for a complete replacement package so presumably there's money coming from somewhere. Luckily we're able to use the original builder and he has a complete set of plans."

"How long are you going to be here?"

"Not sure. I need to talk to Corporate Headquarters to-morrow after I've find out what the police have been doing."

They all went to bed in a very subdued manner.

***

Three days later Mary heard that the *Ocean Salvager* was on location and that she could arrange to be at Broome the following day. She decided to go via Sydney so she got up very early while Andrew looked on and waved goodbye. She checked her car in and caught her flight to Perth. For once there were no hold ups and she arrived at Broome on schedule with her bag. There was a message for her to go to the Toll company's check-in in the heliport at the southern end of the terminal. She crossed the road into the heliport and went to the desk and made herself known. Much to her surprise when she had cleared security she saw Robert Covelli.

"After you left I got a call to look at the wreckage they had just found so I night stopped in Perth."

"What's special about the wreckage?"

"Don't know. Apparently there are quite large lumps."

"That's good, isn't it? You can bring the pieces up."

"Depends on how big the pieces are. We may need a bigger salvage vehicle; that's why I came to-day to have a look."

They took off and flew out to the Ocean Salvager and landed on the helipad mounted on the forward bridge structure of the vessel. Jim Forester, Oceaneering Project Manager met them and explained the situation. "As you know ATSB have chartered this vessel and contracted us to provide a Remotely Operated Vehicle to find the Flight Data Recorder and search for airframe wreckage, We're using one of our Magnum Systems, cage tethered, but we could not find the flight data recorder. With the help of ITAC we found out yesterday exactly where the FDR is attached to the fuselage but to our surprise it wasn't there."

Mary could see Robert couldn't believe what he was being told. "Jim, I don't understand. The FDR wasn't there?"

"Yes. That's right. We couldn't believe it either. It rather looked as if it had been removed and in a rather rough manner."

"That's ridiculous. Perhaps it had never been fitted. I believe the design specification of the two FDR installation allows the aircraft to be dispatched with only one FDR."

"Robert, I'm glad to say that's your problem, not ours. We are now working out the best way to attach lifting cables to the wreckage."

Robert looked to see if there were any aircraft parts on the deck of the ship. "You haven't started to lift anything yet?"

"No. The aircraft is in several parts and we don't want to damage it any more than we have to raising it up. I've been involved in several underwater aircraft recoveries and the parts have always been smaller. Your man here who has been advising us thought you ought to look at the aircraft wreckage before we try to raise it. He's in the control van now working with our guy"

"Good. Where is your control room? We might as well start."

Jim led them to the Control Container which had been 'sea fastened' to the deck of the vessel. It took a few moments for them to get accustomed to the darkness. They went up close behind the two guys sitting down and looked at the eight screens. Mary turned to Robert. "Those two TV pictures of the wreckage are amazing and so stable."

"Well there's not much motion down there which helps and the flood lights are very bright. The range though is not very good." He turned to the ROV operator. "Can you move along this piece?"

The ROV started slowly moving, illuminating what turned out to be part of the fuselage. The operator then moved the ROV to another part of the fuselage which included part of the fin. Mary wasn't expecting to see such large pieces. "Robert, these two pieces look like most of the fuselage." She turned to the operator. "Can we see the nose?"

"I'm afraid not. We haven't found the nose yet."

"Robert, if there was a bomb in the baggage hold wouldn't there be more pieces?"

"Probably. We need to look at the pieces in detail ashore. I imagine that most of the bodies will still be inside these two pieces though there will be some bodies in the nose section of course. We've got to try and get the bodies out and ashore for identification as quickly as possible with minimum damage."

"It certainly doesn't look like an explosion in the baggage hold, not that I have had any experience in this sort of thing."

"Quite correct. It will be very important to examine the wreckage closely, underneath and the front of the fuselage. We will need to get another vessel alongside to be able to transfer the fuselage bits safely to dry land but before that I think we will want to get divers to inspect inside the fuselage pieces and remove any bodies they can easily get from inside. And Jim, presumably you are searching for bodies outside the wreckage?"

There was lot of discussion between Jim Forester and the ROV operator on the best way to attach the lifting cables to the pieces of wreckage and how many cables would be needed. Robert clearly felt that this was not in his area of expertise and so he and Mary left the van. They found their assigned cabins and then found the ship's restaurant. Jim Forester joined them and Robert discussed the timings and what would be needed. In the morning a helicopter arrived bringing supplies to the ship and took Robert and Mary back to Broome. They managed to catch the direct flight to Melbourne and got into Canberra at 10.30pm. Mary rented a car and got back to the Talberts soon after 11pm.

Chapter 8

We were still in bed when Mary messaged from the airport. I could hear Andrew moving so I didn't get up. In the morning we all met for breakfast.

Mary looked a bit tired. "How did you get on? You didn't stay long."

"Peter, it was very interesting but it was a long way to go for a few minutes observation. They examined where the FDR should have been and it wasn't there; it looked as if it had been cut off. The fuselage was broken into at least three pieces and we were only able to look at the two rear sections; they haven't found any part of the front fuselage yet. The bits we saw didn't seem very damaged; they were planning to lift them when we left."

"How are they going to do that?"

"Good question. They will need to get another vessel, a large barge or something that can carry the pieces."

"From what you describe there may be bodies on board."

"Too right. Robert said they wouldn't pull the pieces straight out as it may be better to get some of the bodies out first in shallow water." Mary hesitated. "You can't use any of this info with your Arabian friends. It's confidential."

"If you say so, my dear. The state of the fuselage pieces tends to support a relatively gentle impact with the water and not a dive; maybe a slightly flat rotation."

"Peter, we need to see the underside of the fuselage and see what it looks like. Anyway I'd better be going to the office and find out why the second FDR can't be found."

Breakfast broke up as the children went to school, Andrew went to his office and I took Charlie to hers on the way to mine.

I looked at my phone and saw ATSB was going to make a statement at 1000. I selected ABC radio and Robert appeared; he said that they had not recovered the second flight data recorder from the aircraft and but were analysing the records very closely from the flight recorder they had; so far it had not been possible to isolate the cause of the accident. They anticipated raising parts of the wreckage in the next few days but before that they would probably be bringing the bodies ashore for identification. He was asked about the ISIS video and he said that one theory of the cause of the accident was a bomb on the flight deck but inspection of the wreckage was required before any definite conclusion could be reached and the ROV was still searching for the nose section of the fuselage. Robert pointed out that even if a bomb was thought to be the cause of the accident it didn't follow that ISIS was the perpetrator. He answered a few more questions but there was nothing of note so I switched him off.

I was going down to get a sandwich when Andrew called. "Mike Goldton arrived at the Office late this morning. The police searched all over his house yesterday evening and took him down to the police station for questioning plus his computers and phones. Presumably they couldn't find any evidence to charge him so they released him at about midnight."

"Did you find out who employed him and how long he had been with you?"

"Yes. Derek Courtfield employed him and he has been with us for two months. He seems ideal for the job; I was able to look at his references. As you can imagine he is a bit shaken up. He admits he knew Mary's movements since I had emailed him with all her security details to get into the facility over the phone."

"So we don't seem any nearer knowing who did the deed and why? What are you going to do now?"

"Peter, nothing for the moment in relation to finding out what happened. I'm leaving that to the police. I'll be leaving for Seattle this evening and then carrying on liaising with Camfen; Derek can manage while the facility is being rebuilt."

"That will please Mary."

"I'm not exactly complaining either though we'll have to fish or cut bait sometime, I suppose. Living on opposite sides of the Atlantic, not to mention 3,000 miles across the States is not a really practical partnership let alone marriage."

"Well good luck. That's what Charlie and I had to do some years back, as you know."

"You gave up some senior UK Government appointment didn't you?"

"True but it hasn't mattered and we're good Australians now."

"You mean you've got Aussie passports?"

"No, we haven't done that. Charlie's still a US citizen and I'm still a Brit. We will be able to get dual nationalities in due course. Peter junior has two passports and Francie is just an Aussie at the moment."

"All sounds very confusing."

"You get used to it. If Charlie left her job I don't know what we would do then. We might have to review the situation again. Anyway that's not important at the moment. I think the key to this is to find out why someone wanted your place destroyed."

Chapter 9

Mary sat in her ATSB office looking at the photographs of the pieces of fuselage which had just been loaded on to a barge shaped boat which could accept unusual loads. The pieces were in remarkably good shape in that, though they were twisted and deformed, they hadn't broken up. There was still no news of the front of the fuselage and she couldn't tell what had happened to dislodge the front part of the fuselage but she presumed there was some way of telling if there had been an explosion. Looking at a note Jerry had sent her there had been 241 bodies in the fuselage and they were currently being kept identified in two very large air conditioned hangars built by Rapidwall next to the Broome mortuary. As each body was identified it was despatched to the relevant dependant via the airline but it was a slow and difficult operation.

The phone rang and a business like Charlie came on the line. "Mary I've got to go to Singapore to-night for a few days. When are you going home?"

Mary knew immediately what was worrying Charlie. "Not sure, but I'll get a room in the Novotel until you come back or until I go. It actually will be very convenient because then I won't need a car. I'll be over in a few minutes. Will you be in?"

"Yes, I'm at home now getting organised for the trip."

Mary checked there was a room in the hotel and then drove straight over and started packing. Charlie appeared.

"Jill Evans will be moving in to look after the kids and do the cooking but I thought it would be easier if there was just Peter in the house."

Mary smiled. "Charlie, you don't have to spell it out. Have you told Peter?"

"He suggested it."

Mary decided to make no comment. She didn't have much stuff and the room was soon clear.

Charlie popped her head round the door. "Where and when are you checking the car in?"

"I can take you to the airport now, if that helps."

"OK. Let's go if it's okay by you."

Mary put her bags in the car with Charlie's and as she drove to the airport decided that it would be easier to check the car in later in the day rather than the airport. She said goodbye to Charlie as she was pretty certain she would almost certainly be back in UK before Charlie got back. She returned to Canberra and drove to the ATSB, parked the car and wheeled her stuff to the Novotel which was directly opposite the ATSB on Northbourne. She checked in, took her bags up to her room and then went over to the ATSB. There was no-one in her office and she discovered that photos of the fuselage of RW845 were being shown in the projection room and being analysed by the experts.

She squeezed in at the back and there was a lively discussion going on debating what might have happened. The RAAF was mentioned but Robert said he had checked and there had been only a low level maritime operation happening; apparently all the crews had been questioned and nothing unusual had been observed. Mary remembered her agreement with Peter and didn't disclose what he had learnt; anyway she wanted to discuss it privately with Jerry rather than mention the situation to all and sundry.

She looked at her watch and decided to go by the WorldLink office and collect a parcel that Andrew had left for her. She could have walked but decided to drive and find somewhere to park since she was then going to check the car in. She went into the office and the man there was just locking up. He gave her the parcel. From there she went to Lonsdale

Street to get rid of the car and then walked back to the hotel. She knew Jerry was staying there but she decided to talk to Peter before contacting him.

"How was Stephen?"

"Mary, he was as puzzled as I was about Buster's secrecy but he was going to try to see if Dominic would tell him anything. How did you get on?"

"Everybody was looking at photographs of the fuselage and Robert announced that he had spoken to the RAAF; he said that apparently they had had an exercise on that night but that they were at low altitude and so not involved. I kept my mouth shut but I was thinking of talking to Jerry this evening if he is in as he is staying in the hotel."

"Mary, I'd prefer you kept quiet until I heard from Stephen. I'm nervous that if Robert goes in to the RAAF now then Stephen may not get anywhere."

"But this is a very serious accident. Now is not the time to play soldiers."

"You're quite right but clearly something was going on that was probably top secret and it may take some senior politician or even the PM to agree to release what was happening in the area."

Mary grudgingly agreed. "Alright, if you say so. By the way how many people are in the WorldLink office?"

"One as far as I know. Why?"

"I managed to pick up something Andrew had left for me just as the man there was locking up and he gave me the parcel. The strange thing was that he was not the same man I saw when I first arrived who gave me the key code for the facility and who I gave my office information and timing."

Mary could almost hear Peter thinking. "Mary, did you ask the guy his name?"

"No, of course not."

"How about the first man?"

"No, why should I?"

"Let me think about this. Something doesn't sound right. Look, I expect you are in frequent contact with Andrew. Why don't you double check that there should only be one guy in the office?"

"You could ask Derek."

"No, I don't want to do that. He may be doing something he shouldn't. Your description of that picture of Sophie on his desk may be significant."

"I probably exaggerated the description of the lady in the picture. Of course I'll ask Andrew but he may not know."

"Possibly, but at least we know we can believe him which is more than we can say about anyone else in WorldLink."

"That's a bit unkind."

"Mary, it's the same situation as RW845. Someone's been killed and another person severely injured. We must find out the truth." There was a pause. "Be careful my dear. We are dealing with a murder or murderers and history relates that once they have started they tend to carry on until they are caught. Don't do anything I wouldn't approve of, if you know what I mean."

"You're very strait laced."

"Mary, I'm serious. You may already know more than what's good for you. When are you going home?"

"I don't know. I was thinking of trying to get back to Broome to look at the actual wreckage."

"That might be safer than hanging around here. But UK would be better."

"Are you trying to get rid of me?"

"Yes, I suppose I am. I'm nervous of your being here. I tell you what, why don't you download that app *Find my Friends*? That way I'll know where you are all the time."

Mary was going to be flippant and tell him she didn't want him to know where she was all the time but realised he would be cross if she said that and anyway she didn't mind at all Peter knowing where she was. "Good idea as long as I know where you are in return."

She decided to have a shower and a change of clothes but kept to slacks and blouse. She called Jerry and they agreed to meet in the bar. He was there in a smart short sleeved open necked shirt which she thought was a bit brave in view of the air conditioning. She agreed to a beer which was definitely not her favourite tipple.

"Jerry, where's Tom. Isn't he staying here as well?"

"He was but he's off home this evening. I thought you would like to stay on and get some more experience of dealing with under water accidents. But what are you doing here? I thought you were staying with the Talberts."

"Peter's wife Charlie is a big wheel in the Art Gallery here and she's gone off to Singapore and so I thought it would be more convenient to stay here and I've been able to get rid of the car. The move is working out really well if we are going to Broome or wherever. Thanks very much by the way for agreeing to that. Are we going to actually look at the pieces?"

"Yes, I think we should. Photos are all very well but it is nice to inspect as well, however good the photos are."

"When are we going to Broome?"

"Don't know when the ATSB guys are going but I'd like to wait until bits of the front fuselage have been found. I'm surprised they haven't been found already."

"Jerry, did Robert draw a complete blank with the RAAF?"

"Yes. Why do you ask?"

"Peter Talbert wondered if they might be hiding something."

"I'm sure they wouldn't hide anything if it affects the accident."

"Perhaps. Peter is speaking to the High Commission to make sure."

"Well they wouldn't know anything."

"Of course not but they have contacts in the RAAF and Government."

"Well all help is appreciated."

Mary decided that that was as far as she could go on the subject and they looked at the large TV screen where the Aussies were well on the way to keeping the Ashes. Jerry was clearly a great supporter of cricket and was feeling a bit frustrated. "We've got seventy million people and they've got twenty three million but they're thrashing us again."

"They've got a better climate. It must help a bit."

Another England wicket fell and Jerry shrugged his shoulders in disgust.

Mary's phone buzzed. It was Peter. She decided to take the call outside the noisy bar away from the noisy music.

"What's the problem?"

"Mary, Stephen said that Dominic was very reticent but apparently the JORN has been operating 24/7 for the last month because of some returns they don't understand."

"So what has that got to do with RW845?"

"Well maybe there was a mid-air collision." Mary was quiet for a moment. "Are you still there?"

"Yes, I am Peter, but in that case the loss of the other aircraft would have been reported."

"Depends how clandestine the operation was. However a mid-air collision would explain why the front wreckage hasn't been found. You remember the aircraft did not dive straight into the sea but must have been doing some sort of glide. Perhaps the collision was some sort of glancing blow, if that were possible, and the front part separated. Anyway the ROV clearly needs to look round where the other pieces were found in a fairly large circle, up to twenty or thirty miles."

"But what aircraft could have hit RW845?"

"Obviously a military aircraft; apparently the aircraft were flying every night in that area which means they must be naval aircraft. There aren't many countries that can be doing this. I'm putting my money on the Chinese but I suppose it could be the Russians. I don't understand why the Australians are being so reticent. They should be telling the ATSB what's been going on. There must be more to it."

"I don't understand it but if you're right why should they choose that particular area?"

"A very good question. I wonder if the Australians know. "

"Do you want me to tell Jerry?"

"You can do but I'm going to talk to Robert in just a minute. I think it's sufficiently important to call him at home because ATSB may want to give instructions to the ROV operator and Ocean Salvager. And I'm sure they will want to talk to the RAAF."

Mary rang off and went back to the bar to find Jerry. The Aussies had finished off the Poms and he was looking very bored. Mary saw his face light up as she appeared.

"I thought you'd gone to bed."

"A little bit early for that. I've been talking to Peter. He's heard that the RAAF radar JORN has been operating 24/7 for the last month because of echoes they don't understand. He wondered if there had been a head-on collision with RW845."

"But if that had happened surely there would have been a comment from the operator of the lost aircraft?"

"Yes, it is puzzling. However Peter suggested that if it was a collision the ROV should be looking around in a circle round where the fuselage was found as the nose of the aircraft may have been broken off."

"That's a good point. Has he told anyone?"

"He said he was going to try to call Robert at home."

"But whose aircraft are they?"

"Peter thinks they're probably Chinese but maybe Russian."

"Well if it was a collision we must have a closer look at the fuselage pieces we have got to see if we can spot anything."

Chapter 10

The Australian Minister of Defence, Jack Smithson, called his Secretary into his office. Vin Partridge looked at the papers on the Minister's desk and knew what was coming.

"Vin, you've seen the trouble over that UK aircraft that went into the sea off Broome. `What are we going to do about the UK High Commission and their request to know about military activity that night when the UK aircraft disappeared off the coast near Broome?"

Vin reminded his boss of the flight in question in case he was as[ ] in the House. "You mean the loss of an ITAC 990 operat[ ] y the UK airline Royal World Airways, RW845?"

"T[ ] s the one. Presumably there's no connection betwe[ ] he stuff we've been watching on JORN and the loss of the [ ] aft?"

"V[ ] good question, Minister, if I may say so. We don't know the answer. We will have a real problem if the ATSB ask us if the JORN radar was operating, because they are handling the investigation."

"We will have to say it was operating but we don't believe there was any connection between what we were watching and the accident."

"Minister, we will get crucified if there proves to be any connection."

"Vin, how many unidentified returns have we been watching?"

"It varied between one and six but since that night there have only been two returns."

"Did we send aircraft up to try to establish what the returns were?"

"Yes, apparently we did but I don't know the details."

"Well you had better get Max Wilson over and get him to brief us."

Vin left the office and called the Chief of the Defence Staff, General Wilson, from his desk, asking him to bring the latest information with him. Wilson finally arrived after lunch having had the opportunity to get an up-to-date briefing. They went into Jack Smithson's office.

"Now Max, thanks for coming over. Where are we up to? Have you sorted out the returns?"

"Well Minister, we thought we had but now we are not so sure. We have been watching these radar returns on JORN for many weeks. They are always at night which makes things difficult. We sent up some F18s with long range tanks together with one of our Airbus tankers to have a look but of course with the Jindalee radar it was not possible to vector our aircraft accurately onto the returns we could see. To cut a long story short, one F18 finally managed to get an aircraft in its radar and then get close enough to identify it; it proved to be a Chinese navy plane. They were not breaking any controlled airspace rules as such but such movement should have been notified to the relevant Flight Information Region. We then sent out some P8s low level and with the help of the JORN they managed to locate the latest Chinese Naval Carrier, *Tiangong*."

"Max, how on earth did that carrier get into the Indian Ocean?"

"Not sure but we think it went south of us. It is nuclear powered so it wouldn't have been a problem. Our P8s also saw some support ships without identification markings and we are busy trying to identify from where they came."

"Were the Chinese aircraft anywhere near the commercial airliners flight routes?"

"Difficult to answer that, Minister, as the airliners tend to fly direct great circle routes if they can in order to save fuel. The critical thing is the altitude and there can be little doubt that the Chinese aircraft were on occasions at the same altitude as the airliners, there was no moon and the aircraft were not using their navigation lights according to our F18s."

"Well there is nothing very secret about all this. Presumably we told the Chinese that they should have informed all the FIRs what they were doing?"

"Yes we did that but we didn't publicise the situation."

"Why on earth not? Maybe there was a collision. As I understand it, most of the returns stopped after the night the airliner crashed into the sea."

"We didn't stop because there appeared to be more returns that were significantly different from the Chinese naval aircraft. We want to know what the other aircraft are and whether they are cooperating with the Chinese."

"But Max, a commercial aircraft has been lost. It may have been a mid-air collision. We've got to tell the ATSB what is going on."

"Minister, I expect you've seen the ISIS video claiming they bombed the aircraft. It seems far more likely than a collision. We think that that if there had been a collision we would have heard from either the Chinese or from whoever was operating the aircraft."

"Alright, so you think there hasn't been a collision. But we should still tell ATSB what's going on."

"We need to find out what the other aircraft are and who is operating them. If we announce what's been going on then the chances are that we will never find out who the other people are."

"Does it matter? Could be the Americans, they've got Carriers everywhere."

"In that case if anything had gone wrong we definitely would have heard."

"So Max, what you are saying is that it is so important to the defence of this Country to find out who is operating the other aircraft that we should not tell the ATSB that there may have been a collision?"

"Yes, Minister. I'm surprised you are not aware of this situation. I understand that most of the wreckage has already been found and when the front fuselage is discovered they will know straightaway if there was a collision. Didn't the Minister of Foreign Affairs, Geoff Smith, contact you?"

"No he didn't, but that doesn't surprise me."

He turned to Vin. "Can you get him on this phone, please?"

Vin dialled the direct line and handed over the phone to Jack Smithson.

"Geoff, Jack here. I 've just heard for the first time that you don't want the news of mysterious aircraft over the Indian Ocean to leak out and that we shouldn't tell ATSB."

"Jack, that's quite right. The US Government want us to continue to use our over-the-horizon radar and our F18s to find out what is happening without telling anybody. It won't matter not telling the ATSB because it looks as if ISIS blew it up,"

"Don't trust those ISIS guys. They are very smart with publicity and the internet and will do anything to get some. I think it is more important to tell the ATSB and I guess so would most of the Australian electorate. However, I'll go along with what the Yanks want but I will blame you if the proverbial hits the fan in the media."

Jack hung up immediately and looked at the other two. "Alright, off you go but remember, it is against my advice and Max, you'll be in trouble as well as Geoff if there is a problem."

***

Maureen Chester, the UK Minister of Defence looked at Harry Brown, her Principle Private Secretary. "Harry, what is going on in the Timor Sea? There was that terrible loss of that RWA aircraft due to a bomb in the cargo the other day and now the High Commission tell us that ghost planes are flying in the area. Why are we involved?"

Harry Brown smiled to himself as the Minister deliberately misquoted and exaggerated the situation in order to get him to explain what was going on.

"Yes Minister." Like most civil servants he always liked to start that way to show he was agreeing with his Minister before correcting any mistakes she may have made or making counter suggestions. "I think there may have been a few developments since your last briefing. Apparently the ITAC 990 which was being operated by Royal World Airways on flight RW845 and which was lost in the Timor Sea was probably not blown up by a bomb in the luggage compartment as was first thought. It is now the view of the accident investigators that the most likely explanation was that a bomb was placed on the flight deck before the aircraft took-off. This view is substantiated by the ISIS video that you saw yesterday. However there is another possibility that there was a head-on mid-air collision."

The Minister interrupted, Harry noticing that she was, as usual, identifying the key point. "But if there had been a collision then the operator of the plane would surely have announced that they had lost an aircraft. Why would they keep it quiet? Surely this is a Department of Transport matter?"

"Well Minister, these aircraft are clearly military ones operating unannounced 300 miles or so off the north western Australian Coast. They must be naval aircraft and presumably the Australians know where they come from. They are being very secretive about the whole thing, for some reason. One theory is that one of these aircraft collided with the airliner and whoever is operating them doesn't want to admit that they were flying in the area without notifying the civil FIRs."

"That seems a very reasonable hypothesis, Harry. And what do the Australian accident investigators say?"

"The Australian Transportation Safety Bureau definitely don't know, Minister. They are still trying to find the front part of the fuselage which may be some way away from the main fuselage and also the front flight data recorder. Incidentally Minister, the High Commission security guy who liaises with the ASIO tells me that it was Peter Talbert again who flushed out from the Australians what was happening and got them on the defensive."

"Who is Peter Talbert and remind me about the ASIO?"

"Peter Talbert was the man who discovered that it was a Russian submarine that shot our P8 down a year or so ago."

"I remember now. We gave him a CBE and not a KBE to avoid drawing attention to the fact that what he did probably saved an unseemly armed conflict with the Russians. He seems a very capable investigator."

"Yes, Minister. He was offered a job by the Ministry of Transport but he turned it down. As for the ASIO, it is rather like our GCHQ and stands for the Australian Security Intelligence Organisation. Their Government have been lavishing a lot of money on it."

"I remember now. Didn't they spend a fortune on building a huge building in prime position overlooking Lake Burley Griffin?"

"Possibly, Minister, but I don't think it was quite as much as we spent on the new GCHQ building."

"Harry, stop trying to score points. We should have spent more, Harry. It wasn't big enough."

"Yes, Minister."

"Harry, about Talbert. Perhaps we could offer him a job in the High Commission?"

"Yes, Minister."

"That sounds like a No, Harry."

"Well I don't think he would take it. You may remember he has an American wife who works in the Australian National Gallery as Procurement Director."

"Pity. We need good people in our Government organisations." She paused for a moment. "Well what happens next? We need to find why the airliner crashed."

"I understand everything is on hold until the front fuselage is found. Hopefully then the experts will be able to tell what happened. If there was a collision they may even find parts of the Chinese plane."

"If there was one, Harry, or evidence that there was an explosion on the flight deck."

"Yes, Minister, that was just what I was going to say."

Chapter 11

Mary walked across the road with Jerry to ATSB and they both went up to Robert's office. He beckoned them in while listening on the phone and looking frustrated. He finally put the phone down.

"Hi! Jerry, as you know Peter called me last night and I've been talking to my RAAF contact again about what's been going on. He wouldn't tell me anything. He said RW845 crashed almost certainly because it was a bomb on the flight deck as ISIS claimed. He was sure that this will be confirmed when we find the front part of the fuselage. In fact Peter got more out his contact than I could get from mine.

"However I agree with Peter it makes good sense to move the ROV and *Ocean Salvager* further away from where we found the main wreckage and search for the front fuselage in a wider radius. Fortunately we've salvaged everything we can at the present ROV location. I sent instructions last night to get the boat moving but it is slow going. The ROV tether from the cage is only 500m and it takes time for the ROV to check the area. We'd be better off with another vehicle with sidescan radar attached and a fibre optic cable which can move faster and be steered by a moving ship; something like *Oceaneering's* Ocean Explorer 6000 but we've got to make do with what we've got."

"I thought *Ocean Shield* had *Bluefin-21* with sidescan sonar?"

"Yes it does but it went away when *Ocean Voyager* came on station and we can't get it back."

"Well then, Robert, I agree; there is not much else you can do, I suppose."

"You're right. It would cost us a lot to add another search vehicle assuming we could find one quickly and we'd still need *Ocean Salvager* to lift what was found."

Jerry decided to change the subject. "Now Robert, about our going to Broome. Mary and I were talking last night and I think we should wait a few days before we go there so that, hopefully, by then the front of the fuselage will have been found. If we go now we would be just twiddling our thumbs waiting for the ROV to find it."

Robert smiled. "There are worse places to stay twiddling your thumbs but I know what you mean. Of course, without wishing to be rude you could go back to the UK and leave it all to us."

"Absolutely. You're quite right. Tell you what, why don't we do this? We will go to Broome in a couple of days, look at the fuselage and then wait a day or so to see what is happening. If no progress there are flights from Perth to Dubai and then home."

"Why not wait on *Ocean Salvager*?"

"Great idea if you can arrange it."

Mary went back to her temporary office with Mark Coburn and brought him up to date on their plans. She realised that it was going to be a bit tedious for the next day or so until they went to Broome and so she decided to visit the FDR analysis room, not that there was anything much to see.

Later in the day Peter came on line. "Mary, remind me what time it was when you first visited the WorldLink office. I seem to remember that you said it was quite late."

"It was on my first day. I came in at dawn and went to your place. I sorted myself out, rested a bit and then went to ATSB. While I was there Andrew started organising my trip to the facility and I realised that I needed to go to the office. It was getting late for Australian closing office time; in fact it was about 1730 but I thought it was worth a try. However I was lucky as a guy came to the door and let me in; I gave him my info and he told me the keypad numbers."

"What was he wearing?"

Mary tried to visualise the occasion. "I can't remember but I tell you what, I do remember that he didn't look like he was the office manager and so I assumed he had just changed and was about to go home."

"Well I think it was the previous office manager, John Dixon, whom you met; he must have waited until Mike Goldton went home and then gone in for some reason; perhaps to make sure there was no way he could be traced. Goldton must have taken Dixon's keys but presumably didn't change the locks. As a result of your visit he would have known your car, when you would be going out and where you would be parking the car."

"But that didn't give him a motive."

"I think it might. He was removed by Derek Courtfield."

"That's hardly a reason for blowing up the facility."

"There may be more to his dismissal than we know. When Derek told me about Dixon leaving I thought he was a bit economical with the details. I seem to remember that you told me that you had met another guy on your visit?"

"That's right, Cliff Watkins. I think he was quite badly hurt by the explosion."

"I think I'll call him if I can and get some background to Derek and the lovely Sophie."

"Hadn't you better tell the police?"

"I'm not very popular with them. I thought I might visit and watch that address you sent me myself."

Mary was definitely interested.

"I'm just waiting to go out to Ocean Salvager. If I came too I might be able to recognise the guy."

"True, but I'm not sure Charlie would like that. I think I'd better take a camera and bring you back the pictures."

"I'd be very good."

"Mary, I'm sure you would. That's what I'm afraid of. I'm like Oscar Wilde."

"Not him again. You're definitely not like him. He was gay."

"Temptation is in the eye of the beholder."

"Not sure what that means. I think you're mixing your metaphors."

Mary noticed Peter rapidly changing the subject. "Mary, when are you going to Broome?"

"In a couple of days when hopefully they will have found the front fuselage."

"Alright we'll keep in touch and I'll let you know if I have any luck with that address."

***

Two days later Jerry announced they should go to Broome the next day. The ROV was still looking for the front fuselage pieces but the area to be searched was very large as it was impossible to know the path of the aircraft as it descended. Mary reckoned that they would almost certainly be returning to the UK from Broome so she left at the end of the morning and caught the No 7 bus to do some shopping at Westfield in Belconnen. She went to level three and the Coffee Club where she ordered a Salad Nicoise. She suddenly felt she was being watched and three tables away she saw a man watching her and recognised to her horror the man she had met at the WorldLink Office that first night. Unfortunately she felt it must have been obvious to the man that she had recognised him. She hurriedly asked the lady at the next table to look after her salad which had just arrived and went to the toilet; in the privacy of a cubicle she took her phone out sent a message to Peter 'Very worried. First WorldLink man watching me in Coffee Club third level, Westfield, Belconnen.'

The message was not shown as being delivered so she then copied the message and sent it as an email selecting the receipt and reading options. She returned to the table but became alarmed when there was an automatic reply saying that Peter would not be available for three days. She didn't know whether to be pleased or concerned when she saw that the man watching her had disappeared. Then she suddenly remembered what Peter had said was the name of the man watching her, John Dixon. She didn't know what to do for the best but realised she could be in danger. She rang the Belconnen police station and asked for Commander Martin but was told he was not available. She asked for someone in authority and tried to explain the situation but felt she wasn't getting anywhere so she called 000, explained she was being stalked and asked for protection back to the Novotel.

The lady on the emergency phone said all the right things but clearly wondered if she was dealing with an oddball or a nutter. Mentioning Commander Martin had some effect and finally, albeit Mary felt with some reluctance, it was agreed that a policeman would come to find her in the restaurant. Mary managed to get an email address and sent a photo of herself to the 000 emergency office to help the policeman find her.

Thirty minutes went by and finally she spotted a policeman who was clearly looking for her. He came over and reluctantly agreed to sit down while Mary tried to explain the situation. She discovered he was an ACT policeman and not from the Belconnen Federal police and clearly wanted, very politely, to get rid of her as quickly as possible. They went down to the front of the Westfield Centre where there was a police car parked with a policewoman driver. Mary got in the back and they drove her to the Novotel. Thankfully Mary found that Jerry was in his room and he came down to the lobby to meet her. Mary could see that the policeman was glad to be shot of her and departed with a courteous farewell.

Mary tried to explain to Jerry the problem she was in because John Dixon had recognised her but found it difficult to impart the sense of unease she had felt sitting in the coffee shop with Dixon staring at her. She went up to her room and the next thing she knew was that she was hit violently in the stomach, winded and knocked on to the floor. She struggled but couldn't prevent first her ankles and then her hands being fixed with handcuffs. The assailant had a balaclava on so she couldn't decide whether it was Dixon or a hired assassin; there was no way she was going to find out as she was blindfolded and gagged. She knew she was in great danger but there was nothing she could do.

Her room phone rang several times and it seemed to her several hours went by. Then there was a knock on the door and she realised that someone had come in with a wheelchair. She felt herself being dressed in a burkha and placed in the wheelchair. They went down in the elevator and apparently got outside without being challenged by the hotel staff. They placed her in a car, drove for about an hour and took her into a building, placed her on a bed and left her. Mary guessed they were waiting until it was late and resigned herself to being thrown into the lake or some other similar fate.

***

Jerry rang Mary's room several times when she did not appear in the bar and began to get worried. Finally he spoke to the front desk and they agreed to check in her room. The duty manager appeared and he first knocked on the door and when there was no reply opened the door with a master key. There was no-one in the room but there seemed to have been a disturbance as the carpets were in a mess and the bed looked as a fight had taken place. The manager was clearly worried and turned to Jerry to get advice.

Jerry went over the conversation he had had with Mary and asked the manager to ring Belconnen police station. Jerry could sense that Belconnen were trying to get the manager to ring the ACT police and so he decided to take over and explain about the bomb at the WorldLink facility. He was handed over to someone else who then announced he was going to try to contact a more senior policeman. Finally Jerry found himself talking to Commander Martin which he then remembered was the name Mary had mentioned.

"Mr Masterson, let's go over the ground again. Miss French came back to the hotel with an ACT policeman. She told you she had been worried because she had seen the man who she believed might have blown up the WorldLink facility. She was scared because she thought she was the only person who knew what he looked like."

"Yes, that's absolutely correct."

"Did Miss French go up to her room with the policeman?"

"Unfortunately not. You are the expert but it looks as if there was someone waiting for her in the room and took her away. The room was in a mess and someone had been lying on the bed."

There was a long pause.

"Mr Masterson do you know a Mr Peter Talbert?"

"Yes. He is an insurance investigator based in Canberra."

"To save me looking him up, do you happen to know his mobile number?"

Jerry quickly found Peter's number and passed it on.

***

Mary heard the door open and knew she was in serious trouble. She was put in a car and driven for another hour. The door was opened and she could hear the roar of water. She was lifted out, put on the side of the road and then covered with a blanket. To her horror she felt something being tied round her legs. As the men went back to their car she suddenly sensed a floodlight shining on the scene and heard what sounded like a panicky exchange between her captors. Then she heard car doors slamming and a car, she thought it was the one that brought her, being driven off at reckless speed with squeals coming from the tyres. She heard another car come close, stop and steps coming towards her. The top of the burkha enshrouding her was peeled back. To her amazement and infinite relief she heard Peter's voice.

"Well thank goodness; I got here just in time."

She couldn't say anything as she was gagged and the burkha didn't help. There was a long pause and she felt Peter removing her leg restraints. Then somehow with great difficulty he got her into his car and she heard his phone ringing.

"Mr Talbert. Commander Martin here. I must apologise for waking you in the middle of the night. I'm rather worried about your Mary French. She has disappeared and apparently she recognised the person who she thinks may have blown up the WorldLink facility."

"Commander Martin, you didn't wake me. Mary French has just had a very lucky escape. I've just found her, bound and gagged, about to be thrown into Lake Burley Griffin."

There was a long pause. "I'm not sure I understand you, Mr Talbert. Where did you say you were?"

"Would you believe next to the Scrivener Dam? Mary could almost hear Peter thinking. "This is going to be a long story, Commander Martin. What you need to be doing immediately is finding car NSW registration APR 317, a red Honda five door CR-V with two very dangerous men inside. I've got to rush Miss French to hospital but I think she'll be alright. I'll call you on this number when I've got her sorted. Start looking in the Lady Denman Drive area by the dam and my guess is then towards Belconnen."

He rang off and managed to untie Mary's gag and her blindfold. "Peter, I'm alright. I don't need to go to hospital. Take me to your place and get rid of this burkha and the rest."

He got into the car and started to drive home.

"Peter, call Jerry at the Novotel and tell him I'm alright. Perhaps he could drive over to your place with all my kit."

Peter managed to get through to the hotel while he was driving, hoping there were no police about; the receptionist managed to wake Jerry and he agreed to collect Mary's things. Peter then called Jill Evans who was fortuitously living at home looking after the children and explained the situation. The moment he got home he went in and got Jill, who had by then got dressed, to give him a hand. He inspected Mary's ankles and wrists and went into his garage to get a pair of giant clippers which he had had for years. He also got a large torch which he gave to Jill.

"Mary, I could cut the handcuffs with a saw but it would be very difficult and time consuming and I might cut you at the same time. I'm going to try these large clippers which hopefully will do the job."

He got Jill to shine the torch on the handcuffs fixed to Mary's feet and, after a struggle, managed to get the jaws of the clippers round a link. He tried closing the jaws on the link but couldn't make any impression. He got his phone out and called the Belconnen Police station. It was now 3.30 in the morning and there was a delay before he was answered. He asked for Commander Martin and had to explain the urgency and that he had been talking to him earlier. After sometime he heard Commander Martin's voice.

"I've just got back to my house with Mary French but I can't cut the handcuffs that bind her wrists and ankles. I've got a nurse here so I think if you can get someone to undo her we can get Miss French sorted. Amazingly she seems unharmed, mentally as well as physically."

"Mr Talbert, give me your address and I'll get one of our locksmith experts to come over. I'll be over myself in the morning."

Luckily it was a warm summer's night so Mary was managing alright lying in the rear seat of the car. Jill had got her some water and a blanket and they waited outside for the locksmith to arrive. He appeared after another forty minutes and examined the situation as I held the torch.

"Mr Talbert, the padlocks on these handcuffs are absolutely standard, can be bought anywhere. We'll soon get them undone."

Mary chimed in. "The sooner the better, please. I'm very uncomfortable."

The expert was as true as his word and in about five minutes he had the ankles undone. Peter and Jill pulled Mary up into a sitting position and a few minutes later her hands were free. They helped Mary to her feet and supported her as she went into the house. She wanted to go upstairs but they judged she should wait a bit and get her circulation going again. The three of them sat down in the living room.

Peter asked the locksmith to come in for a drink but he said he would prefer to get home and go back to bed. Jerry arrived with Mary's things looking a bit bleary eyed and only stayed long enough to hear what had happened and be reassured that Mary was going to be alright. Jill took Mary up to her room and then we all went to bed.

Peter was woken up by the children. He got up in his dressing gown to help with breakfast but Jill, looking rather tired, had to get up to take Francie to school. Peter checked that Mary was still asleep and went back to bed feeling very guilty he had not emailed Charlie.

Commander Martin woke Peter at 10.00 saying he was coming over in an hour by which time Peter was dressed and Mary appeared in her dressing gown looking in good shape, a phrase which Peter decided was not one he should use when he got round to reporting what had happened to Charlie. He produced coffee and they sat down in the living room.

Martin waited a few minutes and then started questioning.

"Mr Talbert you seem to have got into the middle of the action again. What's been going on?"

"Have you found the car yet? One of the guys is called John Dixon, I believe."

"No, we haven't and I hope you haven't given us a bum steer."

"It was all a bit of a rush but the number plate I gave you I'm pretty sure was the correct one on the car which had been carrying Miss French; presumably the people inside the car were going to weigh her down and throw her into the reservoir."

"Why would they want to do that?"

"Well John Dixon was the manager of the WorldLink office before the present one, Mike Goldton. Derek Courtfield fired

Dixon and I felt there was something going on he hadn't told me. So I spoke to Cliff Watkins the other day before I went to Melbourne; Cliff was the guy who looked after the facility technically. He was badly hurt when the explosion went off and he had only just been released from the hospital to go home. I asked him about John Dixon and I got a data dump.

"Apparently John Dixon was going out with Sophie Schmidt who was the temporary typist in the WorldLink office. Derek Courtfield took a fancy to her and he contrived to fire John Dixon for allegedly breaching confidentiality. The next thing that happened was that there then was one hell of a row as Sophie decided to leave Dixon and go with Derek who took the opportunity to move Sophie to the facility as receptionist. Cliff told me that according to Sophie John Dixon actually threatened Derek with a gun and he felt sure that she wasn't making the story up. As you probably know she is currently engaged to Derek, apparently with marriage imminent.

"By the time Mike Goldton started work in the office John Dixon had gone and Sophie had left the office; my bet is that Derek didn't tell Mike about John Dixon and Sophie. Understandably therefore Mike saw no reason to change the locks of the City office; consequently in the evenings after Mike had gone home John Dixon was able to enter the office whenever he wanted to, find out what was going on and remove all traces of his employment. He was obviously looking for a way to get back at Derek Courtfield and then his opportunity came. Mary came to the office after it was closed and told him about her impending visit to the facility. Dixon clearly had an accomplice and they managed to get explosives under Mary's car. I guess the plan was just to damage the front of the building and possibly Sophie and Derek but not to kill anybody; clearly they got things wrong. John must have triggered the bomb and obviously he had set the trigger time delay after he had pressed the button so that he had time to get well away and back into Canberra before the bomb went off. Presumably sometime after Mary had gone into the building he pressed the trigger and drove off but the plan went wrong as far as he was concerned as Sophie and Derek were not there when the bomb went off.

"Incidentally Mike Goldton found Dixon's references in one of the office filing cabinets and I see he was in the Royal Australian Engineers, Explosive Ordnance Disposal Squadron. In view of that I'm a bit surprised he got the amount of explosive wrong as he killed one engineer, severely hurt another and virtually destroyed the whole facility. Still it certainly explains his familiarity with triggers.

"Of course he realised that if he was caught he would be tried for murder. He must have been shattered in the Coffee Club in Belconnen to see Mary and know she had recognised him. Like many murderers before him, he realised that he needed to go on killing to prevent being found out."

"Can you prove any of this?"

Mary had been doing her best listening to Peter's explanation despite Jill's attentions.

"I can confirm that the guy in the Coffee Club was the guy I saw at the World Link Office."

"Yes, my dear." Martin sounded very supportive. "But did you see the guy who first attacked you and then the accomplice?"

She shook head. "They were wearing Balaclavas."

Peter took over. "If you can catch the people in the car then surely that would help enormously. The other thing is that I think that Courtfield knew perfectly well who had done the damage but didn't want to admit what skulduggery had taken place over the lovely Sophie. Come to think of it she must have suspected John as well; it would be very interesting to talk to her."

Martin stopped for a moment making notes of Peter's explanation of what had probably occurred.

"Mr Talbert let's leave that for a bit. How was it you managed to be at the right spot at the right time?"

"No mystery about that. I knew Mary here might be in danger from the moment she told me about John Dixon and so I got her to put the *Find my Friends* app on her phone. I was doing a job in Melbourne at the airport when I got her cri de Coeur; I didn't recognise where the phone was and so I immediately caught a plane. I landed at about 22.30 and called Jerry in the hotel as I was going to my car; he was very relieved to hear my voice and explained what had happened. Luckily Mary must have been wearing slacks with her phone in her pocket as I could see the phone in Belconnen. I started to chase the phone and as I got close I realised the phone was moving. It took some time to follow the phone as I kept on having to stop to find out where to go. I made a mistake and got on to the Tuggeranong Parkway but realised I need to get on to Lady Denman Drive. Finally I started to get close to the phone as I approached the Scrivener Dam and luckily I spotted a driveway leading to a car park by Lake Burley Griffin. Jerry had alerted me and I knew Mary must be in great danger so I decided to drive quietly without lights down to the car park where it was pitch black down by the lake; I could make out that there was a car there and I suddenly shone my lights. The car turned out to be a red Honda CR-V with the back door open and there was something by the lake which proved to be Mary; two people were bending over her busily doing some nefarious business. My appearance clearly upset them and I could see them for a few seconds trying to move her but for some reason it was proving difficult; they gave up, ran back to the car and one of them slammed the boot shut. They started the car up and drove past my car at high speed up to Lady Denman Drive.

"I got out of the car and found a body, bound and gagged in a burkha with a heavy stone in a bag next to it; it was already tied round what proved to be Mary's legs. There was also a large ball of heavy twine and some cutting shears. If you find the car my bet is that there will be more stones and bags in the back of it. By the way I've got the shears and I haven't put my fingerprints on it. "

Mary suddenly sat up. "But I didn't have my phone. They took it from me!"

"Then you were very lucky. If they had turned it off I would never have found you."

Peter took his phone out and tried searching again for Mary's phone. "I'm afraid I can't see the phone. They must have realised how I found them and switched it off."

"Well you've given us a good description of the car and there aren't too many of those in red. We have the registration as well which may help.

"Mr Talbert there seems to be a lot of speculation in your story but it has the ring of truth. Hopefully we'll find the car fairly soon. I don't think I can do any more here at the moment. I'll be contacting you and we'll need Miss French to recognise your Mr Dixon when we catch him."

"Well don't leave it too long as she will be going back to UK soon."

Peter gave Martin the cutting shears in a bag and he left. It was too late to talk to Charlie so Peter sent her a long email. Mary went back to bed and Peter decided he had better go to his office. Commander Martin called. "Mr Talbert, I've just heard we caught the car on the Hume Highway approaching Sydney; luckily John Dixon had Mary French's phone in his pocket. They had changed the number plates you saw but you were quite right; there were weights and bags in the car."

***

The next morning Jill was up early dealing with Mary. Charlie called having read Peter's email.

"You seem to have done a great job again. Hope your Commander Martin was impressed. However I don't like the idea of you and Mary alone in the house. She's always had her eye on you."

"Darling she's going to marry your brother."

"That doesn't seem to worry her. Remember the fling she was having with Greg Tucker not to mention that senior guy in GCHQ. She's oversexed."

"Well what do you want me to do?"

"Nothing. Get the message, nothing. Get her back to the Novotel as soon as she's fit." There was an ominous silence. "Remember, nothing. Let Jill look after her."

"When are you coming back?"

"As soon as I can. Hopefully I can catch a night flight to-night."

Charlie rang off and Jill disappeared with the children saying she needed to do some shopping and would be back to give Mary some lunch. Peter went in to see Mary and was amazed to find there didn't seem to be any after effects from the kidnapping. Apparently she had slept like a log and on seeing him she asked for a cup of tea. She decided to get ready for it and sat up in bed with the duvet covering her midriff and her breasts in full view. Peter brought the tea in and put it next to the bed. She could see him looking at her and she felt her nipples hardening and moistening down below.

"Mary how do you feel? You look fantastic but I'd be a lot more comfortable if you would cover yourself up."

"What's the problem? Haven't you seen boobs before? Alright, if you think it might help, get me a bra and panties from my bag and some perfume." However from the way she looked at him it was clear that at that particular moment his being comfortable wasn't what she had in mind.

Peter found the perfume straightaway and Mary used it to good effect but she could see Peter was clearly finding it difficult going through her underclothes; however he finally found the ones she wanted. She didn't rush putting her bra on making sure it fitted perfectly and Peter was clearly appreciating every move. She finally fastened it supporting her breasts but the nipples were not covered.

"Does that look any better?"

She looked at him again and could see that Peter definitely thought it was.

He grinned, "You know damn well the way it looks."

"Pass me the panties, then, and see if that helps?"

She slowly removed the duvet leaving herself fully exposed and used the perfume again before trying to put the panties on. She looked at him but only made a token move before putting her hand lightly on the front of his trousers. "You know, I don't think we need them at the moment. Do you?"

He didn't answer as she pulled him down and kissed him sensuously on the mouth. She knew that this time it was definitely going to happen as he reached down and held her bra, undid it and then, kneeling down, stroked and kissed her nipples. She undid Peter's belt, zip and underpants and stroked him, wondering why some people didn't think size mattered. He started to stroke her thighs and to make it easier for him she sat on the side of the bed as his trousers fell to the floor. She lay back and felt Peter thrusting inside her. She put her hand on his buttocks and pulled him tight so he couldn't escape and they both let themselves go. Slowly they cooled down and lay down next to one another.

Mary whispered "That was wonderful. I've been looking forward to that for ages."

Peter said nothing and got up and went into the shower. Mary followed him and she helped clean him up. "Mary, if you carry on like that we'll need another shower."

"So, are you complaining?"

Chapter 12

I slept well and woke up late. I could hear Jill dealing with the children and also going in to see Mary. She put her head round my door and said she wouldn't be back until lunch time as she had some stuff to get. I got up slowly, showered and went in to see Mary who woke up and asked for a cup of tea. When I took in to her room she was sitting up, the duvet over her bottom part and her breasts fully exposed. They were a wonderful shape and she clearly knew it. I put the tea down and suggested she should put some clothes on but I wasn't convinced that that was going to prevent what she clearly had in mind and certainly I should have been offering some resistance. She asked me to look in her bag to get a bra, panties and perfume; the perfume was easy but I was having a lot of difficulty with the bra and panties as the bag was very full and there seemed to be enough underwear for Mary to change every day for at least a month. I finally found what she was looking for, a minute bra and equally small panties. She took them and I just couldn't stop myself responding strongly as I watched her slowly putting on the bra; I could see that her nipples, which were very firm, were actually above the top of the bra. Any hope of common sense disappeared when I offered her the panties and she slid the duvet off; she made only a perfunctory attempt to put them on and I think we both came to the conclusion that they might be in the way. She pulled me down and kissed me erotically on the lips and I couldn't resist reaching down and holding her bra for a moment before kneeling and removing it so I could stroke and kiss her nipples. I could feel her undoing my trousers, zip and underpants and stroking me. She decided to sit on the edge of the bed while I caressed her thighs. Any thought of stopping half way seemed a million miles away as I, gently at first, went inside her. She clutched my bottom with her hands and we both let ourselves go. It seemed to go on a long time before we relaxed and lay down next to one another.

After a bit I decided it was time to get up even though Jill was not due back for a bit and went into the shower and Mary joined me. We started cleaning each other up with the inevitable result that we went back on the bed again with our towels for another encounter, this time Mary lying on top of me.

As we lay down on the bed again I started thinking of Charlie and what I was going to say. I wasn't sure but of one thing I was sure --- Mary had better go back to the Novotel as soon as possible. She must have read my mind as this time she showered by herself and then started to get dressed. I went into my room, also showered and then got dressed for the second time that day; I was very relieved to find Mary ready, dressed, packed and ready to go when I got downstairs.

"Mary, you are amazing."

"What do you mean?"

"You can separate sex from normal living."

"Of course. I told you before. I just wanted to say thank you for rescuing me and I couldn't think of a better way. There's no way you and I could live together. You've got a happy family and I'm going to start one with Andrew."

I didn't say anything. I had no idea what Andrew would say if he knew what Mary and I had been up to and I dreaded to think what Charlie was going to say.

I dropped Mary off at the Novotel and she told me she would keep me informed of what she was doing. I went to my office and tried to get on with some work.

About two hours later Jerry called me.

"Peter, what have you got planned for the next few days? Mary has decided she needs to go back to the UK and I've got spare seats booked at the hotel in Broome, the helicopter and the boat, *Ocean Salvager*."

"Jerry, you're on. What time and where?"

"You'll need to book your airline tickets but I'll be at the Blue Seas Resort at Broome from 1500 to-morrow."

Jerry rang off and I booked my flights on line before calling Charlie.

"When are you coming home? I'm off to Broome for a few days first thing to-morrow."

"Well that's not very nice. I'll be landing at 0700 to-morrow at Sydney. Are you trying to avoid me?"

"Certainly not but I'm catching the 0900 from here. It looks as if we're not going to meet up for a day or so."

"Where's Mary?"

"She's on her way back to UK. Amazingly she didn't seem to suffer from nearly being drowned."

"Pity. I don't mean that of course. But I'm glad she's gone. One less thing to worry about. She seemed to be determined to add you to her library, collection or whatever the phrase is."

I wasn't convinced 'scalps' was the phrase she was looking for but decided that this was not the moment to find a suitable description; as always on these occasions least said soonest mended though this was the first time I had been in this situation. We rang off and I prepared things for my departure. Back home I told the children the good news about their mother's return and the bad news about my departure but they took it all in their stride. Having Jill was their anchor point and Mary's departure seemed to worry them the most, but not for long.

***

I arrived at Broome on time and took a taxi to the Blue Seas Resort. It was a typical holiday resort and I had come prepared to go swimming if there was nothing else to do. Jerry was already there and we met in the bar. I asked him for the latest news.

"Nothing to report. As you know we are limited on how far the ROV can go searching from the cage position. It's a long winded business as the Ocean Salvager has to keep moving the cage. If only we knew the path the aircraft took while it was descending."

"Well we can guess the maximum distance from where the fuselage was found since there was no power on the engines and we know the rate of descent."

"That's right, Peter. The aerodynamicists reckon no more than 20 nautical miles from where the fuselage and FDRs were found. The ROV must be getting fairly close by now."

"Jerry, you know I'm surprised it didn't dive more quickly as without the nose the aircraft would have been very unstable. Have you had a look at the fuselage bits yet?"

"No, I'm planning for us to have a look to-morrow morning."

"Where are they?"

"They are lying on an old pier. The harbour has been enlarged for new cruise ships and luckily ATSB were able to get permission to put the wings and the fuselage pieces there for a few weeks. The ATSB experts have had a look and apparently there is some evidence of burning which might have been caused by a bomb but nothing definite."

"What about the bodies?"

"They've all been taken to the temporary hangars next to the Broome mortuary. As you know the identification is a very slow process but it is all happening."

We started talking of the cricket and Jerry was clearly a disappointed England supporter.

"Well Jerry, at least it is still only a game and not riddled with graft."

"What do you mean?"

"Well international sports have multi-national organisations like the Olympic Committee and FIFA. They have decision making powers on venues and the like. It is pretty obvious that these decisions are determined by people who are financially involved. I don't believe we have that situation in cricket."

"Yes, you're right there. People are involved mainly for the love of the game though, you know, even in cricket there is some gambling and attempts to get players to influence the result of the matches."

"Yes I know. But that's very different from deciding venues of worldwide sporting events. I think the problem with these international committees is that every country has one vote and for some, being 'persuaded' is the financial opportunity of a lifetime."

We went to bed early and I had a swim before breakfast. When we had finished our not insubstantial meal we put on some working clothes. Jerry got his rental car from the parking lot and we drove to the harbour office to meet the ATSB photographers. They knew the way to the wreckage and had not only a key to get through the guard fence but a radio to the harbour master.

We parked close to the wreckage, got out of the car, put our hats on and just stared, sizing up the situation. There was a lot more bits than I was expecting because the engine, nacelles and wings had all broken up. However, amazingly, the two parts of the fuselage were still roughly in shape. The photographers showed us how to rig the ladders and hydraulic platforms so that we could inspect the wreckage and we started by looking at the mangled front of the front fuselage piece. I was not familiar with inspection of aircraft accidents but to me it looked as if the missing front piece of the fuselage had been torn off. Clearly the break was just in front of where the wings joined the fuselage so that the missing nose would be the crew compartment with the crew rest and galley areas and part of the first class section.

I could see Jerry puzzling over the damage. He was vastly more experienced than I was but he was clearly having trouble trying to visualise what might have caused the damage we were looking at. Luckily there was no wind and we could converse as we inspected each section.

"Jerry, you're the expert but this doesn't look like bomb damage. I reckon the front fuselage has been torn off."

"I agree. Clearly the fuselage pieces would have been torn apart if there had been a bomb in the luggage area and there are no signs of bomb damage from a bomb in the flight deck. I think the ISIS story is just a fabrication and that there has been a collision."

"It clearly must have been a military aircraft or we would have heard by now. I suppose whoever owned the plane does not want to admit liability of flying in the FIR without telling Air Traffic."

"Well clearly ATSB needs to find the front section as quickly as possible."

We checked the rest of the aircraft, wings and engines. The port wing was very different from the starboard wing and it looked as if it had received impact damage confirming our suspicions of a head-on collision with the front fuselage section being torn off. We needed to find the front of the aircraft as soon as possible.

In the bar that night we mused over the loss of the second flight data recorder. I rang Stephen in the morning.

"I've been thinking. How about you getting back to your chums in ASIO and the RAAF?"

"What chums? Wish!"

"Alright, Stephen, your contacts. I think the missing FDR is very significant. I bet they know a lot more about the missing recorder than we think."

"You don't think the RAAF found it, do you?"

"No, of course not. However I think they know a lot more than they are letting on. They won't help us with their JORN radar and what they saw. Why not ask them who they think pinched the recorder and why?"

"Pinched the recorder. Surely it's not that easy to get hold of the recorder?"

"Good point, Stephen, but in fact if the beacon is transmitting and you've got the gear to hand then it can be done. I think the people who pinched the recorder didn't care if they damaged it. They just didn't want us to read the data. It was done so quickly that I think they didn't realise that the aircraft had two recorders and therefore that they were wasting their time."

"But we've read the other recorder. It hasn't told us anything special."

"I agree. It's strange."

"Anyway if someone stole the recorder who do you think would have done it?"

"Stephen, as I told you, the list has to be very short. Russia, China, Japan, USA, France, Germany and UK. Don't think North Korea has the capability, South Korea is too busy making money.

"Wouldn't be us and anyway I don't think we have the capability to grab the recorder in this part of the world. USA definitely could --- just look what they did with that Russian sub and trying to hoodwink the Australians. The Russians got their fingers badly burned losing that sub. I suppose I would go for the Chinese. Anyway let's find out what the Aussies say."

"Alright Peter, I think I'll have a word in the UK to see if they can get any new information from the RAAF or whoever. ATSB don't seem to be getting anywhere with the RAAF."

I reported some of the conversation back to Jerry and told him that Stephen in the Commission didn't seem to be doing much good at the moment with ASIO.

After breakfast we travelled out to *Ocean Salvager* in the second helicopter ferry of the day. We took our bags to our cabins and then met Jim Forester in the canteen; the ROV was covering a lot of ground but so far without success. Jim looked at Jerry. "I think what is really needed is our *Ocean Explorer 6000* with sidescan sonar. I know the water is not terribly deep but the tethered ROV cannot search large areas quickly. If we don't find something soon then ATSB need to contract us to bring the 6000; in my view it will be cheaper in the end."

Jerry nodded. "It's a difficult decision for the ATSB. As you know they had *Ocean Shield* with *Bluefin-21* which could do the job but they lost it. If they go for your *Ocean Explorer 6000* it will cost them more money. As it is they are having to pay the money up front but they will almost certainly get some recompense eventually from the airline and possibly from the UK Government. Having said that it is quite likely that some of the cost will fall on the Aussies. From our viewpoint ATSB do a super job and we will be happy to leave it to them and work with them as required. For example, I'm off home the day after to-morrow if you haven't found anything but will come racing back if anything significant crops up."

"Let's hope we have some success. As you know we work 24/7"

Jim took us along to the Control Van and we stayed for an hour or so watching the ROV swimming along looking ahead and down in the illuminated gloom for some wreckage. We left and went back to our rooms and I was glad I had brought some work with me. Jerry decided he would catch the last helicopter ferry back to Broome that day but I decided I might as well stay on for another day and catch the direct flight which would get me back to Canberra late in the evening.

I was awakened in the middle of the night by Jim who had in turn been woken by one of his people. Apparently the ROV had found some wreckage and the ATSB engineer who was living on the ship was examining the wreckage. We went on to the pitch black deck on the way to the control room using a torch but I made Jim stop for a moment to look up to the sky; there was no smoke or light obscuring the view and the heavens were filled with countless stars all shining down with a brightness unimaginable in any urban environment. Luckily I did not have to speak as I was lost for words.

Inside the control room I could feel an air of excitement. On the main screen I could see some wreckage but it was not easy to sort things out. In my judgement it wasn't a commercial airliner or part of one. It looked like a completely broken military fighter aircraft. The operator in the control room steered the ROV right round the main piece of wreckage as we watched. I turned to Jim who had clearly come to the same conclusion as I had and was shaking his head.

"Peter, we must get the RAAF to look. They might recognise the aircraft. My bet is it is a Chinese aircraft."

"Jim, I suppose we are sure that it did not collide into RWA835."

"I don't believe so. It is all in one piece and there is no sign of what must have been a terrific impact, judging by the other fuselage bits we have. Also I think it has been in the water quite a long time. I'm afraid they need to carry on searching. Of course we will be sending pictures to ATSB in Canberra in case they take a different view."

I went back to my cabin but I paused for a few minutes on deck looking up again at the myriad of stars that illuminated us on the Earth below.

***

The helicopter took me back to Broome and I caught the same direct flight that Mary had caught a few days earlier getting me home at 11pm. Charlie had already gone to bed and I decided not to wake her but use the room which Mary had been using. In the morning I got up and met a very frosty reception from Charlie but nothing was said as the children were fed and despatched to school. I dropped her off at the Art Gallery but the atmosphere remained definitely frigid. Arriving in the office I decided I had better write reports to Al Jazeera and ITAC bringing them up to date. I then tried to work out yet again what had happened to RW845.

Chapter 13

Vin Partridge, Secretary to the Australian Minister of Defence, went in to see his boss, Jack Smithson, holding an urgent message from Max Wilson, Chief of the Defence Force. He gave it to Smithson to read. He read it once, read it again and looked at Partridge.

"Vin, it says here that when that Pom airliner crashed the other day we sent a P8 to the scene of the crash and found both the crash recorders."

"That's right, Minister." Vin reminded his boss of the flight in question in case he was asked. "It was the loss of an ITAC 990 operated by the UK airline Royal World Airways Flight RW845. These days Minister, airliners have two of the latest crash recorders and one of them floats if the aircraft hits the water."

"Well apparently the P8 also heard the second recorder. How did it do that?"

"Apparently it dropped a sonobuoy and heard it transmitting."

"But the report here says that when our Defence Vehicle *Ocean Shield* arrived on the scene it couldn't hear the submerged crash recorder. I thought these days the recorders transmit for 60 days."

"Yes, Minister, that's what I understand. But as you will have read, our over-the-horizon radar was working because there was an exercise on and they saw a return which suggests that there was a boat in the vicinity and may have taken the recorder. In addition the P8 saw a large salvage boat in the vicinity with no markings which might be the one the JORN saw."

"Vin, that's ridiculous. You know it always takes weeks to do get hold of the recorders."

"It's easy enough if the recorder is transmitting and the right ship is on station. Our experts believe that the ship the P8 and JORN saw was a Chinese support ship and it took the recorder away."

"Why would they do that?"

"Because we think they really did lose an aircraft."

"But why would they think taking the recorder would stop us finding out what had happened? And when did they take it?"

"Well our experts think that an instant decision was taken on the spot by whoever was in charge and they just didn't know the aircraft had two recorders. Only the very latest aircraft have them. As to when they did it, they think it was done just after the P8 had found both recorders and had gone home before our patrol boat arrived."

"Vin, I'm no expert as you know but in that case they could have taken both recorders."

"Yes, Minister, but as I said they were only looking for one and remember, the floating beacon was not pinging, it was radiating a radio signal."

"Well didn't you tell me that ATSB has got a recorder?" Vin nodded. "You also said that the ADV *Ocean Shield* found the wreckage of the plane?"

"Quite right, Minister."

"Well then, maybe after all we don't need to tell them anything else at this stage? They are already very lucky to have a recorder and wreckage."

"Minister, shouldn't we tell them everything we know?"

"Vin, we don't know anything. What we think might have happened is pure conjecture."

"Yes, Minister."

***

Maureen Chester, the UK Minister of Defence looked at Harry Brown, her Principle Private Secretary. "Harry, why are we still involved with that terrible loss of life the other day when that RWA aircraft hit the sea off Western Australia? Surely it's time the Department of Transport took over?"

"We seem to be involved because the RAAF and Australian Navy are monitoring military operations. There appears to be a problem, Minister. The aircraft had two crash recorders and the second one has disappeared."

"What do you mean disappeared?"

"Well Minister, immediately after the aircraft crashed a RAAF P8 flew overhead the point where the aircraft hit the water and located the one that was floating and, using a sonobuoy, heard the one that was submerged with the wreckage. However when the Royal Australian Naval Boats arrived they were unable to hear the submerged recorder. Even more curious the second Navy boat had a Remote Observation Vehicle with sidescan radar and it found some wreckage but no recorder. Our aviation accident people are getting worried."

"Are our people trying make out some sort of conspiracy theory, Harry? The recorder probably had a duff battery. Haven't they got a proper salvage boat out there?"

Harry never ceased to be amazed by his Minister's acumen. "Yes, you are quite right. The UK registered *Ocean Salvager* is on station and has already raised most of the wreckage. The experts are saying that the recorder is just not there. If you like, there is a hole where it should be."

"So who took it?"

"We don't know but presumably whoever did it waited until the P8 had gone away and grabbed it. It must have been a very agricultural removal but clearly they didn't care if they damaged the recorder."

"But the boat had two recorders, they were wasting their time."

Again Harry was lost in admiration of his Minister.

"Only the latest aircraft have two recorders, Minister. It is thought they didn't know."

"Harry, a thought occurs to me."

Harry wondered what was coming and was not disappointed. "Yes, Minister?"

"Harry, the P8 crew must have seen the ship which took the recorder, certainly on their radar. They would have reported it."

"Yes, Minister."

"Tell you what. Why don't you get through to your opposite number in Canberra and start spelling it out."

"Yes, Minister, a very good idea."

"And Harry."

"Yes Minister?"

"I know it's nothing to do with us but isn't it time the new guy started reorganising the accident people? You know the AAIB, MAIB and the RAIB. It seems a bit strange to have separate accident investigation organisations these days, duplicating facilities; I thought we were going to reorganise and be like the NTSB in the States and the ATSB in Australia. We shouldn't be involved at all."

"Yes, Minister, it does seem to be taking rather a long time."

***

Harry got up, put a dressing gown on and went into his study. Even though he knew the Government would pay he decided to use Skype to make the call. He selected it on his phone and called Vin Partridge in his office before he went home.

"Vin, hope all going well. We're a bit worried this end on that terrible accident to the ITAC 990 being operated by our airline RWA, flight RW845."

"So are we, Harry. Our ATSB is going flat out trying to sort it all out."

"Of course they are Vin, we know that but they seem a bit short of information and we felt you might be able to help. Our accident people tell us that you had an exercise on that night and apparently your ASIO people have told our people in the High Commission that you can't help at all."

"That's very interesting Harry. I can't believe there's any truth in that."

"Come on Vin, let's be frank with one another. You had your JORN operating and you must have sent aircraft up to see what was happening. One of the flight data recorders was stolen and you must be as curious as we are to know who took it. If you won't tell us at least tell ATSB what you know."

There was a long pause before Vin replied.

"Harry I wish I could help but my hands are tied."

"Vin, you should know better than most that our submarines roam the world so we are not completely blind. We may have to consult advisors and they tend to leak to Av Week. It would be much better if we kept them out of it"

"Alright, Harry," there was a pause, "alright I'll have to consult this end. I'll call you back."

"Thanks, we look forward to hearing from you and your Chinese friends."

**

Maureen called Harry in.

"Morning Harry, bring your coffee in. How did you get on down under?"

"Not terribly well, Minister. In the end I told him about our submarines and I wished him well with his Chinese friends."

"Harry, you're telling me something new. I didn't know we were monitoring the situation out there with our submarines. Someone should have told me."

"Forgive me, Minister, I was just pressurising our friends."

"Harry, I didn't know you had a romantic streak in you. I must be careful in future. Did he believe you?"

"I hope so. It was after that he told me he would call me back."

"Why do you think it was the Chinese?"

"That was Talbert's idea and I think it was a good one. They seem to be the only people who could grab the recorder and Talbert is wondering as an alternative to a bomb if there was a head on collision with one of their naval aircraft which they don't want to admit."

"More romance but possibly Talbert is right. I think we should have been doing what you told Vin Partridge we were doing, that is having one of our subs monitoring the Chinese carrier and the support ships. Presumably we've got one not too far away?"

"I'll find out, Minister."

***

Vin Partridge caught his boss just as he was about to leave the office.

"Yes Vin, what's so urgent?"

"Minister, I've had my UK opposite number on the phone. The Brits want to know what is going on."

"Well they'll have to wait."

"My contact quoted their submarine and the Chinese and threatened to start discussing things with Av Week."

Jack hesitated. "Alright Vin, what do you think we should do?"

"I think we should tell them the truth about the Chinese carrier and the possibility of a mid-air collision. When the front of the fuselage is eventually found it will be pretty obvious if there has been a collision or an explosion."

"What about the Chinese? Are they going to admit a collision?"

"We don't know but does it matter whether they do or they don't?"

"But Max Wilson told us there were other unexplained aircraft flying at the same time."

"Well the time has come to ignore that. There are more important things to deal with and you have to be careful not to be blind-sided in the house, Minister."

"Thank you for that, Vin, I'll have a word with Geoff Smith."

***

"Maureen, Jack Smithson here." Maureen Chester motioned to Harry to pick up the other phone. "We wanted you to know straightaway that the ATSB ROV has found a crashed Chinese fighter aircraft near where your airliner crashed into the sea. We've just had a look at it."

"Jack, thank you for letting us know. Was there any signs of a collision with our airliner?"

"No, Maureen. I expect you know that the Chinese navy has had a carrier operating in the general area for a month or so."

"Yes Jack, of course. What is puzzling us is that we believe your P8 aircraft found and heard both crash recorders when our airliner crashed but when your naval vessels arrived on the scene they could not find the submerged one attached to the aircraft. Did you ever locate the ship that was close by and took the submerged recorder?"

"I'm not sure I understand you Maureen."

"Come on, Jack, your P8 must have seen the ship that was very close to the wreckage and took the recorder."

There was a long pause. "Alright, Maureen. Yes we did see a ship but we don't know for sure if it took the recorder. It was a Chinese support vessel."

"Have you told the ATSB all this?"

"We're going to but we wanted you to be the first to know."

"That's very kind of you, Jack. Much appreciated. Let's hope they find the front of the airliner soon. But Jack, what sort of support vessel was it?"

"Don't know but if we find out we'll let you know immediately.

They rang off and Maureen turned to Harry. "What do you make of all that?"

"I think they had decided that they had better tell ATSB what they knew before it leaked to the press. Mind you, Minister, I'm not sure they planned to tell you about the salvage ship until you launched it."

"It wasn't quite like that, Harry."

"Yes, Minister."

Chapter 14

Stephen rang me. He'd spoken to the UK Ministry of Defence and then to Dominic Brown who had told him about the JORN radar returns and the Chinese carrier.

"Stephen, so the situation is that we think a Chinese support vehicle managed to get hold of the recorder. In addition, the submerged fighter aircraft I saw was indeed Chinese and had been operating off one of their carriers. Moreover, the RAAF experts confirm my view that there was no evidence of a collision looking at the wreckage of the fighter. However, we still don't know for sure if ISIS put a bomb on the flight deck on RW845 but having looked at the wreckage it looks most unlikely." I pondered the situation. "Don't ring off. Another question. I think we need to know a bit more about the ship that might have taken the recorder. Any chance of finding out?"

"What's on your mind?"

"Nothing really, but it is amazing that a routine support vehicle could have been able to get hold of the recorder. Oh, something else, you can ask Dominic if JORN is still operating and while you're about it what happened to the Chinese Carrier?"

"I feel like the middle man. You ought to be talking to him direct."

"Don't think that's possible. At lease you have accreditation. I'm just a lodger."

I drove home and clearly Charlie was waiting to talk once the children had gone to bed. I knew at once this was going to be a full frontal attack.

"Peter, don't bother to deny it. You had it off with Mary. She left her vestigial bra and a pair of panties on the floor. Trust her to find sexy stuff like that."

I decided commenting on her lingerie wasn't going to help the situation. "Charlie, I'm not denying it, though what her leaving underclothes around her room has got to do with it I'm not sure. I thought she would be poorly after what she had been through and she asked me for a cup of tea which I brought. But she wasn't poorly, quite the reverse, and we both knew Jill was going shopping after taking the children to school."

"I don't want to hear a blow by blow account of how you both gave way to your sexual desires. It's bad enough knowing you've ruined our lives without hearing how you did it."

"You're right. I can only apologise. I should have resisted the temptation. It was a moment of weakness."

"A moment of self-gratification, indulgence and selfishness."

I decided that adding 'curiosity' wasn't going to help. Unconsciously I had prepared myself for this showdown ever since Mary and I had had sex. I knew it had been folly and was hoping that eventually Charlie might forgive me but I also knew I deserved everything she was throwing at me.

"Peter, you know damn well you should have gone away. You are as bad as her. You can bloody well stay sleeping in her room while I decide what to do. I expect you thought it was just going to be a one night stand and I'd get over it but I warned you, several times. How she ever got a high security classification with her sexual appetite I'll never know. It wouldn't have happened in my Country."

There was no point in debating the pros and cons of the granting of security ratings in the States and the UK as it definitely was not the issue in hand. I hoped that one day I might be forgiven for giving way to a moment's carnal desire but clearly the day was a long way off.

"Peter, let's be quite clear, if it hadn't been for the children I would have thrown you out straightaway. In a way it was my stupidity as I should never have let her stay in the house; I've always suspected you were like Oscar Wilde." I couldn't help raising my eyebrows. "Don't try and change the conversation. You know what I mean."

"Charlie, we got rid of her when you left but she was kidnapped."

"I got rid of her and you brought her back. You should have taken her to the Novotel."

"With the handcuffs on, tied and gagged."

"Alright then, to the police station."

There was no point in debating the issue. I had 'screwed up' to misapply a phrase and what happened next rested entirely in Charlie's hands. I didn't want to be divorced as I loved being married to her but I knew I had been very unwise and that I was incapable of lying, pretending that I had just watched Mary displaying her boobs to good effect, spraying perfume in all the right places, drinking her tea and then walking away.

Later, I lay in bed wondering about the situation. It was interesting in a way that Charlie, who knew all about paintings, artists and their ways was taking such a strong line, not that I was an artist, just a human being attracted to the opposite sex. I supposed it was one thing for her to be an onlooker and another to be involved. I knew I shouldn't have given way and had sex with Mary but it was just all too easy. She wanted it and, at the time, so did I; the opportunity seemed irresistible but now the moment of reckoning had clearly arrived.

The phone rang at 6.30am and Charlie picked it up. She stormed in and gave it to me saying "We'd better have two lines."

It was Roger O'Kane from Seattle. "We've got a new problem in London, at Heathrow. We've introduced a new modification on the 990 pilots' displays and it affects the way we show the fuel. It conflicts with what RWA have on their iPads and it needs solving. Would you like to evaluate the problem and try to sort things out?"

"Not sure how I'll be able to look after RW845 when I'm in London."

"Well nothing is going to happen until they find the front fuselage and we'll let you know straightaway when that happens, assuming you won't have heard already from your other sources."

"Alright, I'll see what I can do. Send me all the contacts, a video of the display and arrange for me to have an RWA pilot's iPad. I should be able to travel to-morrow night."

"How will you get hold of the iPad?"

"Send it to me at the RAF Club. I'll be staying there."

I got up and we had a very quiet breakfast with Peter and Francie who clearly sensed there was something wrong. Jill appeared and took them to school and, to my surprise; Charlie accepted a lift to the National Gallery.

There was a message to ring Stephen when I got into the Office.

"Peter, I've had a word with Dominic and he's prepared to talk to you off the record. He doesn't want any emails and suggests the small coffee shop Loui in Alinga St at 3pm to-day. If I don't go back to him he'll be there."

I agreed the time and location with Stephen and then booked my flight for the following night with QANTAS. I also booked a room in the RAF Club. Commander Martin came on to me trying to find Mary and I gave him all the contacts he needed. Before leaving the Office I called Telstra and asked them to fit another line in our house though in reality I couldn't see why Charlie couldn't manage with her mobile. At 2.45pm I walked down to Loui and chose a small inside table at the back of the place though sitting at a table outside in the shade would have been infinitely preferable. Dominic arrived without jacket and tie but very smart trousers.

"Peter, good to see you again."

"Dominic, do I congratulate you now you are in ASIO."

"Not really. It's just much better and more efficient to keep us all under one roof."

"It's good of you to see me. As you know I'm acting for ITAC but in reality what I suppose I'm really trying to is to find out what actually happened in parallel with ATSB. I've seen the fuselage pieces and I'm not convinced by the ISIS video. There has to be a reason for the front FDR to have been taken. I'd like to know a lot more about the ship that took the FDR and I'm convinced you people know a lot more than you've told ATSB and for that matter the UK High Commission here and your UK contacts. I'd like to know the reason for your reticence."

"Well, Peter, I'm sure you realise that I'm not able to brief you at all apart from what you know already. However you might be interested to know that the Chinese fighter aircraft which you saw was lost some days before RW845 went into the water and that the *Tiangong* needed several support ships."

This was the first confirmation as far as I was concerned that the Chinese were operating a Carrier in the accident area which was a great help but clearly thanks would definitely be inappropriate. "Well that tells me that you've been watching the area for some time after the aircraft was lost. And that's the bit that worries me. You've been watching radar returns which presumably have not been Chinese fighters. Whatever you've been watching might have hit RW845 and it seems important to let ATSB know."

"Well the Government line is that when the front fuselage is found, as it surely will be, then ATSB will know soon enough if there's been a collision or a bomb. We don't know what happened and if we tell everybody about these returns now then they will almost certainly stop before we know what they are."

"Does it matter what they are? If there has been a collision then there may be another one and quite apart from another terrible disaster and the ensuing loss of life, you people and the Government will be in terrible trouble, especially if it is a QANTAS aircraft."

Dominic looked at me. "I'm not arguing. I don't create policy, unfortunately."

"Have you spoken to the Chinese?"

"All the time. Now we've found their fighter they've asked us if they might recover it. Obviously with *Ocean Salvager* there we don't want another salvage vessel there and though we cannot stop them putting their ship in place, they've agree to hold off for the moment. In fact they've been fairly cooperative agreeing to advise the FIRs in future when their aircraft might be near commercial air traffic."

"And what did they say about the other radar returns."

"'What returns?'"

"Come on, the ones we've been discussing."

"You asked me what they said and I told you, 'what returns'."

We talked a lot more but I could not make up my mind if the RAAF and their JORN radar knew a lot more or if they were also in the dark. However of one thing I was pretty certain, Dominic felt it was time to disclose to ATSB what they knew but presumably this was being prevented by another faction

159

within the Department of Defence and ASIO or the Department of Foreign Affairs possibly being pressurised by the American DoD.

Before going home I called Robert and asked him how the search for the front fuselage was going and he told me that no further progress had been made.

Back home things had not improved. We seemed to be at a stalemate. Stilted conversation through the children was happening but not directly between Charlie and myself. I told Charlie I would be off to UK the following evening and that she'd have to stay in the following morning to get the second telephone line installed.

"That settles it. We'll have to get a divorce. Chasing after that girl."

"I'm going nowhere near Mary. I'm staying in the RAF Club."

"That's my point. You are both members."

"You seem to forget that she and your brother are planning to get married. I don't think you understand Mary."

"Oh yes I do. She's a nymphomaniac. I'm very worried for Andrew getting entrapped."

"Once they work out where they going to live my bet is that they will get married and she will get pregnant, if not before."

"Maybe you've made her pregnant already."

"Don't be ridiculous."

"You've done it before."[8]

"Well we know whose fault that was. If you must know she excused the whole episode by saying it was her way of saying thank you for rescuing her."

---

[8] Peter junior in *Now you see it* by same author

I wasn't sure whether that last remark helped the situation but I never found out as Charlie snorted and went off to bed.

In the morning we had our, by now, customary incommunicative breakfast and then I took Charlie to the Gallery and said a stilted goodbye. I noticed she said no more about a divorce, which I regarded as a good sign.

Checking my mail I saw that the guy renting my house in Kingston in the UK wanted to terminate the lease and I decided that instead of immediately asking the estate agent to look around for a new tenant I needed time to consider the situation when the lease expired in a month's time. I couldn't believe that Charlie would want to divorce me but she clearly could if she wanted to in which case I would need to consider whether I was going to stay in Australia. I liked working where I was but maybe it would be slightly easier working in London. Problem was I wouldn't see the children very often living in London. On the other hand Charlie might go back to New York at any time. It was all very difficult and a problem entirely of my own making for, as she said, just to have a one night stand.

The QANTAS flight left on time and after refuelling in Dubai we arrived at 5.30am. I had been travelling business class and slept well. The driver of the car I had booked was waiting at the meeting point and we were soon at the RAF Club. There was no spare room available so I checked my bags, collected a parcel which I guessed to be a RWA pilot's iPad for the ITAC 990 and went into breakfast at 7am when the restaurant opened. To my horror Mary came on line and I left my table to take the call in the corridor.

"Peter, why didn't you tell me you were coming to England?"

"How did you know?" and then I realised that I had not turned my *Find my Friends* app off. "I'm losing my grip, Mary.

I'd forgotten all about the app. Just as well Charlie didn't know, she would have rung her lawyer straightaway."

"Are you in trouble?"

"In spades. It's going to be touch and go. How about you and Andrew?"

"No problem. He didn't ask. He is being moved in WorldLink so he will be based in Seattle and not travelling to Camfen all the time."

"What are you going to do?"

"I'm trying to get a K1 visa."

"What on earth is that?"

"It's a fiancée visa and you have to get married within 90 days of arrival."

"That's great. Congratulations to you both."

"Haven't got it yet. Andrew has to do some paperwork."

"Mary, I'm really pleased for you both. Has he told Charlie?"

"Trust you to put your finger on the spot. I believe she was not over the moon."

"Let me guess. He broke the news to her about four days ago when the proverbial hit the fan."

"You really are very coarse sometimes but you're right."

"How much did she tell Andrew?"

"I've no idea but I think she said something like 'Are you sure. She's been around a lot'. So he asked me if that was true and I remarked that I clearly wasn't his first conquest from the way he's being performing and that clearly we both have had a lot of practice. I used your favourite phrase 'what's sauce for the goose is sauce for the gander'. I explained that was one of the reasons we got on so well together."

"Mary you are incorrigible. Just as well you didn't use my other favourite 'I can resist anything except temptation.' "

"No I didn't. I'm not about to pry into his past and I'm certainly not going to let him explore mine."

"Well there won't be a problem then though the wedding might be a bit touch-and-go when the guy gets up and says 'If any of you know cause or just impediment, why these two persons should not be joined together in holy Matrimony, ye are to declare it.' Charlie might be compelled to say something."

"Peter, don't even joke about it; the Americans have no sense of humour about things like that. But in fact you don't have to worry as the current version is 'If any man can show just cause why they may not lawfully be joined together, let him now speak, or else hereafter for ever hold his peace.'"

"Don't believe that. Must have been an interim release. The feminists would never allow it. Anyway thanks to the pill and condoms, these days no-one would ever get married if pre-nuptial sex was a blocker. When are you planning the great day?"

"I'm not counting my chickens. I will only start counting when I land in the States. And it won't be in a church so Charlie will miss her opportunity of scuppering the whole thing."

"Well back to business. What's happening on RW845?"

"You should know better than anyone, you've been talking to Dominic."

"And you've been talking to Stephen. But we need to know where the front fuselage is."

"The ROV will find it eventually."

"I wonder."

"What does that mean?"

"I wish I could talk Chinese, I'd love to talk to their Carrier people."

"If you think I didn't notice that you didn't answer my question you can think again. But why don't you talk to the Chinese Embassy in London? I bet they have a Defence Attaché."

"Mary, that's a very good idea but I'd better get on with what I came for. ITAC gave me another job and thank goodness this time it is not an accident but revised crew procedures/displays on the 990. Thanks for calling and keep in touch."

I went back to the dining room and carried on with my breakfast. I decided to keep to my normal procedure and sent Charlie an email advising that all was well. When I left the dining room I went down to the computer room which was empty. I called Stephen at home and asked him if he could arrange for me to be invited to meet the Chinese air attaché in London and he agreed to get someone in the Foreign Office to see what could be done.

My next call was to John Chester, the chief pilot of Royal World Airways who I knew well from previous occurrences.

"Peter, good to hear from you. I knew ITAC had asked you to look at the little problem we're having with their displays. They also told me they've asked you to look after their interests with relation to that terrible accident we had off North West Australia, our RW845."

"Yes, that's right. I'm afraid the ATSB are not getting on very fast at the moment."

"Why don't you come round for a chat and we can discuss both things? Are you free 1400 to-day?"

I agreed and then spent the rest of the morning trying to get to grips with the display problem. I downloaded the video of the ITAC 990 displays which Roger had sent me and then operated the RWA iPad to try to understand the issues. The problem seemed to be the fuel needed for diversion as shown on the displays did not agree with the numbers on the iPad. There was just time for an omelette in the Running Horse and then I took a taxi out to the airport and John Chester's office. Jill Stanton, his long serving secretary collected me from reception and took me up to John.

John looked older than when I saw him last which was hardly surprising trying to maintain hundreds of pilots to the required standard of training plus all the personal problems that occur all the time. I expect he was probably thinking the same thing about me but at least I was spared his level of responsibility.

"Peter, what's it like Down Under? Can you maintain your business so far away…"

I smiled, "from civilisation?"

"No, you know I didn't mean that. But it is not in the centre of development and certification. It must mean a lot of extra travelling."

"Perhaps, but the internet makes it all possible. Incredible when you think it only started in 1989."

"And of course some of the accidents have been in your neck of the woods."

"Yes, you're right though thank goodness I wasn't dragged into MH370."

"But you're in the middle of our RW845."

"Yes, I am. It's a funny business. I'm not convinced by the ISIS video saying they put a bomb on the flight deck though it would solve a lot of problems."

"I know what you mean but what else could it be?"

"Well I think it might be a mid-air collision."

"Surely if there had been a collision we would have heard all about it from the operator of the other aircraft?"

"You would have thought so."

"Well they are bound to find the front of the aircraft soon."

"I wonder."

"I know the area is large but not that large." He looked at me. "Peter, you haven't changed. You've got some theories which you are not sharing with anybody."

"John, I'm not the accident investigator. However, like everybody else I would like to know what really happened."

"Alright then. What about our fuel problem? Why don't the calculations match?"

"I've only had a brief look this morning but I suspect the people who did your iPad need to talk in more detail to ITAC. There's an error in the two procedures somewhere."

"They say they have."

"Of course, but my bet there's a misunderstanding somewhere. I'll have a more careful look but I'm not a performance expert."

"OK. I'll wait to hear from you but meanwhile I'll go back to my people and ask them to try again."

Back in the RAF Club I started looking in detail at the RWA fuel problem display and calculation in the computer room. I had barely started when I got a message to call a Group Captain Williamson. The exchange put me through after checking my name.

"Peter Talbert?" I murmured assent "Group Captain Laurence Williamson here. I gather you would like to talk to the Chinese Air Attaché. Could you give me some background? I believe it's in connection with the loss of the Royal World Airways aircraft that went into the sea on the way to Adelaide --- that's a very sad story. I think it would be helpful if I spoke to the military air attaché first so that he was prepared for your questions."

"Laurence, absolutely. I don't want to waste his time making several journeys. In fact it is the military guy I want to talk to and not the Civil Air Attaché. As I'm sure you know the Chinese have a carrier in the area where the RW845 came down and they lost a military fighter in the same area. They have a salvage vessel in the area and I'm trying to get more details of what it did when RW845 hit the water."

"Peter, excuse my saying so but they are not likely to tell you things like that."

"I agree, but I'd like to hear them say that."

"Who are you representing?"

"The Seattle based Independant Transport Aircraft Company who manufactured the 990 that came down but really I'm trying to find out what happened to the aircraft. ISIS say they put a bomb on the flight deck which would explain the accident very neatly but I'm not at all sure that that's what happened. I think there's more to it than that and in my opinion the Chinese hold the key."

"Surely all this questioning should be being done by our AAIB?"

"Yes and No. They are not in charge of the investigation. The ATSB are doing it because the accident happened in their airspace. AAIB have a team out there and I've been working alongside them and ATSB."

"Peter, really AAIB should be asking for you to talk to the Civil Air Attaché."

"You're right but I'm trying to check on something."

"Well all I can do is to ask if I can see the Military Air Attaché and bring you along with me."

"Laurence, yes please. I really would appreciate it if you could ask and see what happens."

"OK. Give me all your contact details."

"I'll attach my card to an email if you would email me at *petertalbert@canberraaviationconsultancy.com*."

We rang off and I went back to the iPad and the video. I couldn't concentrate and called Jerry.

"What's going on?"

"Not a lot. My boss is wondering what we should be doing."

"What do ATSB say about the front of the rear fuselage? Do they think it was an ISIS bomb?"

"They have an open mind. They are waiting to look at the front section."

"I have a theory that they may never find the front section."

"Don't be defeatist, Peter. It's only a matter of time and money."

"If you say so, Jerry."

We talked some more but without coming to any conclusions. Then Laurence Williamson called me back. "Peter, Kwok Qiáng has agreed to see us to-morrow afternoon. Suggest we meet and have a sandwich together first and then we can get a taxi to Portland Place. By the way I assumed we would see the defence air attaché but we're seeing the head man so you had better tell me a bit more about what is going on so I can ask the right questions."

"Laurence, well done. I'll be at Main Entrance for check-in at noon because it always takes a little time."

***

I was at MoD on time and Laurence Williamson came down wearing a lounge suit and took me to the dining room where we queued and sat down at a table in the middle of the throng. I tried to bring him up to speed on the sequence of events.

"Peter, let me get this right. ATSB don't know why the aircraft crashed, the Chinese lost a naval fighter and the airliner's front fuselage ahead of the wing can't be found. In addition we think a Chinese salvage vessel took the submerged Flight Data Recorder." I Nodded. "So why do we need to talk to the Chinese in the UK?"

"Because I wondered if the Chinese salvage vessel also took the front fuselage. It would be relatively easy to do since the missing piece of the front fuselage is not all that big and they could have taken it when they took the FDR."

Laurence looked at me in amazement. "Are you serious? Why on earth would they want to do that?"

"I'm not sure but there must be something that happened to the flight deck that they don't want us to see."

"So what are we going to say to Kwok Qiáng?"

"I thought we might ask him if he could find out if their salvage vessel took the FDR and also the Flight Deck. Just a spirit of pure enquiry. No criticism. He probably won't know but in the unlikely event that he does I don't imagine he would tell us."

"Forgive me for being rude but why are we going through this pantomime?"

"Because I believe there is a very good reason why they did take the Flight Deck and I want to watch how he reacts."

Laurence smiled. "He will be inscrutable."

"If you say so. Do you know him well?"

"No. Not at all. I've met him briefly but he is normally above my level. That's why I find this meeting so interesting."

"Well if he starts discussing military aircraft you might start talking about UAVs and how they are the coming thing."

"Why would I want to do that?"

"Because I'd like to see if he would discuss them with you."

We took our time and arrived at the Embassy at 2.15pm. We gave in our names and clearly they had all Laurence's details. I had to have my picture taken and give in all my details with my UK passport and Australian address. We sat down in the large entrance for a few minutes and then a very smart obviously Chinese guy in a blue lounge suit appeared and introduced himself as Kwok Qiáng. He did not take us to his office but to a small meeting room on the ground floor.

"Well gentleman, how can I help you?" His English was superb and if we had not known or seen him it would have taken us sometime to work out from where he came. Laurence introduced himself and followed by explaining that I was a civil aviation insurance specialist involved with the loss of RW845.

Kwok looked at me. "Mr Talbert, I think you are very known in accident circles. My information tells me that you were appointed as head of the UK equivalent of the United States NTSB and that you turned it down. It is a pleasure to meet you. How can I help you? Please call me Kwok."

I felt a bit put off balance by his approach as I was expecting him to talk to Laurence, who understandably looked a bit surprised. I explained as best I could the situation as we knew it.

"Mr Kwok, we believe that your salvage vessel took the FDR, perhaps trying to help. It is also a possibility that your vessel also salvaged the front of the fuselage as we have not been able to find it. If that is indeed the case then we would like to examine it to find the cause of the accident."

Kwok smiled and said predictably that he had no idea what had been going on but he would try and find out. He changed the subject to West Orient Airlines and an accident I had been involved with in Hong Kong. It was all very pleasant but we were getting nowhere. Kwok started discussing military matters with Laurence and asking how the F35 was going. Laurence did a great job and remarked casually that UAVs seem to be the way to go these days rather than these very expensive fighters. Kwok agreed and mentioned one of their low level drones that we knew all about. At this point we could both sense it was time to leave and we made our farewells. Kwok turned to us.

"It's been a great pleasure to meet you both and I will try and find the answers to your questions, Mr Talbert."

We made our farewells and returned to MoD and Laurence took me up to his office.

"Peter, what do you make of all that?"

"I'm not sure. It will be interesting to see if he or one of his people contacts us."

"What I found so unexpected is that he was talking to you and not to me. He must have been briefed very thoroughly and clearly knew a lot more than he was letting on."

"Yes, that rather surprised me as well. Hopefully it might be a good sign."

"The other thing was when you suggested that they had taken the front fuselage as well as the FDR. He wasn't in the least surprised; in fact I think I reacted more to that suggestion than he did as I didn't think you would actually ask him. You really believe they have the front fuselage, don't you?"

"Yes, I do. For a start it would explain why the ROV can't find it. I'm hoping the Chinese will admit to taking it and letting us have a look."

We talked a bit more and then I went back to the Club. I sent a routine report to Charlie, not that I expected a reply; I decided not to request a read receipt but just assume the email would go through as normal.

The following morning my phone rang and to my complete surprise I saw it was Charles Simon, Director General responsible for Safety in the UK Department of Transport.

"Peter, good to talk to you. I didn't realise you were in the UK again. I thought you were in Australia."

I had got to know Charles quite well when I was applying to be the new Chairman of the UK Transport Safety Board just before going to Australia with Charlie.

"Charles, it's only a temporary visit."

"Not to do with that aircraft we lost approaching Australia, RW845."

"No, though I am involved. You are clearly very well briefed."

"Well a strange thing has happened. The Chinese civil air attaché came on to us and enquired if you were working for the AAIB?"

"Oh, I think I can explain that. ITAC are employing me to look after their interests in RW845 and we had a chat with the Chinese Defence Attaché, Kwok Qiáng."

"Who is we?"

"Group Captain Laurence Williamson, he works somewhere in the MoD. He arranged the meeting."

"Peter, you do get around. Kwok is a very heavy breather in the Chinese Embassy. I would have thought that you two should have seen the military air attaché, not the head man. What's going on?"

"How much do you want to know? It could be a long telephone call."

"Can you spare the time to come round to Horseferry Road after lunch?"

"I'd be delighted.

I arrived on time and Charles' secretary took me up to his office. I went through the situation as currently understood.

"By the way when we saw Kwok I suggested that they took not only the FDR but also the front of the fuselage."

Like Laurence Williamson he looked very surprised.

"You don't really believe that do you?"

"Yes, Charles I think I do. I'm not quite clear why yet, but for some reason I think they decided to collect it. They had plenty of time as *Ocean Salvager* had to come from San Diego and the ADV boat *Ocean Shield* had to be prepared before it could leave Garden Island near Freemantle. RAN had a patrol boat but it couldn't stay for very long, just long enough to tell us that it couldn't hear the submerged FDR which the P8 heard on its first visit."

"So you know when the FDR and nose was taken?"

"Not for sure but I think the FDR was taken before the patrol boat arrived and the front fuselage was taken the moment patrol boat left the scene and went back to Darwin."

I thought for a moment. "What did you tell the civil air attaché?"

"I said you were working with AAIB on RW845."

"That was very smart of you. How much did you know about the Chinese and their carrier?"

"It was just a shrewd guess on RW845. Anyway it didn't do me any good as he just rang off. Of course I knew nothing about the Chinese situation. What are you expecting to happen next?"

"Good question. I don't know. I'd like to think that we would be allowed to look at the FDR and the front fuselage but I think that's very much wishful thinking."

"I agree. It would involve some embarrassing admissions by the Chinese."

"More than that. There could be some considerable financial considerations depending on what we find."

"Peter, I think you know more than you're saying."

"Charles, there are several alternatives and we are just guessing."

"Alright, you don't have to tell me if you don't want to."

I made my farewells and went back to the Club. That evening Mary rang me.

"Peter, we've had the Chinese Civil Air Attaché on the phone wanting to talk to you."

"Great. What did you say?"

"The call came through to the secretary of the Chairman who is forming the new Transportation Safety Board and she said that you didn't work for the AAIB."

"How on earth do you know who said what and to whom?"

"Oh I'm quite friendly with her and she didn't know I knew you. Apparently she was told to say that you had nothing at all to with AAIB in a very firm manner."

"I'm not surprised. You know I warned you when you applied for the job not to mention my name as I wouldn't be very popular with the new man having turned the job down."

"Doesn't matter anymore as I'm about to give my notice in and emigrate to the States. My visa has come through."

"Congratulations. That seems very quick. Don't forget to invite us to the wedding."

"You bet. Will you need two invitations?"

"At the moment, yes. But your departure for the States might help. I'll let Charlie know straightaway. When do you leave?"

"In a few weeks. I've got to put my flat on the market and tidy up all sorts of things."

"Better let Rupert know. You'll be persona non-grata."

"I have and I won't."

"Give me a farewell call. By the way thanks for info on Chinese civil air attaché. I'd better try to contact him to-morrow."

When she rang off I brought Charlie up to date and got an immediate reply. 'Andrew told me the news. Don't even think of a fond farewell.'

The thought hadn't occurred to me but in a way I thought it was a good sign as well as a warning.

In the morning I contacted Charles Simon and told him about the Chinese civil air attaché call to the AAIB.

"Peter, that hasn't helped, has it? What are you going to do?"

"I thought I'd ring him if you could give me name and number."

"Good idea. It is Guan Jìng and the number is 020 5476 99997"

I rang the Embassy on the direct line but in fact I got intercepted by the operator. After a struggle I got through and found I was speaking to Guan Jìng who had a really excellent American accent.

"Mr Talbert, thank you for calling back. We thought you were working for the AAIB."

"No, Guan, I work as an independent insurance investigator and currently I'm employed by ITAC to look after their interests on RW845."

"Well by mistake our salvage vessel did take the FDR. We have worked with you before on that accident in Hong Kong and we are happy to give the FDR to you."

"Guan, it might be easier if you gave it to the ATSB direct."

"Arrangements have already been made for you to get the recorder."

"Very well. I'll be back in Australia in three days time but how do I contact you?"

"We are getting special permission for one of our small working vessels to land in Broome and give it to you. I will send you an email; then please tell us when you will be in Broome 48 hours before you arrive. There will be a senior naval officer for you to talk to."

He rang off and I thought through the whole ridiculous scenario. The Chinese had finally admitted they had taken the FDR but why they wanted to give it to me and not the ATSB I could only guess. I wondered what to do and finally decided to tell Robert what was happening in the morning. I thought about telling him my suspicions that the Chinese also had the front fuselage but decided to wait a little longer until things hopefully would become clearer.

ITAC sent me a message saying that they had arranged with the designers of the RWA iPad how they should alter their software to be compatible with the ITAC display modifications. They thanked me for my help but in reality I had done very little. Still the job had been very useful to fund the trip to UK and unearth the missing FDR.

I arranged to visit John Chester the following morning and then booked my flight to Perth with onward connection to Broome; I left my return flight to Canberra open. I then used Tripit to send the whole itinerary to Charlie.

In the morning I was woken by Robert who came on the phone from his home. "Peter, glad I could get hold of you. Our Department of Foreign Affairs have had a request from the Chinese to allow one of their small support naval vessels to dock at Broome to give you the FDR of RWA945."

"Yes, Robert. I was about to email you. Their civil air attaché here enquired for me from our AAIB and I called him back. He volunteered the information that they had taken the FDR by mistake and would like to give it back."

"A likely story. But why give it to you?"

I decided not to tell him about our visit to the Defence attaché.

"That's easy. I had worked with them before on an accident in Hong Kong. I did try to get them to give it you direct but he told me it was too late and arrangements had already been made."

"Well our Foreign Affairs people don't like it and we're not over the moon about the situation ourselves. However I persuaded my boss that we need the FDR and that we need to co-operate with the Chinese so he convinced the Foreign Affairs people to agree. We need to know when you will be at Broome."

I gave Robert the information and when he had rung off I went on-line and booked a room in Broome at the Blue Seas Resort again. Then I rang Jill Stanton, John Chester's secretary and managed to shift my appointment to the afternoon so that I could stay at the airport after seeing him and catch my flight to Dubai and on to Broome. After breakfast I went up to the Cowdray Room and started reading The Times. It had the Appointments supplement and I started looking through to assess UK current salaries which at the senior level had clearly got out of hand compared with the people at the working level which understandably was causing some social unrest. I thought I'd check people in Charlie's area and saw that Southeby's were advertising jobs in New York, which made me feel rather uncomfortable since she still had her flat in New York.

The meeting with John Chester went well and I was able to tell him that I was going to collect the missing FDR from the Chinese in a couple of days. John's reaction was the same as everyone else's, why were they giving me the FDR, a sentiment which I shared though I didn't explain about seeing the Defence Attaché in London which might have had something to do with it.

The flights to Broome were uneventful and thanks to ITAC funding my trip I felt fresh on arrival since I was travelling business class. When I checked in I got a message from the Harbour Master saying that a Chinese naval vessel would be arriving ETA 1000 local time but would not be 'landing' so that I needed to go through customs and immigration to meet the boat and the same on my return.

In the morning I made my number with immigration at 9am and showed my passport. I then went into a small waiting room by the harbour master's office to await events. While there I planned for success and booked a seat on that evening's flight direct to Canberra. One of the berthing masters then appeared and told me that the Chinese vessel would be tying up in 45 minutes. Sure enough I could see a boat flying a Chinese flag of sorts being moored alongside; the berthing master then reappeared and took me to the companionway which had been placed between the docks and the boat.

I went on board the vessel and someone who I took to be an interpreter led me to a small room which might have been the captain's cabin. There was a rather larger box than I was expecting on the floor in the room and shortly after I had sat down a man in uniform appeared with a rank I judged to be a Commander, since I had taken the precaution of looking up Chinese naval ranks on the internet. He had no English and I had no Chinese so we had to converse through the interpreter.

"Mr Talbert. Very pleased to meet you. Please call me Duanmu. We are glad to give you this Flight Data Recorder which we took by mistake from the crashed British airliner. The crew from our salvage vessel thought at first it was from our naval aircraft which had crashed."

"Duanmu, thank you very much. The box looks bigger than I can carry."

"We propose to help you to the customs area."

"Thank you."

I pondered over my next question but decided to have a go. "Duanmu, when will you be returning the front fuselage of the airliner? I assume you salvaged that as well, thinking it was your crashed aircraft."

There was a long pause and Duanmu asked the interpreter to repeat the question and I had to ask the question again. Clearly Duanmu was searching for the best answer which convinced me that I was on the right track. However, there was still a long pause after the repeated translation.

"Mr Talbert, I cannot answer your question."

"I understand your difficulty but I am sure you understand our need to see the front fuselage so that we can determine why the airliner crashed."

"Mr Talbert, may I be rude enough to enquire if you have a recorder on you."

"Duanmu, no I don't but please search me."

"We know you and trust you which is why we wanted to give the recorder to you. There are reasons why we cannot allow the Australian investigators to look at the front fuselage."

"Can you tell us where you found the wreckage? That would be a great help."

"I'm afraid not."

"Could we do a deal? We let you rescue the wreckage of your aircraft and you let us have the front fuselage?"

"Mr Talbert. We don't need to do a deal. We can rescue our aircraft whenever we like."

I felt that I made some progress in that I had established they had the front fuselage but clearly I had not established if they would let us have it.

"Duanmu, in the end everybody will find out why you don't want us to have the front fuselage."

To my surprise he nodded. "Mr Talbert, I think that is far as we can go at the moment. I look forward to meeting you again"

A sailor appeared with a trolley and we went ashore and made our way to the customs area. The sailor handed the FDR to the customs officer and went back to the boat. Understandably the lady on duty was very suspicious and I did my best explaining what it was but she didn't like the look of my British passport. She asked one of her team to prise open the box to expose the recorder and part of the structure from where it had been cut-off. I invited her to phone Robert at ATSB which she did and after a fairly lengthy conversation she got the box reassembled and let me have it.

I phoned Robert and asked him what to do with it and he said the easiest thing would be to bring it with me and ATSB would pay any excess charges. I called a cab and with the help of the driver we got it into the boot of the car. At the hotel I left it with the concierge, organised a 6pm check-out and went up to my room.

My next move was to re-confirm my flight and then email Charlie. I also emailed Robert asking him to get someone to meet my flight and rescue the FDR. I packed up my things and with the help of the concierge got the FDR into the taxi. At the airport I checked-in the car and managed to get the box loaded into the shuttle bus. At the terminal the driver helped me get it on to a trolley and I finally managed to reach check-in. To my surprise it was accepted without a demur and no excess baggage charge, one of the benefits of travelling business class. The flight got into Canberra as usual at dawn and to my relief there was someone from ATSB to take the FDR. I took a taxi home and collapsed onto the bed in the spare room, leaving until the morning the decision on how I should communicate my supposition that the Chinese had the missing nose of the aircraft.

In the morning the children were delighted to see me and we all had breakfast together. Maybe it was wishful thinking but Charlie didn't seem quite as frosty as she had been. I took her to the National Gallery and then drove on to my office. I decided to call Stephen and I gave him a complete account of my meetings in London and on the boat in Broome.

"Stephen, I haven't told anyone anything yet. You are the first."

"Well Peter, I will tell the High Commissioner here and you had better tell your contact at ATSB, not to mention AAIB. The fact that the Chinese are holding the front fuselage is likely to cause a diplomatic incident unless they return it straightaway."

"Stephen, we don't know they have the nose but the Commander didn't deny it.

"I'll back your hunch."

Chapter 15

Maureen Chester looked at Harry Brown her Chief Secretary in the MoD. "Harry, this guy Peter Talbert gets around. The High Commissioner tells me that Talbert thinks the Chinese navy has salvaged the nose of that airliner that crashed into the sea off Western Australia."

"Yes, Minister. The problem is that the news is bound to leak out and I understand that the head of security in the Commission thinks you should tell Jack Smithson. It is obviously very important for the accident inspectors to find out what actually happened."

"But Harry, what makes Talbert so sure that the Chinese have the nose of the aircraft?"

"Well, Minister, when he was collecting the crash recorder from them, you remember the one they said they took by mistake," Maureen Chester nodded, "he asked the Chinese naval Commander who was giving him the recorder if they were going to let the Australians have the front fuselage. Apparently he wasn't expecting the question but after checking that Talbert didn't have a recorder on him he didn't deny the possibility."

"So Talbert obviously reckons the ball is in their court." She paused and Harry wondered what was coming next. "Harry, if they did recover the front fuselage won't they have a lot of bodies? Crew and first class passengers perhaps?"

"Yes indeed, Minister." His mind was racing. "I wonder if anyone else will have thought of that aspect of the situation?"

"I'd be very surprised if your man Talbert hasn't thought of it. He seems to drip feed the problems and the possible solutions as things develop. Pity he didn't take that accident job."

"Well Minister, as I mentioned, Stephen Wentworth in the Commission thinks you should talk to your opposite number, Jack Smithson. Since the Australians are doing the accident investigation, the initiative to look at the front fuselage should come from then."

"What time is it in Canberra?"

"8.30pm. May we try to set up a conversation to-morrow morning the moment you arrive?"

"Excellent."

***

Jack Smithson wanted to leave his office and go home but he knew he had to speak to Maureen in the UK first. He could have taken the call at home but he wanted Vin Partridge to listen in. He was pleased when the call came through promptly.

"Jack, Maureen Chester here, thank you for staying at the Office late. I thought we ought to discuss the accident to our Royal World Airways Independent 990 off Broome and the recent visit you had at Broome from a Chinese naval vessel. They handed over the crash recorder they said they had taken by mistake."

"Maureen, I know the one. They insisted on giving it to one of your insurance advisers for some reason."

"Hardly one of our advisors, Jack. Maybe they gave it to him because he was the one who worked out that the Chinese had taken the recorder. His name is Peter Talbert and you may remember he was the one who helped sort out those P8s that were shot down a year or so ago. Apparently he had done a job at Hong Kong and they trusted him."

"Well hopefully that's the end of the matter. We don't want him poking his nose in any more."

"Not quite, Jack. Haven't your people told you? Talbert thinks they also have the nose of the aircraft which we can't find."

"Why on earth does he think that? That's ridiculous."

"Because he asked the Chinese Naval Commander to give it back and apparently the guy was completely unprepared and then said no they wouldn't. He thinks that for some reason the Chinese don't want us to look at the front of the fuselage."

There was a pause as Smithson realised Maureen was way ahead of him.

"Well what do you think we should do?"

"Can't you ask for it to be returned or does that have to be done by your Foreign Affairs people?"

"Geoff Smith, Foreign Affairs I imagine."

"Well your ATSB are in charge but obviously we are helping as much as we can. We need to know about the accident. Of course I'm only involved because of the military aspect."

"Maureen, that goes for me too. It's the Department of Infrastructure that deals with civil aviation and the accident people. I'll tell them what you said about the front fuselage section and leave it to them."

When the conversation was finished Jack told Vin to pass the news on to his opposite number in the Department of the Infrastructure in the morning since he was off to Perth the next day; that way Infrastructure could make the running with the Foreign Affairs Department. Vin made the call and found that the front fuselage news had already been passed up from the ATSB and that they had asked the Foreign Affairs people to talk to the Chinese.

Chapter 16

Laurence Williamson called me from UK just as I was getting up. It was nearly four weeks since I had come back from Broome with the flight data recorder with the suggestion that the Chinese naval salvage vessel had the front fuselage of the crashed RWA airliner but I had heard nothing. Nearly all the bodies had been recovered except the pilots, the first class passengers and the front crew; there was enormous pressure on the UK accident investigators to find out what had happened and recover these thirteen bodies. The UK Minister of Transport had said that everything was being done to establish the facts but so far it had not been possible to find the missing front fuselage.

"Peter, I don't know what's going on but the Chinese military attaché called me and said Kwok Qiáng would like to see us."

"That's great. Any idea of when?"

"I got the feeling fairly soon. I was asked to ring back with suggested dates. You obviously made a hit with Kwok Qiáng."

"It's to do with the front fuselage of that crashed Royal World Airways aircraft they say they haven't got."

"How do you know?"

"I don't, but I can't think of any other reason. I'll have to look at my diary tomorrow and call you back."

I decided I'd better bring myself up to date before committing myself to going to London. I called Robert and luckily he was in.

"Robert, any news. Are you making any progress?"

"Peter, the Chinese are still saying they haven't got the front fuselage of the aircraft."

"What's happening then? Are you still searching?"

"You bet we are. Costing a fortune."

"Presumably you got nothing from the recorder I brought back?"

"You are absolutely right."

"Well I'm glad I'm not in your shoes. All very difficult."

"Peter, Jerry tells me he is getting a lot of stick as well."

"I can imagine. Anyway thank you for bringing me up to date. I might have some news for you."

"Such as?"

"The chief Chinese air **attaché in London** wants to see me again."

I could hear Robert thinking. "Peter, without wishing **to be rude we are not over the moon with these** *tête-à-têtes* **you have with the Chinese.**"

"I well understand that. Presumably your Foreign Affairs people have told them it should be direct communication."

"You bet they did."

"What do you want me to do?"

"I think my boss would say nothing but we've got to get **this thing settled and we need every bit of help we can get.** Forget we've had this conversation and let's **see what the deal is.**"

"OK, thanks. If necessary you might remind your boss this **conversation in London is going to cost** thousand dollars as I'm not prepared to go steerage. I'm spending my money because I want to help."

"Peter, I well understand the position but equally I'm sure you understand the sensitivity of these people."

"Fine. I'll let you know what happens."

I went home feeling discouraged with lack of progress on RW845 though the Chinese invitation could be good. Things weren't helped by Charlie who was still keeping me in the sin bin. She was already at home and gave me my mail. I looked at one very smart envelope that clearly had come from Seattle. It was an invitation to the celebration of the wedding of Mary French to Andrew Simpson. It was in ten days' time and I was surprised that it was to be in New York until I remembered that Charlie's parents lived in Upstate New York. I looked at Charlie who was having a drink and watching the television with Peter junior who she rapidly despatched to bed. I showed her my invitation. "Did you get one?"

"What do you think? I know you're lecherous but didn't know you were stupid. Seems a lot of expense for what will only be a temporary affair."

"Come on. It is going to be great. Mary is very determined. It will be a long and happy marriage with a large family. You've got it in for that girl."

"I've got it in for that girl? You got it into that girl!" She almost frothed at the mouth. "No wonder I'm cross. Goodness knows where she'll go after Andrew."

"Give it a rest. She wasn't marrying me. We just had sex."

"We just had sex! I see. If I go and just have sex with a guy it's OK? Fine. Now we know the rules. I had better try and draw level as you're currently one ahead."

There was no answer to that so I didn't give one. I tried another tack.

"Anyway it shouldn't be that expensive, it's not going to be a white wedding according to the invitation. It's just a get together, parents and special friends at the Soho Grand Hotel, West Broadway. The actual wedding will be like ours was, getting the marriage certificate witnessed in City Hall. We've been asked to be the witnesses and be there before going to the hotel which is very nice of them and very special."

Charlie said nothing.

"Do you need to go to London? I've unexpectedly got to go to London which in a way is good news. I'm thinking of doing a round the World trip."

She looked at me speculatively.

"What's that got to do with me? I'll do the short leg across the Pacific to Dallas, thank you. I don't want to waste my money."

We both knew that that was the longest leg of any airline but to get to New York it was probably shorter than going via London.

"Fine. Meet you in New York."

Somehow in spite of that lively exchange I didn't feel too downhearted. I got myself a drink and started making my bookings. Charlie was watching me. "You can tell your Mary, I plan to arrive two days before. If she's making the reservation we'd better share a room to save comment but forget about double beds. Ask her to get a small suite."

I made my flight booking and messaged Mary with arrival date and flight. She came straight back. 'You must be winning. At least not two separate rooms. I was going to gamble and book a twin bedded room for you both but I think the hotel has small suites which won't break the bank. Much more exciting.'

My reply was short and to the point. 'We've had enough excitement, thank you.'

In the morning I contacted Laurence, explained I was planning to be in London on the way to New York and suggested a date so I could go straight on the following day. He emailed a reply the following day. 'Peter I can't believe it but we have a 10am appointment with the man himself the day you wanted. You had better explain to me what is happening before we go in.'

I replied straight back. 'That's very good news. Come and have breakfast in the RAF Club and we can go through it all then.'

I made my reservations on line and told Charlie what was happening. She listened as if she didn't care but I knew she was taking it all in. "You'd better start learning Chinese so you can have it off with the secretaries."

"Charlie, cool it. I know I was stupid but I don't make a habit of it."

"I'm not sure. I'm told it's like a disease once you start."

"What had you in mind? Chicken Pox?"

"Something like that, but afterwards."

* * *

Laurence joined me for breakfast as arranged at the RAF Club. I explained that I had collected the crash recorder from the Chinese Navy at Broome but no progress had been made on finding the nose of the aircraft.

"Well Peter, he must be going to make a proposal or suggest something."

"I hope so but why do it all through me instead of the correct way? It makes me unpopular with the accident people, certainly in Australia and also the head man here and I'm unpopular enough with him anyway."

"Yes, Peter, I can imagine. I didn't know until Kwok Qiáng mentioned it that you had turned down the chairmanship of the new accident investigation organisation. They are clearly doing it this way in my opinion because they don't want to admit formally they've got the front of the aircraft."

"Laurence, you're probably right."

We went up to the lounge to read the papers and then caught a cab to the embassy. At the check-in we knew we were definitely in their system as our badges were produced immediately with excellent photographs. Exactly at the appointed time Kwok Qiáng appeared by himself and took us into the same meeting room as before; I supposed he was able to come by himself as the room would have a microphone recording all conversations, not to mention hidden cameras.

Kwok was the soul of politeness welcoming Laurence first and then myself. He had a discussion with Laurence about Rosetta, the comet lander, which unexpectedly had started to transmit some information though there wasn't enough power apparently to do some analysis work. He clearly wasn't in a hurry as he went on to discuss the latest drones in the Middle East and their new capabilities not that Laurence gave anything new away. Finally Kwok turned to me.

"Mr Talbert it is very good of you to come all the way from Australia to have this chat. We wondered where your ROVs have been searching. Though of course we are not involved in any way with the Royal World Airways accident, we did have a carrier close by. Some of the experts on the carrier have suggested you should be searching in this area." He put his hand into the inside pocket of his jacket and passed me an envelope. I hesitated. "Please, have a look inside."

I did as instructed and all I could find was a stiff piece of card with a latitude and longitude printed on the card in degrees and minutes to three decimal places.

"Kwok, thank you very much. What an excellent suggestion. Perhaps our ROVs have missed this area." I smiled at him so that he would be certain that I knew what had happened but that I was not going to discuss it. "I know the Australian investigators are desperate to find the front fuselage of the aircraft so that the cause of the accident can be ascertained. The UK investigators and the airline are waiting anxiously for some news so that the relatives of those that were killed can be informed. I wondered when you were searching whether you found any bodies?"

We continued chatting for a bit and then Kwok made his farewells. We caught a cab back to MoD and Laurence found a vacant meeting room to save going up to his office.

"Peter, what was all that about?"

"My guess is that they have put the nose fuselage back in the water somewhere close to the position on the card. We will then find it and the Chinese will not be involved. They clearly don't want to admit they had the nose all the time. By using me as the intermediary there is nothing on record. "

"That makes perfect sense. Why have they taken so long to put it back?"

"Good question but a better ones might be 'why did they take it in the first place?' and 'what have they done with the bodies?'

"And what is your guess?"

"I don't know yet but I shall be very interested to look at the nose."

I left Laurence and went back to the Club. My flight wasn't until the following day which gave me time to consider how I was going to promulgate the information from Kwok Qiáng. I looked at the lat/long of the position Kwok had given me and then went to the Club Library to see where it was relative to the positions I knew; I could see straightaway that the ROV must have been over the Chinese position at least once; their salvage vessel must have put the front fuselage in the position he gave me while *Ocean Salvager* was some way away.

I spoke to Jerry first and brought him up to date and suggesting that the Chinese had put the nose back in the water.

"Jerry, would you like to try to formalise the situation by passing this lat/long to ATSB? I'm suggesting this way of doing things as it will not bring me into head-on conflict with the Australian Public Service."

"Peter, they are bound to ask me where I got the information from.

"No worries there. You can give a truthful answer, from the Chinese. Keep me out of it. Clearly you will suggest that the Chinese salvage vessel may have put the nose back."

"Great. I'll pass the information on straight away. Do you think they will relook at this Chinese position?"

"They will be mugs if they don't. I'd bet money they will find the front fuselage straight away."

I started to relax since the ball was no longer in my court. I sent a message to Charlie bringing her up to date though I wasn't sure when she would get it. Then Mary called me.

"What are you doing in the RAF Club again?"

"I've definitely lost my grip; I still haven't removed you from my app. Just as well Charlie doesn't know. Still unfair as you've stopped me looking at you."

"I should think so too. A girl about to be married doesn't want to be stalked by other men. And as usual you haven't answered the question."

"The Chinese have just told me where they have put the nose of the aircraft."

"Just like that?"

"Not quite. They've had an inspired guess where it might be."

"And they had to tell you? I suppose they didn't want to make it official."

"Right on but not everybody likes me interfering."

"Surprise me."

"Anyway how are you getting on? Everything arranged?"

"Pretty well. You do know we want you and Charlie to witness the marriage certificate?"

"Honoured and I'm looking forward to it."

"And she who must be obeyed?"

"Don't know. You know she hasn't forgiven you. Not sure how things are going to work out. Anyway she's nearer you than me. In fact hasn't she arrived already?"

"I expect so but haven't checked yet. Andrew should do her. Friends of the groom. You're friends of the bride."

"Not sure Charlie would classify me that way."

"Alright, good friends of the bride."

"Very good friends."

"I think you are exaggerating. Are you still in the sin bin, my love?"

"You bet and you can leave out the 'my love' bit. It will be interesting to see how things go."

"I shall be watching with interest."

"Don't you dare. You concentrate on the job in hand."

"That's not the most elegant way of putting things."

"Seriously Mary, I wish you every happiness and lots of children. I know you are going to be really great together. You'd better get back to what you are doing. All my love."

I hung up and watched the television for a bit before going to bed. In the morning while I was still in bed Robert came on line.

"Peter, Jerry has just sent us a Chinese estimate of the position of the nose we can't find. As you can imagine we've looked there before. My boss thinks it is a waste of money going back but I've managed to persuade him we ought to do it. You can guess he doesn't like getting help from the Poms. I detect your fairy hand."

"Well done. Just as well your boss doesn't know I'm involved; the air attaché gave me the co-ordinates suggesting we may have missed searching there. By the way I'm very keen to look at the front fuselage when you find it; don't suppose the bodies will be there but I suppose they could be. Where are you going to take it?"

"Broome again where you and Jerry saw the rest of the fuselage."

"Fine. Could you email me if and when you find the nose?"

He rang off and I dressed and packed before going down to breakfast. On my return my mobile rang and I saw it was Charles Simon.

"Charles, good morning. What can I do for you?"

"Peter, that's a very good question. I gather from the head investigator at AAIB that you've seen Kwok Qiáng again, that they may have had the nose of the aircraft all the time and that they have put it back."

"Charles, it's only a guess but obviously by telling me a possible position it can be all unofficial."

"Well I'll back your hunch. Would they have told you if you had been a member of AAIB?"

"I don't believe so. Why do you ask?"

"Well we have a problem. The re-organisation of the UK's accident investigation boards is not going at all well and the Chairman of the Transport Safety Board has asked to be allowed to resign."

"I had noticed that nothing seemed to be happening but I put that down to ignorance because I was on the other side of the World."

"Well Sir Philip Brown has asked me to contact you and enquire whether you would be prepared to take the job on after all?"

I was completely unprepared for his question and didn't reply for a moment. Had it not been for my current marital problems I would have refused straightaway but clearly I needed time to think.

"Charles, you've caught me unawares. It is a great compliment that you are asking me but I am sure you understand I can't answer immediately. Apart from anything else I need to ask my wife."

"Of course. We weren't expecting an answer straight away. Take your time. Don't email me on this matter, of course, but give me a call when you are ready."

I completed my check-out almost automatically as I started to wrestle with the problem and opportunity that Charles had given me. The private taxi I had booked to the airport that undercut the standard taxi fare arrived on time. The flight to New York was uneventful and thankfully a lot quicker than going to Australia; I called Charlie from the cab on the way to the hotel who grunted. I arrived at the hotel at 5pm, checked in and went up to the room.

Charlie was sitting down on a sofa in the lounge part of the suite with a drink looking very smart and relaxed. She allowed me a greetings kiss and indicated my bedroom to dump my gear. I decided to have a quick shower and then joined Charlie for a drink. She made it plain that I could sit next to her on the sofa.

"Any news of the team?"

"Yes, we're having a meal in the Algonquin Hotel at seven o'clock."

"Great. How are Jill and the kids?"

We discussed their various commitments for a bit and then I changed the subject.

"Charles Simon called me to-day and offered me that job again."

There was a definite silence as Charlie took it all in.

"When do you start?"

I couldn't help smiling and nor could Charlie.

"Haven't decided yet. It all depends."

Another long pause. She looked at me carefully.

"Sotheby's in New York are advertising for a director."

"I know. I saw it in the Times Appointments section. Have you applied?"

"Haven't decided yet. It all depends."

"Charlie, we don't want a divorce. I love you. I love being with you. You're fun."

"You should have thought of all that before you had it off with that tart."

"You mean your **sister-in-law**?"

"Don't rub it in. Anyway you're warming the bell to use your limey expression, it's not consummated yet."

"Now there's an interesting statement."

"You know what I mean."

"Charlie, please be reasonable. We don't want your brother asking you to-night why you are treating me like a leper. They are made for each other."

"I really hope you're right, my love."

I wasn't sure if she meant that but I said nothing.

"Well I'd better get changed if we're going out. You don't need to, you look great already."

"Thank you, but I shall get changed as well."

We got up and went to our separate rooms to get ready and I felt I was making progress towards being re-admitted to our marriage but that wasn't helping my Charles Simon problem, quite the reverse.

The evening went well. Charlie's and Andrew's parents had come down from Upstate New York and were staying in the hotel as were Mary's parents; I knew Charlie's parent quite well as they had visited us a few times in Australia. No-one except Mary would have detected that there was a problem between Charlie and me and I did wonder if she thought that Charlie had relented. We broke up early and went back to the hotel where Andrew and Mary joined us for a drink in the bar. Mary couldn't resist talking shop.

"Have they found the front fuselage yet?"

"Hardly, they will have to move *Ocean Voyager* first before they can start looking."

"You will be very popular if they find it."

"I'm not sure about that. They think I go to places where I shouldn't."

Charlie joined in keeping an expressionless face. "I can well understand that."

Mary came straight back. "Peter, that's nonsense. They should appreciate your first rate skills."

I definitely wasn't sure how Charlie would take that and I certainly wasn't going to look.

"Thank you, Mary. We shall have to see how things go."

We only had one drink and went to our rooms.

"Charlie, that went well."

"If you say so. You've been talking to Mary behind my back."

"She called me because I'd left my app on my phone and she saw I was in London."

She looked at me.

"Have you disconnected from her completely."

"I have now, thank you. If you're interested she wanted to know if the front fuselage of the RWA aircraft had been found. And she wanted to know if you had forgiven me."

"What did you say?"

"Not yet, twice."

"Good."

"But we need to find the nose and you need to forgive me."

She thought about that.

"Are you going to take that job in UK?"

"That depends on you."

She went off to her room but in the middle of the night I suddenly felt Charlie getting into bed with only my favourite perfume on.

***

We decided to have breakfast downstairs. We got our food and sat down.

"Peter, you needn't think I've forgiven you. I was just cold and trying to get warm."

I wondered why if she was so cold she didn't put a nightdress or some pyjamas on but somehow I didn't feel it was the right time to mention it.

"I did try and warm you up."

She looked at me and clearly was deciding what to say.

"Well clearly you have been having plenty of practice."

"You're right, when is our tenth wedding anniversary?"

She almost smiled but managed to suppress it. "There isn't going to be one the way you've been carrying on. And you haven't told me yet, are you going to take that job in UK?"

"I definitely don't know. We're settled in Australia, the children love it, you've got a good job, why should we move?"

"It's a prestigious well paid job and you wouldn't have to travel all over the world all the time. You need to live a more normal life."

"And it's pensionable. But what about you and the kids?"

She smiled.

"That's no problem, I can stay in Canberra."

"Yes, dear, but it would be rather a long commute."

She decided not to continue the discussion.

"We'd better get changed if we're going to get to City Hall in time."

Charlie looked really great in a smart suit and I too had bought a new suit for the occasion. We arrived on time as did the bride and groom. We soon got through the formalities and shared a cab back to the hotel. Andrew and Mary looked really happy and I detected that Charlie was relaxing. They had booked a private room and we slowly all assembled. There were quite a few people we didn't know but there was one guest I did recognise, Wendy Greengrass, Charlie's boss at Westfield Insurance when we first met in St Anthony. She was obviously delighted to have been invited.

We had a few speeches including one from Andrew's best man who I didn't know but I think Charlie had met in the distant past. When the meal was over a small area was cleared for dancing and Charlie agreed to dance with me after Mary and Andrew had led the way. Later Andrew asked Charlie to dance so I found myself dancing with Mary.

"Mary, have a wonderful marriage. It's been a lovely day. Where are you off to?"

"It's not polite to ask a girl where she's going on her honeymoon. We're renting a catamaran from Tortola in the British Virgin Islands."

"Sounds great. I wish we were with you."

"The cat's big enough but it would be a bit unconventional."

"That's never worried you."

"How's things with you?"

"I think it's going to be alright but I have another problem. They've offered me that job again in the UK."

"That's great. Third time lucky. If I hadn't married Andrew I'd be working for you. Are you going to accept?"

"I wish I knew. If Charlie had chucked me the decision would be easy but now I'm definitely undecided. I like Australia and the lack of pressure in Canberra. London is much

much worse than Sydney and probably equals New York. On the other hand there would be a lot less travelling but a lot more man management."

"You would get someone to do that for you. You need to do the thinking."

The music stopped and she took me over to Andrew who was with Charlie. Mary looked at her. "Peter's just told me about the new the job in London. Sounds great. What are you going to do?"

Charlie smiled. "What am I going to do? What is Peter going to do? It's his job."

"You could get a job in London. The National Gallery or the Royal Academy."

"My sort of job comes like hen's teeth. Anyway why would I want to move? I'm very comfortable in Canberra and so are the children. It's Peter who has the problem."

Mary said nothing and I could see that she had decided she had probably said more than enough. Later she and Andrew disappeared on their honeymoon. Up in our suite Charlie decided she would like a gin and tonic so I got two and we sat on the sofa again.

"Well that's that. Let's keep our fingers crossed. Why did you tell her about the job?"

"Did in matter? She was very supportive and I thought concerned."

Charlie admitted grudgingly. "I suppose so. Maybe she isn't all bad. I wonder where they're going on their honeymoon?"

"Tortola and they are renting a catamaran."

"Trust you to ask. I'd like to go to Tortola and have a few weeks sailing."

"She did say there was lots of room on the boat but she thought it might be a bit unconventional."

"Surprised that worried her."

"That's what I said."

"Well we'd better get some sleep as my flight is quite early to Dallas."

"So is mine. 1100 hours."

"Sounds **familiar**. We can share a cab." A pause. "I suppose you'd better share my bed as well so we don't oversleep."

"That's a good a reason as any."

"But you needn't think I've forgiven you."

***

Back in Canberra we caught up with our work. At home I was still kept in Mary's bedroom but otherwise we were pretty well back to normal. The arrangement suited the kids as they had no hesitation in rushing into my room early in the morning and waking me up for a chat or to read to them; they knew Charlie wouldn't allow it except on special occasions. However I wasn't sure **that** Charlie wasn't a bit put out with my obvious rapport with the kids; it clearly made the separate room arrangement rather unsatisfactory from her viewpoint.

A few evenings after our return we were sitting down after the children had gone to bed when the phone rang, mine not Charlie's.

"Peter, Robert here. We've found the front fuselage quite close to the position your Chinese friend said. It's an amazing sight apparently, the front completely bashed in. No bodies unfortunately."

"Probably good news about the bodies; hopefully the Chinese will be keeping them dry and cold. What are you going to do?"

"We should have it ashore in Broome in a couple of days."

"Well don't touch it without looking at it very carefully and be very careful moving it. Also make certain that the salvage people look very carefully on the ocean bed underneath the nose when they've moved it."

"Peter, you sound as if you suspect something."

"Well it certainly sounds like a mid-air collision and not a bomb. You need to know what hit it."

"Well it can't have been the Chinese fighter; we've looked at that."

"You're assuming that the Chinese have given us everything back. Sounds to me as if they've kept the aircraft that hit RW845."

"Peter, you seem to be able to guess what the Chinese have been up to. Did your UK Chinese friend tell you anything else?"

"They didn't tell me anything except the lat/long. They clearly don't want to admit that one of their aircraft hit the RWA aircraft. Think of the liabilities. That's why you need to collect everything you can find. I think they will have tampered with the nose to remove any tell-tale traces of the other aircraft but it must have been difficult underwater. When you get the nose ashore it will be much easier to search for bits."

"Would you like to have a look yourself?"

"Thank you. I'm not an expert as you are at looking at bits but it would be nice to look at it."

"OK. I'm going to be in the hotel not to-morrow evening but the one after. Bye."

Charlie had clearly been paying attention. "That sounded good. Thinking about the UK job, it would be right up your street. For example you clearly have sussed out the whole of the Royal World Airways situation and then you are advising Robert what to do. There really is no need for you to look at the thing yourself since, as you said, you are not an expert at looking at crashed and bent pieces of metal. Your strength is in working out what happened and, if applicable, who the rogues are."

I looked at Charlie and went over, held her and kissed her. She looked pleased and surprised. "What was that for?"

"Well you really understand and sympathise with what I am doing."

"Of course I do. I'm your wife. I wouldn't have married you if you weren't very smart but I hadn't anticipated you having an affair to spoil our marriage."

"I haven't had an affair. It was just an unfortunate set of coincidences."

"I take it that's a plea in mitigation."

I nodded. "Well **Charlie**, now you've decided that I'd be good at the new job, what are we going to do?"

"Well I take it you've worked out why I can't divorce you?"

"You could but since Mary would be the co-respondent your brother wouldn't be over the moon."

Charlie smiled ruefully. "Bingo. So what am I going to do, since you seem to be an ace at forecasting what is going to happen?"

"You are going to forgive me and together we are going to wrestle with the problem of what we should do together."

"Yes, you're right. But you better leave your clothes where they are for the moment as I've taken over your wardrobe."

She pulled me towards her as I clearly showed my relief. We were both quiet for a bit holding each other. Then she let go and we sat up.

"It's too late to discuss things to-night. Let's try to do it after breakfast."

And after breakfast we wrestled with the problem. Clearly one solution would be for me to take the job and Charlie could try and get a job in the UK. The situation would be complicated by having to move the children. The other solution would be the simple one, stay put with no changes but we both thought that that was a bit unimaginative. I suppose I was definitely tempted to try something new but I was worried about what job Charlie could find; maybe UK firms and galleries wouldn't want to employ an American. We didn't come to any definite conclusion and we decided to let things run for a week or so; I had got the feeling from Charles Simon they were prepared to wait a bit for my answer.

Back in the old routine I dropped Charlie off at the Gallery and went to my office. There was a lot of mail to go through and a lot of work that needed my attention. The ATSB was about to announce the finding of the nose section of RW845 and I sent a situation report to Jeremy Prentice. I also did the same to Roger O'Kane at ITAC explaining that apparently there had been a collision of some sort and not an explosion. I decided to leave at dawn for Broome the following morning and got home early to sort things out.

Jeremy Prentice, after reading my email, came on line and wanted an interview so I setup Skype. He called me asking a load of questions some of which I answered and some I ducked. I agreed to another interview from Broome after I had seen the wreckage though I was mindful that I'd have to get permission from Robert so that I wasn't ahead of the Australian media.

Charlie came home full of excitement. "Christie's have a job and also there is one at the Tate Modern." I wrinkled my nose. "You may be too old for the Tate Modern but I'm not. It's well paid and I'm eminently qualified. I think I'd prefer it to Christies."

"Why don't you apply for both and see what happens? If you don't get what you want we can stay here."

"I'm glad you said that as I've applied for the application forms – I had to give them both a brief résumé and they will only email them to me if they think I'm a serious contender. It's a sensible way to proceed rather than letting everyone apply and having to sift through miles of paperwork."

"The problem is that the firms advertising use head hunters who are not in a hurry and want to make as much money as possible recommending a candidate. The pre-sifting looks good but may not mean anything."

"I think you're biased."

"Almost certainly."

"Have you packed? What time are you leaving?"

"My flight leaves 0625 which means I'd better leave here soon after five."

"That sounds a bit tight. Quarter to five would be better."

"I'm business class for a quick check-in but you're probably right. Shall I sleep in the sin bin to avoid waking you?"

"No, it will be alright but we'll go to bed early."

I got up at four fifteen and arrived at check-in wishing as usual that I hadn't got up so early. Coffee in the lounge revived me but then I had to endure changes at Melbourne and Perth. However the flight arrived at Broome at 1420 which was good and the Blue Seas Resort almost felt like home. I didn't call Robert straightaway but went down for a swim. Later I contacted him and we agreed to meet in the bar; he had overnighted Perth and had arrived lunchtime.

"Robert, did you go out this afternoon and have a look?"

"No, as they were still unloading the nose. However I've got a few photos."

He opened a folder in front of him and passed a few photos over. It was a horrible sight as the nose was completely crushed and the whole section was not very long; the crew must have been killed outright. The force of the impact had clearly torn the nose away from the rest of the fuselage just in front of the wings. The main fuselage descent from altitude until it hit the water must have been a very rough ride indeed and absolutely horrific for the passengers and crew.

"That's awful, Robert. Never seen anything like it. What do you think happened?"

"Looks like a **head on collision** but at an angle I think which separated the front section."

"The main fuselage must have broken up on impact and filled with water and they were all drowned. But think what it must have been like on the descent for six minutes and thirty seconds."

"I'd rather not thank you. I'm afraid as accident investigators we often meet terrible situations though I agree this is worse than most as the passengers were alive for some minutes knowing they were going to die. The pilots must have known nothing. A completely dark night, no warning, a bolt out of the blue or something like that."

"You say that but shouldn't TCAS have alerted them?"

"You've got a point there. I'm not sure if Chinese military aircraft carry TCAS."

"Well hopefully you will find some clue on the front of the fuselage, perhaps metal pieces or fragments. What instructions have you given your people?"

"I've taken your advice. Have told the team not to touch the nose until we've examined it very carefully. We are also looking all round the sea bed where we found the nose."

"Just under the nose is where to look. If there is anything to find it will be there, in my opinion."

We didn't stay in the bar late and met for breakfast. Robert had rented a car and we drove out to the harbour and parked by the pier which had the nose and the rest of the wreckage. I recognised a couple of the team from ATSB who had helped us when Jerry and I had looked at the fuselage; they let us in through the gate and we drove along to the wreckage. The nose section was obvious though it didn't look much like an aircraft nose; as the photos we had looked at last night had shown, the front had been crushed flat. We looked at it very carefully and clearly the nose had been torn off the rest of the fuselage by the impact. However the front where it had been hit was a mess. It was just possible to see part of both pilots' seats and it certainly looked as if the pilots' seat belt straps were missing. My assessment was that the Chinese had interfered with the front of the fuselage and possibly removed the bodies, perhaps cutting the straps. Looking more carefully I wondered if the Chinese had removed bits of the aircraft that had hit RW845. To me it seemed most unlikely that the aircraft could be hit, the front fuselage completely torn off and yet there would be no sign of the colliding aircraft. I looked at Robert and he was a speaking into his phone making a lot of notes, relying on the ATSB photographers for the pictures. We spent three hours moving around looking at the nose section and then we went back to the hotel and changed from our working clothes into short sleeved shirts and shorts. We met again in the cool of the bar which was almost empty. We both decided that water was what we needed and then Robert asked me what I thought of the front fuselage.

"I think the Chinese have interfered with it. The first thing that needs doing is to get the bodies of the pilots and any other bodies they managed to rescue."

"But the Chinese haven't admitted that they had the fuselage, Peter. How can we ask them?"

"That is a real problem and at the moment I have no suggestions."

"I'm struggling with how we are going to treat this in the accident report. Clearly we can now say that there was a head on collision but we need to know what hit the aircraft."

"The ROV hasn't found any bits, I suppose?"

Robert shook his head. "I'm afraid not."

"Well I can't do anything more here, I'm afraid. I think I'll overnight Perth and catch first flight to Canberra in the morning. Thanks for letting me look."

"Well I've got to stay here and go through the whole situation in detail with Mark who is coming in this afternoon. We will have to do a preliminary report I think and then negotiate with the Chinese to see if we can get them to admit they had the front fuselage." He smiled at me. "If you were working for us I'd send you back to talk to your Chinese friend but my boss would not like you doing it. He's the head man and very correct; however he's retiring shortly and I'm thinking of putting my hat in the ring."

Robert's last comment was news to me but I said nothing. I guessed he wouldn't be exactly delighted if I decided to apply in competition. I left the bar and went up to my room to check the flights and pack. I made a reservation, booked a hotel in Perth for the night, emailed Charlie and then got a cab to the airport. In the morning while still in my room I called Stephen and brought him up to date. I also made an appointment to see him just before he went home the following day.

***

At Canberra I dropped my bags off at home and then went on to see Stephen.

"Peter, what wild suggestion have you got now?" I must have looked surprised. "You do tend to push the limits of credibility sometimes."

"Well Stephen, you know the problem. We don't know what hit RW845 but I think it must have been a UAV."

"I didn't know they could fly at that height."

"You need to read the intelligence reports you circulate. The latest Russian military ones can easily fly that high, and it won't be long before Boeing or Airbus will be floating the idea of unmanned freighters. It makes very good commercial sense but of course the rules need to be defined so that the aircraft can be certificated. This may be the holding factor before commercial operations start since the rules have to be agreed globally. The aircraft will have to transmit their position all the time so that they can be 'seen' not only by air traffic but also by neighbouring aircraft."

"Sounds a bit alarming to me as a passenger flying in the same airway. Still I'm not worrying as the pilots' unions will never agree."

"They won't be on the aircraft so their agreement won't be necessary."

"They can refuse to fly on airways which have the crewless freighters."

"You may be right, but don't rule it out. I know it seems unlikely but remember we don't really need any new technology. It could be done now. The commercial pressures will be great --- no crew to worry about with their restricted duty hours; the design of the aircraft should be cleaner not having to worry about the crew being able to look out."

"How about flight testing?"

"Very good point. To take full advantage of not having any crew it will be necessary to make all flights including test flights automatic."

"Maybe the Chinese are doing just that."

"No, Stephen I don't think so. I've read the latest issue of your technical assessment and my bet is that the UAVs are Russian built. However, whoever built the UAV, somehow we must make the Chinese admit that it was a UAV that hit RW845 and of course we want any bodies they may have."

"Have you told ATSB about your idea of UAVs?"

"No, they probably think it is a fighter, and of course it may be. We need to be watching their carrier operations because I think the UAVs must be operating off their carrier."

"I wondered why you wanted to see me. You're here because you want the UK to send a submarine to have covert looks at what's going on? But Peter, how do you know we haven't sent a submarine anyway?"

"That's a good point. Maybe we ought to ask."

"Anyway surely this is a civil matter?"

"Not at all. The UK needs to know what the Chinese have got."

"Well I can ask but don't hold your breath." Stephen thought about things for a moment. "Anyway how do you know the Chinese are still there and operating the UAVs?"

"Very, very good point. I'll go back to the RAAF and check. Hold your fire until I call you."

When I got home Charlie was buried in paperwork. "Peter, they both sent me application forms. It will take me a long time and a good memory to fill the forms in. Typical recruitment agencies. In fact, there are only two pages that matter."

"Good news about the forms. When do they have to be in by?"

"Christie's to-morrow; I've asked and got a week's extension. Tate, I've got ten days.

"Sounds good but I'll probably have to reply before you hear, unless of course you're not short listed in which case I'll turn the job down."

"We've got time to think about it for a day or two. What would we do about schooling?"

"Well luckily they are not into secondary education yet. We've got to decide where we want to live. You will be operating from London I'm sure. Problem is I'm not sure where my office is going to be. I assume London but the AAIB is in Farnborough, the MAIB is in Southampton and the RAIB is in Derby. I need to talk to Charles Simon to find out what's been done and what the Ministry of Transport have in mind."

"Can't we live in your house?"

"Possibly but you would spend a lot of time travelling."

"I thought you were going to integrate the Boards or Branches or whatever they're called. London seems the obvious place."

"I'm not arguing but the previous guy must have done something; he must have had an office. As I said I'll talk to

Charles. By the way are you sitting comfortably? Robert's boss is retiring shortly."

Mary considered the information.

"Are you interested? Would they take a **Pom**?"

"Not really but yes, I think they might."

"Well that's settled then. What happens next?"

"We have some supper."

In the morning I called Buster Stone. "Can you tell me if you are still operating your Jindalee radars 24/7?"

"Not sure if they are and not sure if we can tell you? I'll call you back."

He was as good as his word; apparently the radar has just gone on to an 'as required' basis but he had no details. I called Stephen on the special phone he gave me.

"You can relax on the submarine request. Sub wouldn't see anything."

"What are you going to do?"

"Not my concern but I'd like to get the bodies back if I could. However I do have some ideas."

Chapter 18

Vin Partridge came into his boss's office. "Graham Smith wants to talk to you urgently, Minister"

Jack Smithson looked at Vin. "Do you know what it's about?"

"I think it's something to do with the Chinese and their aircraft carrier."

Jack shrugged. "Alright, get him on line and listen in."

A few minutes later Jack picked up the phone. "Graham, how can I help you?"

"It's the Chinese, Jack. A couple of days ago they requested that we take our salvage vessel out of the way as they would like to search the area themselves."

"Did they say what they wanted?"

"No, but in accordance with our foreign policy, good relations and promoting trade and that sort of thing, I think we should agree."

"Graham, hold on. I have a feeling things are more complicated than it seems. Let me call you back."

"Jack, I can't see the problem. I've told them it should be alright and I'll confirm."

"Well I'm pretty sure there is a serious problem. As I'm sure you know they took the flight data recorder of the crashed UK airliner when they shouldn't but I think it's even more serious. You'll have to tell them there will be a delay."

Jack rung off and Vin came into the office. "Vin, remind me of the situation."

"Minister, I'm not up to speed on this one but I know you were absolutely correct in hesitating. Of course it's a civil airliner but as we know there's more to it than that. We haven't found out yet what the aircraft were that apparently were not Chinese fighters."

"Well get briefed as soon as you can and you had better get Max Wilson over as well when you're ready."

Vin decided to ring the ATSB but the head man was not in. He asked for the guy dealing with the crashed UK airliner and was put through to Robert Covelli. He explained what the Chinese wanted and Robert had to think fast.

"Vin, I don't think we should agree at the moment. From our point of view the Chinese have been very deceitful. They took the recorder, pretended they hadn't and finally gave it to us with some weak excuse. Then we couldn't find the nose section of the crashed aircraft and suddenly it appeared."

"Why blame the Chinese for that?"

"Well it's a long story. There's a British insurance investigator who suspected the Chinese had salvaged the front of the civil aircraft because they didn't want us to see it. They wouldn't admit they had the nose but all of a sudden they called this Pom to London and gave him a latitude and longitude to search, saying that's where they would look if they were looking. And guess what, when we searched there for the second time the missing piece was there; clearly the Chinese had the bit all the time."

"Why bring this Pom into it?"

"Well the Chinese won't talk to us because they don't want to admit anything and by going through this guy they think they can't be blamed. The current situation is that if they did have the front section, which they almost certainly did, then they probably have the bodies of the two pilots and the first class passengers with crew; obviously the ATSB and the dependants want these bodies. Meanwhile to cover all the options we need to carry on searching not only for the bodies but for the aircraft that hit the UK airliner. If the Chinese would admit they had the front fuselage then we could negotiate but clearly they don't want to admit they were to blame because of the liability they would assume."

"Robert, the problem we have here is that there are several organisations involved, RAAF for a start, you people, the Brits and our Foreign Affairs people. Can't we use this Pom to negotiate with the Chinese so it's all informal?"

"Vin, this guy is first rate but our Foreign Affairs people and my boss can't abide what he's doing. It's not the correct way of doing things."

"Bugger that. We've got to sort this thing out."

"Let me have a think and I'll call you back. Give me your direct line. Off the record we need to do this thing quickly while my boss is away."

Robert decided he had better bring Peter up to speed and arranged to go to his office.

"Robert, it's strange how things work out. I was already thinking of going back to London and working out an excuse with the Chinese for them to admit they had found the bodies. However someone must pay for my ticket.

"I think this new request puts another dimension on things. Something must have happened and it sounds as if the Chinese may have lost something --- perhaps another aircraft. My advice is that we should definitely say no to the Chinese and start searching the whole area again."

"Peter, my boss would go hairless if we spend any more money searching the sea bed; it's costing us a fortune."

"Well get the RAAF to pay. My guess is that we're looking for a military aircraft."

"It's alright for you to say that but you know damn well it's a lot more complicated than that."

"Well have a think. I think I'll try to get the AAIB to pay for my ticket but the senior guy is like your guy and doesn't love me."

When the conversation stopped Peter rang up Buster Stone.

"Were you aware the Chinese now want to search where the ATSB vessel is searching?" Buster indicated it was news to him. "Well apparently two days ago they approached your Foreign Affairs people and made the request. I know you don't like giving me information but this could be very important. Can you find out when and why your JORN radar suddenly stopped its 24/7 watch? I think it may relate to the Chinese asking to do a search."

"Peter, you shouldn't be involved in all this."

"Tell me about it. Nobody's paying me but I seem to have the only hot line to the Chinese."

Chapter 19

Laurence called me at 7am as I was getting up. "Would you believe your man wants to see you again and said you can travel by Air China? His aide said they have booked you to-morrow night if that would be convenient."

"Laurence that sounds as if he really does want to see me. I'd better contact Air China and see what's going on. Will you be able to come in with me when I've got an appointment?"

"Peter, I wouldn't miss it for the world. It's the most exciting thing that's happened to me since I learnt to fly."

"I'll email you with my flight details and ask for a meeting."

After breakfast Charlie persuaded me to try to sort my travel out before we went to work. I rang Air China in Canberra and asked them if a reservation had been made in my name. The reservation lady asked for my date of birth and then gave me the flight details which turned out to be first class with an open return. She asked if it would be alright if she could send the tickets to my office and I agreed, telling her the lady at the desk would sign on my behalf if I was not there. Charlie was listening in to all this and clearly was impressed.

"My love, they really want you. What on earth is going on?"

"Not sure but hopefully we can organise something."

I rang QANTAS to arrange my flight to Sydney. The man doing the reservation was clearly confused as he told me I already had a reservation with an onward connection with Air China. Charlie overheard and shrugged her shoulders. I gave up and emailed Jerry, giving him my flight details and asking him not to bother with trying to get funding for my ticket. I got the car out of the garage and dropped Charlie off on the way to my office. I had barely got seated when the tickets arrived and I signalled Laurence with my ETA asking him to arrange the meeting with the Chinese.

I called Buster Stone for a bit more detail on the timing of the JORN shut down. "Peter, about two days ago all targets disappeared and so the order was given as I told you to shut JORN down."

"Well Buster, almost immediately after the targets disappeared the Chinese requested to search the area. What does that tell us?"

"That we should be searching for what the Chinese have lost."

"I imagine so but the searching is not as simple as that as ATSB won't see why they should pay for the extended search."

"Good point, needs the heavy breathers to sort it out between them."

"By the way, nothing to do with me but you should be aware the Chinese Defence attaché in London has just given me a free ticket to travel to London to meet him again."

"How do you mean 'nothing to do with me'?"

"Well I didn't ask them. Apparently they rang up Group Captain Williamson from MoD, the guy I go in with to see the attaché, and told him to let me know."

"Peter, that's could be very important. Any ideas of what the attaché wants?"

"No. I wanted to see him to see if we could dream up a cover story so they could return the bodies which I'm sure they must have, the pilots anyway but probably the first class passengers and the crew as well. I also believe they have the aircraft that hit the airliner RW845. Now we've got the new problem of a possible Chinese aircraft loss. My feeling is that you people must try and find the lost aircraft so a deal can be struck."

"How are we going to be able to communicate with you securely?"

"Suggest you use Stephen Wentworth at the High Commission or Group Captain Williamson but I don't know which department he is in. However Stephen might know how to contact him --- he seems to be able to find everybody from the Ministers downwards."

"Fine. I'll start with Stephen. Good luck on your trip."

I spent the rest of the day doing my routine work and in the back of my mind trying to decide what the air attaché was going to propose. Back home Charlie was completing her application forms and looking at schools in London.

"You seem to be planning for success, darling, and hoping my office will be in London."

"Of course I am. You've already got your job but I haven't."

"When I'm in London I'll talk to Charles Simon to find out what's been done and what the Ministry of Transport have in mind for my office."

In the morning I phoned Stephen telling him about the Chinese search request, my trip to London and that I'd given him as the UK contact for Buster Stone.

"Peter, be careful. They wouldn't have given you the ticket unless they've got a definite plan. This is high security stuff. You need to be able to talk to someone to clear any agreements even though they will be off the record. That phone you've got from me is Australia only. You might go through your man Laurence Williamson if he agrees or if it's a civil matter through AAIB."

"Thanks for the advice. For reasons I'm sure you'll understand I think I'll use Charles Simon in the Ministry of Transport Head Office if he will agree. I've got to talk to him anyway about another matter. Will Simon know how to contact you securely? How about Buster Stone?"

"I'm sure he will but for Buster Stone it will be easier to use your man Williamson."

"Where does he work?"

"Don't know but probably foreign air forces liaison. I'll find out and leave a message with him to contact me should you ask. I think it may be quicker to get decisions through me than Stone but either way it will take time. Expect several meetings with your man Kwok Qiáng."

I phoned Charlie to say goodbye and to tell her not to expect me back in a hurry. I then started the long trip to the UK from Canberra to Sydney and onwards to London via Beijing. The only good feature was the superb First Class service from Air China; I felt really spoilt and almost rested when we arrived at Heathrow at dawn.

At the RAF Club I checked my bag and had breakfast, not that I needed any but it helped to pass the time. I took a copy of the Times as I went in and in the Appointments section there was an advert from the Royal Academy. I messaged Charlie and got an immediate reply.

'Must be a new one. I've already replied and been short listed.'

'How long ago was that?'

'Shortly after you broke the seventh commandment.'

'But Charlie I hadn't been offered the job then.'

'What had that got to do with it? However it may work out after all despite your transgression. My interview is in three days' time but I wasn't going to tell you.'

'Just as well I'm in a double room.

'I know. I checked the moment I heard yesterday.'

Still shaken by Charlie's news, I took a cab to MoD; Laurence collected me after I had got my pass and we went to his office. The meeting with Kwok Qiáng was not until the following day and I spent some time bringing Laurence up to speed and discussing secure communications.

Laurence let me use a small empty office to phone Charles Simon. I explained the situation as it affected ATSB ad asked if I could come round to his office if it proved necessary in order to phone Robert. He was very supportive and when I had finished arranging that I went on to discuss the job he had offered me.

"Charles, if I accept your offer where would my office be?"

"Well the present incumbent was thinking of having his office in London and not moving any of the accident branches. However he has not made a lot of progress and you would be starting with a clean sheet of paper. Obviously the whole point of the change you would be making would be to make accident investigation more efficient and ensure that all three boards and branches use the latest technology. Having your office in London would be expensive and probably frowned on by the Treasury."

"My feeling is that the right thing to do might be to pull everybody in to Farnborough. Not so convenient for the Marine side and I'm not clear how it would affect the Rail people. I would need to talk to all concerned. My immediate concern is a personal one as I want to know where to live and where to educate the children. Furthermore my wife is quite a high flier in the art world and would probably get a job in London."

"Well it seems to make sense for you to work in Farnborough but your wife would have to be prepared to travel."

"Charles, that's fine. Obviously we're going through the pros and cons of moving and we'll have to discuss this."

"Of course, take your time. However we'd like to know in the next couple of months."

I went back to the RAF Club and checked into my room. I emailed Charlie and told her about Farnborough. After lunch I walked to the Royal Academy and used Charlie's Joint Friends card to go into the Keeper's House for a cup of tea. I looked at the current exhibition and decided it was not for me.

In the morning Laurence came round for breakfast and once again we took a cab to the Chinese Embassy. Everything worked like clockwork and Kwok Qiáng took us to the meeting room. He went through all the pleasantries with us both but then he rather ignored Laurence and addressed me.

"Mr Talbert, let me start by saying that we are so pleased that our guess was correct and that the Australian salvage vessel found the nose of the airliner.

"However, we apologise but there has been some confusion with our salvage ship; the crew thought that the bodies they recovered were Chinese but we now realise that they came from the Royal World Airliner that tragically crashed."

"Well Mr Kwok, it is very unfortunate that the bodies were taken and have not been returned to the airline much earlier. What are you proposing?"

"We are going to deliver the bodies to Broome in two days' time if you wouldn't mind informing the Australian accident people so that the bodies can be delivered to the people who are dealing with all the other bodies."

I decided I had better start exploring the situation.

"Of course, I would be delighted but Mr Kwok, people will wonder exactly how you had these bodies since apparently you did not have the nose of the aircraft."

Kwok Qiáng did not hesitate as he was clearly expecting my question.

"Mr Talbert we were looking for another aircraft near where you found the nose of the Royal World Airways aircraft but we did not find the aircraft. It is for this reason we have asked for our salvage vessel to look where the Australian salvage vessel is looking."

I considered the situation for a moment and then decided to go ahead.

"Mr Kwok, I will have to consult with the accident investigators because they are still looking for bodies and will want to check whether your people managed to find all the bodies."

I decided to go for broke. "Mr Kwok it is quite clear that there was a head on collision between the Royal Airways Aircraft and another aircraft. May I ask you to ask your salvage people whether they found it? It may be that it was an unmanned aircraft which would explain why there has been no announcement of an aircraft loss."

Kwok Qiáng looked at me, in my view trying to decide which of the many lines he had planned he should use. However, I made it clear that we could go no further and Kwok Qiáng got the message straightaway. We made our farewells and went back to Laurence's office.

"Peter, that was fascinating. What happens next?"

"It's not too late. Let's ring Stephen Wentworth at home if you can do that."

"No problem. I spoke to him earlier and he has a secure phone at home."

He made the connection, explained the situation to him and handed me the phone. I explained first the way I had handled the dead body situation and how I proposed to ring Robert from Charles Simon office. "It's the UAV situation that we need an answer for. Whether he will admit that they have the remains of the aircraft that hit RW845."

"Isn't that a civil matter? Can't you sort that out with Robert?"

"Not sure. I thought the RAAF wanted to know what sort of aircraft they were. I'm sure the UK would as well for that matter."

"I'll ask Dominic but from a liability point of view it's a civil matter."

"Robert won't care about who pays but he will need to know exactly how the accident occurred. Alright I'll talk to him while you're sorting out whether the RAAF want to be involved."

I decided to ring Charles Simon's office and his secretary said that Charles had several appointments but he had said I could use a secure phone in his meeting room. I left MoD and took a cab to Horseferry Road. Charles's secretary collected me and she managed to get Robert at home on a secure line.

"Peter, how are you doing?"

I explained the situation as best I could. "Robert, the bodies are going to be delivered to Broome in two days but I've no idea how many and whether you and the airline will be satisfied. It's quite ridiculous but I seem to be negotiating with the Chinese."

"Well Peter, there's no way that we ought to agree to removing *Ocean Salvager* until we know a lot more and have the colliding aircraft."

"How's the search going?"

"Well we're administering the search but really the RAAF are driving it now we are looking for the Chinese aircraft."

"What is to prevent the Chinese salvage vessel coming into the area anyway?"

"Nothing I suppose. All very difficult."

"Well we are clearly in a holding situation until the bodies have been examined and counted. If you need to contact me then email me and if it needs to be secure I'll have to go to MoD or Department of Transport."

After I had finished talking to Robert I had lunch and then went to visit Jerry. I brought him up to date but somehow I felt that his attitude towards me had changed slightly and was slightly more cautious. I wondered if it was because I was doing all the negotiating with the Chinese or whether the bush telegraph had been going reference my being offered the new job but I decided not to explore. Back in the Club I checked they were aware that Charlie was coming at dawn.

Before it was light I took a cab to the airport and waited at the dreaded Terminal Three. Charlie sent me a message saying she was waiting for the baggage and would catch a cab. I broke the news that I was right outside at the information desk and she just sent me sent me a string of exclamation marks. In fact I did not have long to wait and we stood in line for a cab. My phone rang just as we were getting into one which didn't help the baggage handling. I could see it was Robert but I could not answer in time. However once we were settled I messaged him asking him to try again.

"Peter, they've found a crashed UAV but the Chinese know we've found it and saying it is their aircraft and they want it."

"How are they communicating?"

"Through our Foreign Affairs people who want to roll over and say 'help yourselves' but I believe our Defence Department are saying 'wait a moment'"

"Robert, how closely has the UAV been examined? I have a suggestion to make but I don't want to do it on this phone. I'll go to MoD as soon as they wake up. Thanks for telling me what's going on."

I put the phone away and Charlie poked me. "Remember me?"

"My love, I got up dawn to meet you. Stop scoring points."

"Alright, I was only joking. It all seems to be happening. Who's paying you?"

"Bingo. I was wondering about that. Just as well you're working or we'd be broke."

"Slight exaggeration but it is all getting ridiculous. You are working flat out for nothing."

"You're absolutely right but I don't see how I can withdraw from the situation."

Charlie unloaded her bag in what had been my room and had a shower. We went down to breakfast.

"What time is your interview?"

"10am to-morrow. I decided to come a day early."

"Tell me, when will you know the result?"

"Not sure. They may select straight away."

"What will you say if you are selected?"

"I'll have to say yes since they will have asked me that at the interview."

"What about travelling from the Farnborough area every day? It will be a nightmare. I was wondering if it wouldn't be better if we lived in London and I travelled out."

"Can we afford the housing and the schools?" We discussed the matter and put it into a 'to be discussed later' folder. Charlie decided she might have an unofficial wander round the Royal Academy and she went back up to our room. I then telephoned Charles Simon and explained the UAV problem. He suggested I came straight over so I also went up to our room, got the stuff I needed and got into a cab. I was able to go straight up to Charles' office.

"Peter, what is your suggestion?"

"Well I think it is absolutely vital to find out who made the UAV. I have a theory that the UAV that hit the Royal World Airways aircraft and the one they have just found must be Russian. Reading the state of Chinese technology I don't believe they have UAVs that can fly at 40,000ft with such long ranges. Maybe the Russians were trying to sell their UAVs to the Chinese and operating off their carrier. It would explain why the carrier was operating where it was and not from their own bases."

"But in that case why aren't the Chinese admitting it and blaming the Russians."

"Maybe they were operating the UAV when it hit the airliner. However, at this stage I believe the Australians should examine the UAV that has just crashed very closely and then let the Chinese have it back in order to avoid an international incident. How are we going to penetrate the corridors of power?"

"I think you had better brief Sir Philip Brown, you remember the Permanent Secretary, and then let him do it. I'll see if he is available. However I'm not sure that the UAV is anything to do with us. See what he says."

Charles asked his secretary to try to contact Sir Philip; the only gap that he had was at lunchtime so at the appointed time I went down to reception. He appeared at 1230 and we went down to a small restaurant down the street.

"Peter, it's great seeing you again and I do hope you will be able to accept the job. I gather you have a tricky problem with the Chinese and the crashed Royal World Airways airliner?"

In as short a time as I could I made him aware of the whole scene. "Sir Philip, first of all let me say that I shouldn't be involved at all with the sad loss of the Royal World Airways aircraft. However the Chinese are using me as the intermediary because they don't want to admit to anything if they can avoid it. So far they have admitted to having taken the recorder and the bodies from the front fuselage, allegedly by mistake of course. My current assessment is that the

Chinese have the UAV that hit the airliner and that it is probably a Russian one since we believe that they have such high flying drones and we are pretty sure the Chinese don't. At the moment there is a rapprochement between Russia and China so I think that the Chinese have been testing the UAVs from their carrier trying to decide whether to buy some or not. What we don't know is who was operating the UAV which hit the airliner, was it the Chinese or the Russians? The operator of the UAV at the moment of impact is liable to have to pay damages to Royal World Airways and all the dependants; it will be a fairly large sum consisting of a payment for the hull plus a minimum of about $170K per passenger. Moreover as you know, because the accident was no fault of the airline, the Montreal Convention says that passengers will not be able to claim a larger amount and for dependants who have lost a breadwinner this is a severe limitation."

"But Peter, won't the insurers have to pay the damages to the airline and the passengers?"

"I imagine so but in the circumstances the insurance company will want to be recompensed. Furthermore, because of the Montreal limitation, in my view we should try and get the perpetrators of this terrible accident to pay the dependants a realistic amount above the 170K maximum where it is required."

Sir Philip was silent for a bit as we ate our lunch. "Yes, Peter, it is a real problem but it has to be solved. Forgetting legal implications I would have thought that both China and Russia are liable and should share the damages. Neither should have agreed to operate where they did without notifying the FIR controllers. Problem is that we have no way of leaning on either Country to get them to pay up." He looked at me. "What would be your recommendation? I suspect you've been thinking about this for some time."

"Well how about getting both Countries to put an agreed sum into a kitty to pay out the claims without admitting liability? It would save an enormous amount of time and legal fees. It will never be possible to satisfy all the claimants but it might be a possible way forward."

"You're right. It would be a good solution but it would need selling to the Chinese who would have to persuade the Russians and of course we would have to get the Airline and their insurers to agree."

"Well if someone would give me a figure I don't mind having first go with Mr Kwok. The deal would be that they don't have to produce the UAV which hit the Royal World Airways aircraft and they can salvage the other UAV which has been found but they would have to provide the compensation money. The ATSB would then complete the findings saying that they had been unable to ascertain what had hit the aircraft."

"But Peter, how is the money going to be declared and handled?"

"I suggest the money should be paid to some form of international account which needs to be administered separately from the airline. Part of the money would be to RWA for the loss of the aircraft and crew; the rest would need to go to the passengers with an agreed formula but the real trick is somehow to keep the passengers' lawyers out of it, if that is possible. The passengers would have to agree to abide by international arbitration."

"How would the airline explain where the money is coming from?"

"Don't know. Maybe the Chinese could say that they were operating in the area and though they didn't lose any aircraft they were prepared to help. All I can hope to do is to get the money agreed and for you or someone to arrange an account to hold the money."

"Alright Peter. I clearly need to get some advice from ICAO or IMF or the Airline or elsewhere. When I've got an agreed sum then I'm happy for you to have a go. Certainly someone has to negotiate with the Chinese and you seem to be the best placed to do so."

"Well Sir Philip, I believe that speed is of the essence right now while they seem agreeable to talk to me."

"Agreed. By the way who is paying you for all your time and work?"

I paused trying to decide what to say.

"Sir Philip, thank you for asking. No-one is paying me. I got my most recent fare paid by the Chinese but I'm working for nothing."

"Maybe you should be paid out of this international sum?"

"Don't like that idea even though it would only be a minute amount of the total amount. Hopefully I can get the sum agreed but obviously I can't afford to sit here much longer waiting."

Sir Philip came to a decision. "OK. This is what we'll do. Obviously it will take time to get the necessary sum agreed. You go home to Canberra and, since it is a UK airliner, we will pay for you to come back and to do the negotiation. We'll also pay you for your time in the future. You will have to explain to the ATSB that they are never going to find the plane that hit RW845."

We shook hands on the deal and I felt very relieved as I went back to the Club. Charlie was back but before going to the Cowdray Room I called Laurence and explained the deal.

"Peter, what are we going to do about Kwok?"

"Well you remember I did ask him about the UAV that hit the airliner. We need an answer. As you know his email address, I suggest you write saying that I will be contacting him when I've spoken to the ATSB people. No need to tell him I'll be back in Canberra. Hopefully when we see him next we can propose a deal."

I rang off and we went down to the Cowdray Room. Charlie made herself comfortable. "Peter my dear I really love your funny old British custom of afternoon tea."

"Well you're a member so I don't have to be with you when you want to splash out."

"But we do have to be married."

"Well I'm not complaining. How was the Royal Academy?"

"Great. It would really suit me if I could get the job, though it would be slightly less money than Canberra. How did you get on?"

I explained about my talk to Sir Philip. "Peter, at last someone is going to pay you for your altruism?"

"Looks like it. Mind you it is probably an encouragement for me to take the job."

"Doesn't matter. We will need all the money we can get to educate the children."

"You're right there. Don't know yet what schools are available near Farnborough but there is bound to be something."

"Maybe we could afford a pied à terre somewhere for occasional overnights. Anyway we'd better have a quiet night to-night and good luck in the morning."

In the morning Charlie looked at her emails and found she was short listed at Christies.

"If I get offered the RA job I shall probably take it."

"Well take your time. Remember we don't have to do anything. When are we going home?"

"To-night. I'm booked already."

"Well I've got to go back with Air China so we'll meet at home."

"All right for you, you're first class and I'm only premium economy."

"But you'll be home first."

Charlie went off for her interview and I booked on the Air China flight. I decided not to talk to Robert until I got home. I was reading the papers in the Library when Charlie messaged me saying she wouldn't be home until mid-afternoon. I went to the desk and arranged a late check-out and then wished her Bon Voyage explaining that I would have leave the Club for the airport at 1500.

After a light snack in the Running Horse I packed and was on my way spot on time. As we approached Heathrow I got a message from Charlie 'They've offered me the job of Director of Overseas Planning and I accepted.'

'Have you signed a contract?'

'Yes, but I can withdraw up to fourteen days to allow my lawyer to read the fine print.'

'When do you start?'

'Two months' time.'

'Great I'll let Charles Simon know the moment you're satisfied.'

I checked in and remorselessly got sucked into the system. I escaped twenty three hours later as I collected my bag at Canberra after a painless but lengthy trip. Charlie hadn't gone to work but had waited for me to appear. We discussed the situation and her contract and agreed she should email the Royal Academy accepting the post and give her notice in at the National Gallery. On my part I would accept the Transport Safety Board offer but I would make it four months to fit in with the kids schooling at both ends; Charlie would start in London in two months and look for somewhere for us to live.

That way hopefully we could start them in the summer term in the UK.

Charlie went off to work and I knew that I would then have to tackle Robert but I decided to talk to Stephen first. I explained the plan. "There are two problems as I see it. We have to persuade the Australians that they can't have the UAV and also persuade ATSB they can't have the aircraft that hit RW845."

"Peter, how are om earth are we going to do that?"

"Well someone needs to brief Jack Smithson on the UAV that's been found. I could talk to Buster Stone but I'm not sure that will work."

"I think you should brief him yourself with perhaps Max Wilson, Chief of the Defence Force. Have you ever met him?"

"No, but if you can arrange it I can meet him first before we go and see Jack Simpson. I might be able to make that task a little bit easier for you."

"Not following you, Peter."

"Well I'm about to become Chairman of the new UK Transport Safety Board so that may help by giving me some status but give me a few hours as I've only just decided to take the job."

"Isn't that the one you've turned down twice already?"

"Well it wasn't quite like that but I know what you mean."

"However it was, it will certainly make it easier in your negotiations as well as mine. Particularly with the ATSB. Incidentally the head of ATSB is nearing retirement; I'm surprised you didn't go for that job."

"I did know but on balance we preferred the UK job which was a certainty while the Aussies may not want a Pom."

"Well I shall miss you but congratulations."

"Thanks. Coming back to the ATSB, I'll talk to Robert and see if he can produce his accident report without having the

UAV. I'll let you know when to arrange for me to meet Max Wilson."

"Peter, this isn't going to be easy so the sooner I can start the better."

I emailed Charlie asking if it was OK for me to tell Charles Simon I would take the job and she said she had that moment handed in her resignation. It was too late for me to call Charles so I sent him a simple email saying 'OK, four months please, will phone.' which I reckoned was safe enough. Having done that I went back to Stephen and asked him to go ahead.

My next move was to talk to Robert but I felt that it would be better to be face-to-face. He was in and so I walked over to Northbourne Avenue and tried to explain the problem. I could see he was having difficulties with my position so I thought I'd better explain.

"Robert, I know you're worried that I seem to be a one man band but if it helps I've been offered and accepted chairmanship of the UK's Transport Safety Board."

"Isn't that the one you refused?"

"Yes, you're right but the present incumbent hasn't really managed the amalgamation of the three existing branches and has resigned."

"You should be applying for the same job here. You wouldn't have to move, nor would your wife, and your children wouldn't have to change schools."

"I thought you were applying for the job here."

"I am but I reckon you're better qualified."

"I don't believe that and I can't tick the Australian citizen box."

"That won't matter. It's quite fashionable to have overseas appointees occasionally like your wife at the National Gallery."

"You would be talking yourself out of a job except that I'm committed and so is my wife. She's resigned and got a job at the Royal Academy so hopefully we've done the right thing."

"I'm sure you have but we will be sad to lose you."

"Thank you. Now let's review the situation. Did the Chinese return the bodies they had taken and are the identification team satisfied that you have them all?"

"Well I'm advised by the airline that the numbers are correct and the long and difficult job of identification is now taking place."

"Well that's good and it's got one of the stumbling blocks out of the way. What about the wreckage?"

"We've got all the bits of the crashed RW845 and it clearly has been hit on the nose by something."

"Robert, the problem we have is that we believe the Chinese salvaged the remains of the aircraft which was almost certainly a UAV and they won't admit they have it, they won't give it to you nor will they admit liability. What I'm suggesting is that you accept the situation and you write your report saying that it has not been possible to find the remains of the aircraft that hit RW845 but you think it was a UAV."

"Not very keen on doing that even though it happens to be true."

"I'm pretty sure the AAIB and Royal World Airways will be happy with that as long as there is a fund provided by the Chinese to pay for claims by the dependants of the passengers, the crew and hopefully the airliner."

"Why would the Chinese provide a fund if they are not admitting they caused the collision?"

"Well they lost another UAV and they or, more likely, the Russians want it back. The deal hopefully will be to let them salvage it and also not insist on exposing the whole UAV situation. Of course, I've got to try to do the deal so nothing is definite."

"Peter, why shouldn't we insist on getting the crashed UAV and publicise the whole thing?"

"Two reasons, nobody wants to have a spat with the Chinese if it can be avoided, particularly your Government, and if we do the deal the relatives will at least be able to get more money than the minimum laid down by the Montreal Convention."

"Well the news is bound to leak out and how is the fund going to be administered?"

"Not sure yet. The Transport Department in London is dealing with that and hopefully will brief me before I go in to see my Chinese negotiator, Kwok Qiáng."

We agreed I would keep in touch with him and let him know how things proceeded.

Chapter 20

Jack Simpson looked at Vin Partridge. "Who's this Pom coming here with Max?"

"He is going to be the new head of the UK Transport Safety Board and has been doing all the negotiation with the Chinese. He has a plan to settle the ATSB report problem on the Royal World Airline aircraft crash and also these unknown aircraft that we have seen flying around on our JORN radar."

"Why do we need him to tell us how to run our business?"

"Well Minister, the Chinese are only prepared at the moment to talk to Peter Talbert, that's his name by the way, in this matter because they don't want to admit to causing the civil airliner to crash and at the moment he has no affiliations. I don't know all the details but apparently he has a proposal he hopes you will agree to so that we can try to wind this affair up."

"Alright Vin, bring them in."

Max came in, introduced Peter to Jack Smithson and then they sat round the conference table.

"Alright Max, let's have it."

"Well Minister, as you know we have found a UAV that has recently crashed and the Chinese are saying it is their aircraft and want to salvage it. We believe it is one of the aircraft we have seen flying around using our JORN radar and was probably Russian made. We are very keen to salvage the aircraft ourselves and examine it but Peter Talbert here wants to do a deal with the Chinese which would result in letting the Chinese salvage it themselves. Perhaps you had better let Mr Talbert explain the situation."

"But Max, we want the aircraft." Jack looked at Peter, slightly belligerently. "Well Peter, you'd better try to convince me why we shouldn't have it."

"Minister, as you know we believe a UAV operating from a Chinese carrier hit RW845, the UK airliner, head on and all the passengers and crew were lost. The Chinese won't admit it directly and the problem is that money is required to reimburse the airline for the loss and also all the dependants of the lost passengers."

"But Peter, there's no problem there. The insurance will pay."

"Well Minister, dealing with the passengers first, the amount of money that the airline has to pay is defined by international agreement and is not very large. In a situation like this relatives of the dead tend to start very long claims against the airline, normally with very little hope of success and even if they are successful the lawyers get a very large share of the awards. With regard to the hull and crew, the insurance companies will get absolutely nowhere with the Chinese since they are admitting nothing. You may take the view that that is what insurance is for and why should the insurance company be recompensed but it is my view that the Chinese are liable and should pay. If the insurance company has to shoulder the whole airline claim the effect will be to raise the premiums on all airline travel covered by this insurer.

"Now with regard to the UAV which has been found I'm sure there have been a lot of photographs taken and you must be well aware of the manufacturer which we have assumed is Russian. We would like you to forgo actually salvaging the aircraft and in return for letting the Chinese salvage the wreckage and not insisting on their giving ATSB the remains of the aircraft that hit the airliner, we want the Chinese to provide a special fund to recompense the airline and the passengers."

Jack looked at Max. "Is it really necessary to land and examine the actual UAV we've found?"

"Well Minister we've examined it very closely with our divers underwater. It would be nice to have the wreckage ashore but it won't really matter if we don't have the hardware. The UAV is extensively damaged but my experts tell me that despite that they can judge the performance of the aircraft pretty well and what weapons it can carry. They also know the details of the engine. If it is going to help international relations then I would advise that we should let the Chinese have it."

"Well Geoff Smith will definitely be pleased if we do that,"

Peter came in. "Minister, as I explained, we don't want an agreement to let the Chinese salvage the UAV until they have accepted the financial deal though of course it may be difficult to stop them; luckily the ATSB salvage vessel is over the UAV so it should be alright. At the same time the ATSB need to agree that they will not insist on looking at what's left of the UAV that hit the airliner. With both agreements I can then go back to London to meet the Chinese Defence Attaché again, Kwok Qiáng."

"Peter, you will have to keep in touch with Max here and keep him fully briefed. But, to be frank, it all looks a bit of a long shot financially."

"Yes, Minister, of course. I've been working with Sir Philip Brown the Permanent Secretary of our Transport Department and I'm sure he also will let you know the state of play as well as your Ministry of Transport and the ATSB."

"Alright Peter, we will wait to hear from the UK. Meantime we will do our best to keep our Foreign Affairs people on side and the Chinese at bay."

Max and Peter left and Jack asked Vin to let Geoff Smith know what was happening.

***

Maureen Chester called Harry Brown into her office.

"What's going on with the accident report on that Royal World Airliner that crashed on the way to Australia? I'm getting pressurised by some local dependants in my constituency. Apparently not only is investigation taking a long time but so is the identification of the bodies."

"Well Minister, you may remember that Peter Talbert has been seeing the Chinese Defence Attaché in connection with the accident. He went back to Australia but is shortly coming back to see Kwok Qiáng again. He is hoping to do a deal with the Chinese to get them to provide money to settle claims without them having to admit it was their fault that an UDV hit the airliner head on."

"Harry, that seems a most unlikely thing to happen."

"Well another UAV operating in the area was lost and the Australians found it. The Chinese seem very keen to get it back and Talbert is hoping that if the Australians agree not to salvage the UAV and leave it for the Chinese to salvage then it might be possible to do the deal."

"But Harry, what's to prevent the Chinese just moving their salvage vessel into place regardless of the Australians?"

"Very good point, Minister. However the Australian salvage team is already in position and there is the matter of their UAV hitting the airliner. The Australians will agree not to pressure the Chinese to admit their UAV hit the airliner if a deal can be struck."

"I thought you said it was a Russian UAV. Why should the Chinese pay?"

"That's another reason why Talbert is hoping the Chinese will agree. It is not clear who was operating the UAV at the time of the accident and it may well be that the Russians were doing it in which case one imagines that the Chinese will lean on the Russians to contribute to save having the Chinese saying exactly what happened."

"Well it all seems a very long shot to me, Harry. Maybe the insurers will have to pay and that's an end of it."

"I think your constituents would be keen for the Talbert solution, Minister. It would provide a real financial help to the dependants that need it rather than a nominal help."

"You're right there, Harry. Let's hope he is successful."

"By the way Minister, Talbert has been offered the chairmanship of the new Transport Safety Board and has accepted."

"I thought there was a chairman."

"I understand that he has resigned as things were not going too well."

"It will be interesting to see if he will be as good an administrator as he is an investigator."

"Yes, Minister."

Chapter 21

I was back in the RAF Club, Kwok Qiáng having agreed to see Laurence Williamson and myself the following morning. I had made appointments to see Sir Philip Brown and Charles Simon to be briefed. Life was very hectic at home as we prepared to move halfway across the world. One of my jobs on this visit was to try to look at schools as well as sorting out my house but the school situation was proving impossible until we knew where my office was going to be.

Before leaving Australia after seeing Jack Smithson, I had called Mike Mansell to try to find out which insurers the Chinese and Russian airlines used and luckily he had come straight back with detailed information which I printed out in the Club and put in my bag.

My first visit was to Charles Simon, primarily to sign on the dotted line and discuss administrative details. He had the paperwork ready; it looked identical to the contract I had signed previously though the salary had been increased a little and I signed straightaway; we also discussed the funding I would receive for moving from Australia. He had told the three accident branches of my appointment and had told AAIB to arrange for me to have a separate office. I decided to raise my concerns.

"Charles, clearly the AAIB building is not large enough for the amalgamated Branches. If we try to extend the existing building it will take a long time and I feel that speed is important. We need to get a move on. Is it feasible for us to rent a building on a long lease that has enough space? It will probably be cheaper."

"I'm glad you said that, Peter, because that was our view but we wanted you to have time to works things out. We need to discuss things as soon as possible but, for the moment, I expect your head is full of RW845 and the Chinese."

"Well is it possible for some government organisation to be given a specification and told to look for possible accommodation? I think it needs to be somewhere near London and the main airports. But you're right, I need to talk to Sir Philip to settle a few things." I added as I got up to go, "Have you announced my appointment externally yet?"

Charles smiled. "Going out now. I thought I'd better wait until you had actually signed. Good Luck with Mr Kwok."

I went up to Sir Philip's office before the appointed time and while waiting I looked at Mike Mansell's information on airline insurance. In fact I was shown in to his room a little early and couldn't help noticing the splendid view of the Thames and London to the South. "Well Peter, how did you get on?"

"Sir Philip, the Australian Minister of Defence agreed to forego salvaging the second UAV and the ATSB are not going to insist on badgering the Chinese for the first UAV, though of course the Chinese have not admitted anything."

"Presumably the agreements are subject to the Chinese agreeing to provide some money?"

"Absolutely, I should have said that."

"Well Peter when I heard from Charles Simon what has happening and your involvement I had a word with Harry Brown, my opposite number in MoD who was up to speed with the whole situation. He has just called me back. The Navy positioned one of their subs in the area the moment you discovered from the Australians that the Chinese were involved; it could not find the Chinese carrier in the position that it was when it was found by the Australians but it has found not only the Chinese salvage vessel but also a Russian vessel close to it with lots of radar antennae and a large helicopter sitting on a landing pad towards the ship's stern. Perhaps what is more important, the sub's captain reports that there appears to be two large drones ahead of the helicopter under some sort of cover, presumably to prevent aerial reconnaissance from spotting them; however the captain reports it is difficult to be certain and he has to be very careful not to be spotted. He is worried that the helicopter might take-off and drop a sonobuoy so he only surfaces infrequently to keep the use of the periscope to an absolute minimum. He is also concerned that there might be a Russian sub in the vicinity so besides listening to the ships the sub is keeping as quiet as possible."

I thought about this new piece of information. "I suppose we could accuse the Russians of causing the accident with RWA845? We know it's one of their drones and the Australians have one that crashed. However, my guess is that neither the Chinese nor the Russians will want to admit they caused the crash of RW845. Look how the Russians refused to admit their involvement in the shooting down of the Malaysian aircraft over the Ukraine."

"Well we still haven't got a way of dealing with the money yet should the Chinese agree to provide some."

"I've been thinking about that, Sir Philip. Not surprisingly both the Russians and the Chinese use Aviation Insurers Ltd for a lot of their Western made aircraft since they are the World's biggest aviation insurers. Now Aviation Insurers are also the Royal World Airways insurers. If the Chinese agree we could get them to make the money available to the insurers with a joint committee for the administration of the account but keep the money in a Chinese bank; that way the airline could settle with the passengers through the insurers without anything unusual appearing in their accounts. The Chinese sum of money would not appear directly in Aviation Insurers' accounts either but clearly there would be a small number of people in Aviation Insurers who would be privy to the arrangement but the company would be so relieved in not having the find the insurance money themselves that it should be possible to come to an arrangement."

"But Peter, the auditors should spot the situation."

"True, but that will be some time later and hopefully Royal World can persuade them to hide the situation in some way. And if the news does leak out, so be it. Everyone can deny it."

"Peter, the other problem I foresee is that there is nothing to stop the Chinese going back on the agreement."

"Yes, that is a worry but if that happened Aviation Insurers could refuse to carry on insuring the Russian and Chinese aircraft and my guess is that it would then cost both countries a lot more to transfer elsewhere."

I could see Sir Philip weighing up my suggestion. "Alright Peter, it's a possibility. You see your man Kwok Qiáng tomorrow. All I can do is to wish you good luck."

As I returned to the Club I realised that I would indeed need a lot of luck. I called Laurence Williamson and reconfirmed breakfast he was coming to breakfast in the morning. I sent a long message to Charlie and went to bed early.

At breakfast I went over the current situation and we departed for the Chinese Embassy. Everything worked like clockwork and we soon found ourselves in the same meeting room with Kwok Qiáng. There was not much pretence of talking to Laurence as in the earlier meetings since I sensed he wanted to get down to brass tacks or whatever was the Chinese equivalent. "Mr Talbert, let me congratulate you on your forthcoming appointment to the UK Transport Safety Board. It will be a pleasure for us to be able to meet in the future without your having to come from Australia."

"Thank you Mr Kwok. I am looking forward to starting my new job."

"Will you be bringing your family here as well?"

I was a little surprised at his remark and was pretty sure that I was not inscrutable. "Yes indeed. In fact they will be here before me as my wife has a job at the Royal Academy starting in two months." I decided to start exploring. "Let me start by thanking you for returning all the bodies that were taken by mistake. The numbers are correct and identification is currently taking place."

"That is good, Mr Talbert. Can we help you any further?"

"Mr Kwok, the Australian Transport Safety Board is still looking for the UAV that hit the Royal World Airways airliner and I believe that you or Russia, who are making these UAVs, have lost one which the Australians have discovered. Apparently you are proposing that your salvage vessel which is close by should recover it and are asking for the Australian salvage vessel to move out of the way rather than let the Australians recover it?"

"You seem to be very well informed, Mr Talbert."

I couldn't help smiling as I looked at Kwok Qiáng. "I do my best, Mr Kwok. What concerns the airline is that a lot of the dependants of the people who have died have lost the breadwinners of their family. Does that translate into Chinese?"

"Very clearly, Mr Talbert, but surely the insurance company will reimburse both the airline and the dependents?"

"Mr Kwok, I'm sure you know that the airline liability in this sort of situation is covered by the Montreal Convention and the individual sum for each dependant is not nearly enough in many cases. In fact in this case the airline is only responsible up to 170K per passenger since there is no way that the airline could be held responsible for this accident."

Kwok Qiáng looked at me carefully. "It is a shame that the aircraft that hit the UK airliner cannot be found and we feel very unhappy on behalf of the dependants. So much so that we are prepared to make a sum of money available to try to mitigate the situation even though we have no liability. However we would like to be able to help the Russians and recover the UAV the Australians have found."

"Mr Kwok, that is very kind of you. Maybe you could set up an account in a Chinese bank which could be accessed by Aviation Insurers which is the insurer used by Royal World Airways. When you advise them of the account they could then tell the bank the sum of money required. It may be quite large but no doubt the Russian manufacturer of the UAVs will wish to help. I understand that with suitable financial arrangements the Australian Transport Safety Board will stop searching for the UAV that hit the Royal World Airways airliner and the Australian Defence Establishment will agree not to raise the Russian UAV they have found."

"Mr Talbert, Aviation Insurers need have no concern in this matter. I am sure that the dependants will be able to be adequately recompensed."

"Mr Kwok, Aviation insurers will also need to be able to pay for the loss of the aircraft and crew."

"Mr Talbert, that all seems very straightforward and satisfactory."

"Mr Kwok, this agreement will be a great relief to Aviation Insurers. They were so concerned that they felt that without the agreement they would have to restrict the scope of their business and stop insuring Chinese and Russian airliners immediately."

I looked at Kwok Qiáng and as I finished my sentence I felt I could detect a wink but I knew I must be mistaken.

Chapter 22

The phone rang and I picked it up. "Peter, Mary here."

"Hello, Mary, great to hear from you."

I was visiting Charlie in London and staying in the flat she was renting until I and the children moved from Canberra. I sensed her flinch out of the corner of my eye; I put the loudspeaker on. "Did I tell you that I've got a job with the NTSB?"

"No you certainly didn't. Well done."

"We've just received the ATSB report on the RW845 accident. Do you have a secure phone line?"

"Not at home."

"Well let's hope no-one is listening. It's all old hat anyway. Did you see that there were some Russians on the aircraft?"

"No, I never looked at the passenger list."

"Well the report was sent to you or your team. What have you been doing?"

"It's only just arrived. Jerry is dealing with it. I can't look at everything straightaway. Anyway there were probably lots of different nationalities. What was so special about the Russians?"

"Well the Russians were in the first class compartment; a complete family, Batischev by name."

"Mary, the name rings a faint bell with me. Were the names listed in the report?"

"No, actually the names were not in the report. The passenger list was simply broken down into nationalities but wearing my NTSB hat I asked the airline for the actual passenger list and the name Batischev really got my attention. He used to be a great friend of the current President but they must have fallen out as one day when he was on holiday with his family in London he suddenly asked for political asylum."

"I remember now. Wasn't he involved with getting the President into his Office? It all looked rather dodgy at the time. Weren't hidden bank accounts mentioned? It was quite a while ago. Don't remember the political asylum bit."

"You're right. Some years earlier while the President was manoeuvring to get appointed to his present office, Batischev was quite well known to Russian watchers and was clearly a key man to the President. Maybe I shouldn't be telling you this bit but when he applied for asylum it was a great surprise and a cause célèbre in GCHQ. He was interviewed at length by MI6 and we got involved. The stuff he told MI6 was unbelievable and clearly nothing had changed in the way the Russian secret police behaved. I think I knew more about what was going on than most people because of my relationship with Rupert. The whole affair was kept away from the media. The Russians wanted him back to be put on trial and told us of some murder that he was said to have organised. Not surprisingly our Government refused and he was permitted to stay.

"When I saw his name on the passenger list I rang Rupert to see what he would say."

"Hey, you're an American now. Does he still talk to you?"

Mary ignored my remark. "He made no comment when I told him that Mark Batischev was on RW845 and I couldn't decide if he knew or not that they were on board. It wasn't a secure line and he sounded very cagey."

"Mary, I bet he did know but he probably felt he couldn't confide in you anymore. You are making me think hard, young lady. Bit surprised the newspapers didn't get hold of the story; I would have thought it would have hit the headlines."

"Remember, Peter, when he came to UK and asked for asylum the whole operation was kept quiet. He didn't change his name but he didn't use it in the UK. He used Bozanov, keeping the initials the same. For once the media didn't get hold of the story; he kept a low profile unlike a lot of the wealthy oligarchs who are living in the UK and own football clubs and the like."

"Well the accident was all very convenient for the Russian President. Are your people suggesting that the collision may not have been accidental?"

"Peter, this is just me talking. When you get round to reading the ATSB report you will see there is no mention of Russian UAVs or the Chinese carrier so the people here have no idea of what went on. Incidentally, there were some Americans on the plane and they say they are going to sue the airline above the Montreal limit."

"They will be wasting their money as there is no way the airline can be held liable."

"Peter, I know that but the lawyers may decide to have a go."

"Mary, I'd like to think about what you've told me. Do I know how to contact you?"

"My gmail address hasn't changed and I'm sure Charlie knows how to contact Andrew. I'll send you my new iPhone number as well."

I was glad to put the phone down as I wasn't expecting to have to tackle RW845 again. Charlie looked at me. "She gets around, NTSB no less."

"Why not? She must have a US passport by now and is clearly employable."

"What are you going to do about the Russians and RW845? Do you think the collision was deliberate?"

"Mary clearly does. Maybe I should talk to Rupert."

"Not to-night you won't. We had better try to sort this house out to make it livable in."

***

In the morning I got my secretary to call Rupert. I reminded him that we had met in Canberra when we were dealing with the shooting down of the P8s. "Peter, I remember very well but I hadn't realised you were back in UK. How can I help you?"

"Mary French called you the other day from the States and asked you about the Batischevs."

"Peter, do you have a secure phone in your office?" I grunted that I did. "I'll call you back."

Rupert was back in five minutes. "Peter, I did wonder whether to tell somebody about the Batischevs being on board the Royal World Airlines plane when it crashed but I decided to let things take their course. Presumably you, like us, are trying to decide if the collision was deliberate?"

"It would be nice to know. From the President's point of view it was a very convenient accident and I'm afraid I'm not a great supporter of coincidences. But Rupert, you people should know if it was a coincidence. Tell me if you can, when he was in the UK was he being continually tracked? Were you aware he was off to Australia, presumably on holiday?"

"Yes, we knew what he was doing as he had applied for a resident's visa in Australia and they had consulted us. We were delighted that he was going because it was just another problem being removed."

I noticed that Rupert ignored my question on whether the Batischevs had been watched in the UK and I decided not to press for an answer. "Do you think the Russians knew he was leaving?"

"Good question, Peter, and I'd rather not give you an official answer but as everyone knows they do track their 'dissidents' overseas in London. It would be surprising if they weren't trying keeping an eye on him, especially as he knew so much. We think that is why he decided to emigrate and get further away from Russia."

"Rupert, let me ask you an associated question. Did you know about what was going on with the Chinese carrier and the Russian UAVs?"

"The MoD asked for our help some time back since they were aware of the UAVs and were trying to get more info. Luckily, for fast communication to their mobile units when they needed a quick response, the Russians were using the WorldLink network so we had some idea of what was going on until that Australian Army idiot blew the Oz facility up and the Russians changed to a different communication network."

"But you couldn't read the WorldLink network?"

"You clearly are well informed but remember the NSA could. The Russians made a mistake there. Judging by what the NSA heard the collision could well have been deliberate. Apparently the Russians knew the likely track and timing of the Batischev plane and were fed the take-off time from Singapore."

"How?"

"Don't know for sure. That's what the NSA told us."

"Why didn't someone try to stop the Russians?"

"Peter, you must appreciate that the NSA could only read the communication exchanges some time after they had taken place; when time was not crucial the Russians used their normal fully coded satellite links. By the time we got the material over here it was far too late to do anything."

"The Russians must have had an airline contact. Without knowing when the aircraft was due it would have been impossible to arrange a collision. The UAV needed to take-off from the carrier in time to climb to height and go into orbit a few minutes before RW845 was due. However, it would still require great judgment or a clever computer program to get the UAV going towards the airliner. Fortunately for the operator, but for no-one else, it almost certainly had all the latest 'bells and whistles' as it was being demonstrated to the Chinese."

"What do you mean, Peter?"

"Well the UAV probably had a homing device to lock on to targets and my bet is that it would have been used in order to intercept RWA845; in my opinion it wouldn't have been possible without it to guarantee a hit steering the UAV manually from the ground."

"That makes it a very expensive missile."

"Apparently it was a very valuable target. You people must know what Mark Batischev knew; I'm surprised he was ever allowed to leave Russia, particularly with his family."

"Peter, do you really believe that the Russians would deliberately destroy an airliner just because of one man and what he knew. There were 253 other lives in the aircraft."

"Rupert, you know more about these things than I do but look what they did in Ukraine. The World is changing. ISIS and similar organisations kill thousands for reasons that we find hard to understand. However, I must say that this 'accident' seems incredibly ruthless."

"I agree."

"Well why don't you blow the whistle?"

"A good question but the Russians will deny it. They didn't admit the Ukraine one."

"Did you ever check the passenger list of the Malaysian aircraft they shot down?"

"You're embarrassing me. No I didn't."

"Well on another tack, have the Chinese bought any of the Russian UAVs? "

"No they haven't as far as we know and we're pretty certain they are not going to as rapprochement seems to have cooled a bit; perhaps because of the accident."

"You're absolutely right there. The Chinese were meant to be evaluating the UAVs by operating them and clearly the Russians flew this sortie. Rupert, let's keep in touch on this thing. I don't believe we've come to the end of this story yet."

My hunch to Rupert proved more accurate than I was expecting. Half an hour later Kwok Qiáng came on the phone. "Mr Talbert, good to talk to you. We have been reading the ATSB report on the Royal World Airlines accident."

"Mr Kwok, then you are ahead of me. My staff are reading it now. Is there a problem?"

"We were expecting a passenger list."

"I'm sure we can get you one if you think it is important."

"Thank you very much."

I called Jerry on the phone and asked him to get hold of a copy of the passenger list and send it to Kwok Qiáng at the Chinese Embassy. "Peter, we don't normally do that unless there is a good reason. There is a nationality breakdown in the ATSB report."

"Jerry, there is a very good reason. I don't think we've heard the last of this accident." Jerry rang off but clearly wasn't happy about my decision.

A few days later on a Sunday morning Jerry called me. "Hope you don't mind my calling you but have you read the Sunday Times to-day? You were right about not hearing the last of this accident. There's an article about RW845 and some Russians called Batischev. The article mentions the ATSB report on the accident and the fact that the aircraft that collided into RW845 was never found. The article points out that there was a Mark Batischev on board the plane with his family and that Batischev at one time had been a very close friend of the Russian President. Apparently the paper had rung the President's office in Moscow and there was no comment. The article finishes by pointing out that if Batischev knew any secrets it was convenient for the Russians that he was no longer available to divulge them. Furthermore, the aircraft that collided with RW845 had never been found so it was impossible to determine if the collision was an accident or not." His voice changed as he finished telling me about the article. "Peter, do you think the collision was deliberate?"

"Jerry, it must be a possibility." I didn't wasn't to discuss the matter with him though I was very pleased that he called me. "Thanks so much for the call. I haven't seen the paper yet but from what you tell me we're bound to get some follow up questions and the BBC will be trying to stir things as much as they can. Do me a favour, please ring Simon Greensmith and get him to call me."

Simon was the media communicator I had appointed for the new combined Transport Safety Board who had been with the AAIB. He called me a few minutes later and I asked him to play a 'dead bat' to all enquiries saying that we had nothing further to add to the ATSB report on the accident.

Charlie meantime, while this had been going on, had collected the Sunday Times from where it had been delivered on our front doorstep and had found the article which occupied two full pages in the main newspaper. There were pictures of the Batischev's, an ITAC 990, the *Ocean Salvager* and me as the newly appointed head of the UK Transport Safety Board. As Jerry had pointed out, the article stressed that the aircraft that had collided with RW845 had never been found and how convenient the accident had proved to be for the Russian President.

Charlie looked at me. "What are you going to do? It's a clear cut case of a deliberate collision."

"Nothing for the moment. Let's see what happens."

***

Simon was waiting for me when I got to my office with a copy of The Australian; their Prime Minister had been questioned in Parliament about the accident and the loss of the cricket team; he had explained that the magnificent Australian JORN radar had seen the aircraft which almost certainly had caused the collision and it was believed to be a Russian UAV which was being evaluated by the Chinese. However it had not been possible to find the UAV. He was questioned about the Batischev's but said he knew nothing about them which I felt was probably true.

I rang Robert at home who was full of apologies about the PM's statement. Apparently the elections were approaching and he had made the announcement to try to get some votes. There was no point in complaining to anybody so we just commiserated.

The next thing that happened was not altogether unexpected, Kwok Qiáng came on the phone. "Mr Talbert, as you will have gathered we were not flying the UAV when the collision occurred. We had no idea that the Russians flew the UAV deliberately into the airliner; we thought it was an accident. We are very upset and there will be a statement from Beijing explaining what actually happened and pointing out that the Russians were flying the UAV. In the circumstances I'm sure you will understand that the agreement on finance can no longer be continued since it was entirely the fault of the Russians."

There was nothing I could say. Apparently over half of the money had already been recovered by the insurers and now they would have to pay the rest. Clearly I was going to have to get Jerry to write a full statement explaining and in effect corroborating the Chinese statement.

That afternoon Simon came round to my office with a statement from Aviation Insurers saying that with immediate effect they were no longer insuring Russian commercial airliners. There were two other news items, one from Moscow saying that the Russian Government would be insuring all Russian airliners and that no-one need be concerned; the other was a cutting from the London Evening Standard saying that there was complete confusion on international flights to and from Russia as many passengers who were booked on Russian airlines were trying to transfer to other carriers which were becoming overbooked.

Just before I went home Sir Philip Brown called me. "Peter, well you've really started your new job with a flourish. Thank goodness you were in post. However I'm not really clear how the truth came out."

"Sir Philip, I can't take any credit for working it out. By a strange coincidence it was the girl who was shot down in the P8 in Australia some time ago who realised that the collision may well have been deliberate. She had left GCHQ and had got a job with our AAIB and by complete chance she spent some time with the ATSB working in Canberra on the accident. Then she married an American and started work with NTSB so of course she knew all about the Chinese and Russian involvement when the ATSB report finally came out even though it wasn't mentioned. She decided to get hold of the full passenger list and she spotted that the Batischev's were on board; only then did she realise what might have happened. I'm not clear what took place next but somehow the Sunday Times got involved, probably thanks to a very smart Russian watcher or aviation expert or both. As a result the Australian

PM got questioned and jumped straight in, presumably without getting properly briefed. The rest is history."

"Well Peter, I think it is all for the best that the truth is out. People need to understand that terrorists who kill people ruthlessly are not confined to young men who have grievances but in some countries they can also be found in the corridors of power."

Epilogue

We watched the removal van drive off and then sat down, exhausted, but with a feeling of relief. Charlie had been renting a place for three months in Wimbledon close to where we had just bought our house and she had been able to start at the Royal Academy; she had arranged primary schools for the children starting in the summer term. I had arrived with the children two weeks earlier and Jill had agreed to help out for six months. We had chosen Wimbledon as a convenient place to live as our game plan was to send the children to local secondary schools in a few years time though we knew we might have to pay privately which was going to make our eyes water.

The move we had just completed involved not only moving Charlie out of her rented accommodation but also moving furniture from my house in Kingston which I had sold. I had just finished my first week in my temporary office in Farnborough and approval had been given for the new combined headquarters to be in brand new offices just east of Hurlingham near the River Thames. The Treasury had needed some convincing but the builders had got the site cheaply as it was next to the Thames Water super sewer and was not considered suitable for expensive residential accommodation. From an operational viewpoint it was a good site since it was close to Heathrow, the Thames docks and all the London rail terminals not to mention the corridors of power.

The telephone rang. It was Mary. I put the loudspeaker on. "Peter, NTSB have asked me to see if I can work with your new organisation for three months, meeting your key people and learning how it is going to work. Do you have a spare room? It would be so much nicer than a hotel." I looked at Charlie whose face was a picture, definitely not an inviting one. There was a long pause. "Peter, are you alright? It's gone very quiet." She laughed. "It's alright. You can tell Charlie not to worry, Andrew will be with me, he's working with Camfen." Charlie started to relax. "Oh, and by the way we've just heard, we're expecting twins, two boys."

Charlie looked at me. "That's let you off the hook!"

Printed at Repro India Ltd.